A Ghost of a Second Chance

By

Kristy Tate

A Ghost of a Second Chance

Smashwords Edition

Published by Kristy Tate

Copyright 2012 by Kristy Tate

Table Of Contents

CHAPTER 1

The Chinook wind stirred the fallen leaves and tossed them around the deserted street. *An eastern wind carries more than dust and ashes,* Laine's mother had told her; *it uproots secrets. And everyone knows once one secret is told, no secret is safe.*

Hers included.

Laine paused in front of the Queen Anne Hill Chapel doors. The sun, a faint pink glow over the eastern hills had yet to shine, but Laine hadn't any doubt that it would rise to another scorching Indian summer day. She looked out over sleeping Seattle. The dark gray Puget Sound stretched away from her. On the horizon, distant ships bobbed and sent quivering beams of light over the water.

She turned her back on the ships, on any dream of sailing away, and inserted the key into the heavily carved wooden doors. They creaked open before Laine turned the key. *Odd.* The chapel, built in the 1930s, had a musty, empty smell. She stepped into the cool shade of the foyer and the door swung shut, closing with a click that echoed through the cavernous room. The morning sounds of birds, crickets and insects disappeared when the doors closed. Laine's sneakers smacked across the terracotta tile, her footsteps loud.

She had thought she'd be alone, which is exactly why she'd chosen to come near dawn. Not that she'd been able to sleep. She hadn't slept for weeks, which may explain why at first she'd thought the girl standing in the nave, facing the pulpit, her face lifted to the stained glass window, might be a ghost—or, given her surroundings, an angel.

Although Laine couldn't see her face, the way the child's head moved, it looked as if she was having a conversation with the Lord trapped in the glass, or one of the sheep milling about His feet, giving Laine the uncomfortable sense of interrupting. The meager morning sun lit the glass and multi-colored reflections fell on the girl, casting her in an iridescent glow. Slowly, she turned and Laine realized she wasn't a child, but a young woman, around twenty, maybe half her own age, wearing the sort of thing her grandmother would have worn. Vintage clothing, Laine noted, incredibly well preserved.

"Good morning," Laine said, smiling. "I'm sorry to intrude. I wasn't expecting anyone..." She let her voice trail away. Laine had certainly never felt any peace through prayer, but that didn't mean she wanted to interrupt on anyone seeking grace and Pastor Clark had given her the key, so naturally she'd assumed the chapel would have been locked and that she'd have this time to practice alone.

"Well, where is he, then?" the girl-woman demanded, placing her balled fists on her hips. She had yellow blonde hair, cut in a curly bob, and wore a pale blue sleeveless dress that fell straight to her knees. Laine considered the young woman. Given the scowl and hostile eyes, she didn't look like a humble Christian follower, but she did seem oddly familiar.

"I'm sorry—who are you looking for?" Laine tucked her hands into her pockets, feeling inappropriately dressed. She'd thrown on Ian's sweats, one of the few sets of clothes he'd left behind. Perhaps he didn't exercise at the hotel, or, more likely, he'd just bought himself a new pair of running clothes. Now that her grandfather had died, making Ian The-Man-In-Charge, Ian could afford new running clothes, the hotel suite, and room services of all sorts. Which didn't explain, really, why Laine wore his cast-offs. Just because he'd left them behind didn't mean Laine should wear them. And yet, she did. Frequently.

"Sid!" the woman spat the name. Her gaze raked over Laine, making her uneasy.

Laine tugged at the drawstring holding up the sweat pants, wondering why this woman would be looking for her grandfather. "He's still at the funeral home." She swallowed. "They won't bring the casket here until tomorrow morning. There's the viewing tonight at the house…" She heard her own sadness in her voice.

"Then what are you doing here?" The woman's eyes matched the color of her dress and as she drew closer, Laine saw she wore a necklace of the same steely blue. Laine's hand instinctively crept to her own necklace, a gift from Sid, an emerald he'd said matched her eyes.

"I've come to practice the organ." Laine shifted on her feet. A tingle of déjà vu ran up her spine. Looking at this woman was like watching a rerun of an almost forgotten and yet beloved television show. They must have met some other time at some long ago, forgotten place; Laine was sure they'd been friends. Although, at the moment, this woman was not a friendly person.

The woman looked at the massive organ and then back to Laine. "Why are you playing the organ? I'm sure Georgie could spit out the money for an organist. No need for freebie-family members to play."

Laine opened her mouth to ask how this woman knew her father or her relationship to Sid, but then remembered her family had never lived a quiet life. Well, except for her. Her own life had been, until now, ungossip-worthy. Her breath caught in her throat and then she let it out slowly, bracing herself for the difficult weekend. She'd weather the rumors and the chit-chat. She could be strong.

Even if she'd never been before.

"I wanted to play," Laine told the woman, lacing her voice with resolve she didn't feel. "As a gift to my grandfather."

Why are you here? How did you get in? How do I know you? Laine wanted to ask, but years of social training held back her questions.

The woman snorted. "Not much of a gift, that."

"Yeah, well, it's something I want to do." Laine let a little of her social training slip and she brushed past the woman. She marched up the aisle toward the organ, lifted the massive cover, turned on the switch and adjusted the bench.

"A gift to your grandfather, or an excuse not to sit by your husband?" The woman appeared beside her.

Laine squared her shoulders and bit back a rude retort. She'd have to get used to the questions. Even if they weren't asked so bluntly, they'd still be asked. Maybe not to her face, maybe behind her back, but the questions would be there, either in people's eyes or on their lips. Laine would *not* provide answers.

The woman stood at her elbow. "If you've come to practice, where's your music?"

Laine gave her a tight smile as she settled onto the bench. "I memorize."

"If it's already memorized, why are you practicing?"

For the first time Laine caught a hint of the woman's French accent. "Who did you say you are again?"

"I didn't say and you didn't answer my question."

Laine began adjusting the stops. "Every instrument is different. A pedal may be broken, the bench could wobble... I've learned from sad experience that it's best to give every instrument a test run. I mean, an organ's not like a violin. You can't just bring your own."

The woman cocked her head. "What would you know of sad experiences?"

Most people would say her life was charmed, but if she lived such a fairytale, why was she so sad? *Because the prince she'd been kissing for most of her life had turned into a toad?*

"Do I know you?" Laine asked, her fingers pausing above the keys.

The woman leaned against the organ. "I don't know,

do you?"

All of Laine's politeness drained away. "I'm sorry. I *don't* know you. And because I don't know you, I don't feel I need to share." Laine hit the keys, a D minor chord, and music reverberated through the deserted chapel.

"Good for you." The woman chuckled and hitched herself up on top of the organ. She had reed thin legs, pale as porcelain and covered with silky hose. She swung them back and forth, like a child pumping a swing, her heels rap-tapping the organ.

Laine lifted her fingers, horrified. The sudden cessation of music filled the room. "You can't *sit* on this organ." Her words echoed.

The woman cut her a sideways smile. She wore bright red shoes with ribbon ties on the ankles and the red heels continued bumping rhythmically against the organ. "No?"

"*No.* It's a 1930's Wurlitzer, solid walnut. It's extremely valuable, and you're *kicking* it."

"You're very rich." The woman smiled, but didn't budge or stop swinging her legs. "You could replace it."

Laine hated being reminded of her money. It made her feel guilty and dirty. She supposed that's why she worked so hard at the foundation. She pounded out the first line of *Pie Jesu* and said, through gritted teeth, "Get off!"

And to her surprise, the woman did. Laine almost stopped playing, but after watching the woman wander down the aisle, her hands trailing along the pews, Laine turned her full attention to the music swirling through the chapel and, for a moment, she felt better than she had in weeks.

***

Walking down Lily Street past the turn-of-the-last-century mansions, Laine pulled her blazer close, as if by buttoning it she could hold in all her broken pieces. The suit hung on her. She'd had to pin the back of the skirt to keep it from sliding off. *At least wool breathes*, she told herself, refusing to consider that wool, heat, nerves and sweat could, and most assuredly, would, cause a smelly combination.

When had she lost so much weight? How had that happened? Had she discovered the miracle weight-loss program? Could she market it? The *Lose Your Guy, Lose Your Gut* diet?

Because she'd walked, she'd worn her flats, but stopping at the gate, watching her relatives, friends, and business associates climb from their cars in their suits, dresses, and heels, she considered going home and changing into something less worn. It'd seemed ridiculous to drive such a short distance, ridiculous to walk the three hilly blocks in heels, and it would be equally ridiculous to walk back and forth just to change her shoes. Of course, she could walk home and then drive for the return trip. But—then where would she park?

I'm stalling, she thought. Her eyes flicked over the cars lining the tiny street. This was supposed to be a private viewing, family and close friends only, and yet, somehow, her stepmother had managed to turn it into a celebrity photo opportunity. She told herself she wasn't looking for Ian's Mercedes, but she stopped checking the cars when he pulled up.

She stepped behind a mammoth rhododendron, and through the petals and branches, she watched him climb from his car. Despite the suit and graying hair at his temples, from a distance he looked nearly the same as he had in high school. Which just wasn't right. She'd aged, why hadn't he grown old beside her? The sprinklers had recently shut off and Laine's flats sunk into a patch of mud. Her feet slipped slightly in the muck and she felt off balance and shaky.

A voice spoke in her ear. "Why are you hiding in that bush?"

Laine jumped and put her hand on her heart to slow its

beating. She turned and scowled at the tiny woman at her elbow. "You!"

"You've got mud on your shoes and plant rubbish on your jacket."

Laine looked down at her shoes and brushed twigs and petals off her blazer.

"I thought your outfit this morning was perhaps the ugliest thing I'd ever seen, but now," her gaze swept over Laine, "I can see I was wrong."

Laine cast Ian another look to make sure he hadn't noticed her standing behind the bush and then whispered, "What's wrong with my suit?"

"You mean besides the fact it's ugly and must be incredibly itchy and hot? Well, for one thing, it doesn't fit you. Where did you find it?"

"In my closet."

"That explains a lot." The woman fingered the pleats on her own blue silk dress. She'd changed her shoes. The red heels had been replaced with a pair of black pumps that would have been sedate if not for the faux diamonds on the toes. "You obviously need a new closet."

"This is a viewing, not a fashion show." Laine folded her arms, studied the woman and used the voice she only trotted out when donors tried to renege on their pledges.

"Who are you? Did you work for my grandfather?"

The woman looked sly. "Sometimes." So, that's who she was—one of her grandfather's girls. Laine didn't deserve abuse from one of her grandfather's ladies. She looked too young for even Sid. And she thought that it had been years since Sid's Romeo days, but with her grandfather—it was hard to know who was who in his revolving love life.

Sid hadn't been a paragon of virtue, but Laine had tried to live her life by a strict code. Insulting grieving granddaughters at funerals breached that code.

"Oh hello!" Ian called.

Laine's head snapped up. Even from a distance, the timber in Ian's voice made her quiver. She'd thought he'd seen her, thought he was speaking to her, but now she saw him cross the grounds, his arms open, his eyes kind, warm and generous—he could afford all those emotions now—as he approached a girl in a white sheath dress. Mary or Marie somebody from the reception desk. So much for family and close friends. But then Laine remembered, vaguely, something about Mary or Marie being related to Denis Openheimer, of the Openheimer Weiner fame. Of course, her stepmother would invite an Openheimer.

"Who wears white to a funeral?" the woman asked,

before bringing her gaze back to Laine. "Although, it's better than your frumpy suit."

Laine turned away from Ian, not wanting to watch him embrace Mary or Marie, and looked at the woman just in time to see a fistful of mud flying.

"Hey!" Laine called out as the mud splattered across her chest. Clods of dirt stuck to her blouse as she pulled it out of her waistband, trying to prevent the mud from running down her skirt.

"I think the proper response would be 'thank you'."

"*Thank you?*"

"You're welcome." The woman brushed off her hands, spun on her heel, and headed toward the back entrance of Sid's house. "Now, follow me."

Laine looked down at the disaster of her shirt. "I will not follow you."

The woman stopped in the driveway by the white catering van. "What, you're going to walk three blocks to change into something equally dowdy? You're going to risk being late or possibly even not showing your face at your grandfather's viewing? Think of the gossip, the rumors. Everyone will know for sure that Ian's left you. *He* will think you weren't brave enough—"

"Stop it!" The words and emotions flew out of Laine's

iron-clad control.

A teenager holding a large pink pastry box stepped from around the corner of the van. "Ma'am?" He had freckles dotting his nose and he looked hurt and surprised by her outburst.

"Not you," Laine said, her voice sounding weak. "I wasn't talking to you. I was talking to—"

She looked around, but the tiny woman had disappeared.

The kid edged toward her, as if she were a wounded Doberman in need of help and yet still capable of doing serious injury. "Can I help you? Get you some water or something?"

Laine sighed and put her fingertips on either side of her temples. "Look, I hired your company."

The kid began to back away from her. His hands, clutching the pastry boxes, turned white around the knuckles.

"I just…" Laine swallowed, following him. "There's a short, blonde woman hanging around here. She's about this high." Laine held up her hand so it was even with her chin. "If you see her, I want you to come and get me immediately." *She's going to pay,* Laine thought, *for at least my dry cleaning.*

The mud seeped through her blouse and felt cold and oozy. What to do? Totter home, change into something, anything, clean? Go into town and buy something? She didn't have her purse. She glanced at Sid's house. It had rooms and rooms and closets full of stuff.

She looked out over the lawn. Ian stood on the front porch, pumping hands with Uncle Harry. Ian had on a dark, well cut, custom-made suit. Even as a teenager he'd been fashion conscious. Other girls had shopped with their boyfriends, selecting their clothes, dressing them as if they were the Ken to their Barbie. Laine had always been too busy studying, working on the student council, organizing the next fundraiser. Even then, she'd been raising money for somebody, or something else.

Laine stomped into her grandfather's kitchen and the catering staff, who had been bustling around the counters and mammoth oak table turned to stare at her, their conversations and chatter coming to sudden and stunned stop.

"There's a crazy short lady here," Laine said. "If any of you see her, I want you to tell me immediately."

Most of the staff gave her blank stares, but a few turned away, smirking. *Short, crazy lady,* Laine thought as she kicked off her muddy shoes. *Yeah, right. Short and*

*crazy are both subjective adjectives and could just as easily
be applied to me.*

Laine ran up the back stairs and turned into what was
once her aunt Claire's room. The room still smelled of
violets, her aunt's smell, and Laine's heart clenched with
the sudden memory. Softly, she closed the door behind her
and went to sit on the bed. The room hadn't been
redecorated since the eighties. Tiny yellow and blue
flowers covered everything—the walls, the bedspread, the
host of pillows, the dress of the Cabbage Patch doll resting
against the brass headboard.

What would happen now to Sid's house, to Claire's
things? Why hadn't she thought about this? Had anyone?
Perhaps her stepmother and her dad had plans. Although,
thinking and planning had never been their fortes.

Ian would now officially run the company. He'd been
Sid's puppet for years, until slowly, almost imperceptibly,
he'd begun pulling the strings as Sid had aged. No one had
expected Sid to live to ninety-seven, especially not his
string of ex-wives. He'd outlived all his spouses and two of
his children.

Thinking about spouses, exes and current, Laine
unfolded from the bed and went to the closet. She had
known her aunt Claire as a fussy old lady and didn't expect

to find anything other than flowery muumuus, Claire's favorite daywear. A muumuu or a dirt crusted suit? Laine had to find something without mud clinging to it and she didn't need a whole outfit. Her suit was fine, thank you very much. She just needed a blouse.

She glanced out the window and saw Ian talking to a circle of her employees from the foundation. Marie laughed and placed her hand on Ian's sleeve. White heat flared through Laine and she closed her eyes against the pain and anger.

When she opened her eyes she saw a dress hanging in the closet. Long sleeves, high neck, black lace over a strapless taffeta under-bodice, a pleated band at the waist. The sort of thing she'd never buy.

And yet.

She looked back out the window. Marie had on an impossibly short skirt, something no one over the age of thirty should ever wear. Allison, a mother of four children, had on a blouse that lifted when she moved her arms and exposed a bright strip of white belly. In a world of inappropriateness, Laine, the good daughter, the philanthropist, could wear a black lace dress.

She took off her suit, kicked it into the closet's corner, and stepped into the dress. To her surprise, it didn't smell of violets or mildew, but of Chanel Number 5. The lining felt luxurious against her skin and the lace clung slightly as she moved.

Considering her reflection in the mirror, she decided she couldn't wear the muddy flats. Tearing into the shoe boxes on the closet shelf, she discovered black lace shoes with pearl buttons and three-inch heels. She couldn't. She wouldn't be able to walk. With the shoe box tucked under her arm, she went to the bed, sat down and slipped on the heels. They fit perfectly. *Odd.*

Looking at her herself in the mirror, she wondered when and where her aunt had bought the dress and matching shoes. She tried to imagine the woman she'd known, the wearer of shapeless muumuus and of the collector of Cabbage Patch dolls, wearing such a dress, wearing Chanel Number 5 perfume. *There are so many things we don't know about the people around us, even the people we love*, she thought, *and we pass so quickly through our lives, briefly colliding before sailing away.*

On an impulse, she reached up and took the pins from her hair. Her curls spilled down her back. Remembering the handkerchief in her suit pocket, she drew it out and promised herself that she wouldn't use it. No one would see her cry, but if they did, they would think she cried for Sid.

Not Ian. Perhaps Ian would cry and she could magnanimously lend him her handkerchief and give him a condescending smile, accompanied by a conciliatory pat on the shoulder. She smiled at her reflection, braced her shoulders, and left the room.

CHAPTER 2

She took the front stairs. Pausing on the landing, looking out over her grandfather's closest friends, family and anyone else her stepmother thought worthy of socially cultivating, Laine immediately knew something wasn't right. Like a fluttering flag without a breeze, something was off. It tickled in the back of her mind, indefinable and yet there.

The front door gaped open and the eastern wind circulated, whispering. Laine felt it twirling and tightened her grip on the banister. Ian looked up and caught her gaze. His lips tightened as he took in the lacy dress and his eyes came back to hers, serious. He set down his drink on the piano and stepped toward her.

"Darling, there you are!" Trudy's voice cut above the crowd. Laine heard the panic beneath the trill. Her stepmother loved drama. Perhaps her habitual theatrics were residual from her days as Marla Cassel, betrayed wife of Dr. Darren Mead, the lusty lead of the *The Passing Days,* a soap opera whose days had certainly passed. "This is soooo terrible!" Trudy's hands fluttered over her impressive breasts.

Sid was ninety-seven years old. He'd enjoyed a life of debauchery and indulgence. By all medical accounts and statistics, he should have died thirty years ago. Of course, Laine's social training kept her thoughts from becoming comments. Instead she said, "As funerals, even lovely ones, usually are."

She tried not to look at Ian, weaving through the crowd toward her. She willed herself to focus on Trudy's watery eyes. Her stepmother did look genuinely upset. Given that Trudy hadn't seemed overly sad since Sid's death nearly five days ago, this burst of raw emotion surprised Laine. She took the stairs quickly and slipped her arm around Trudy's shaking shoulders. "Where's Daddy?" she asked, squeezing her stepmother in a sideways hug, angling her away from the approaching Ian.

"He's gone to the mortuary," Trudy said in a ragged whisper.

"The mortuary?" Laine looked out over the clustered mourners. They stood in huddled groups of black, their heads down, their eyes averted from hers. She heard their murmurs and felt the gossip tingling up her spine. Laine led Trudy down the hall, close to the kitchen. Even the caterers had stopped bustling. An eerie quiet had descended on the house like a heavy, smothering cloud. Where was the music? She'd hired her friend, Bette, to play Beethoven and Bach, among others. Where was Bette?

"An awful mistake—" Trudy stuttered, her nose running.

Trudy never stuttered and her nose never ran—at least, not in public. Could this be more than a show from a practiced and perfected drama queen? Had something terrible, even more terrible than Sid's death, happened? Laine handed Trudy the handkerchief, but Trudy wiped her nose on her sleeve, a sure and telling sign of extreme anxiety.

"Sid…." Trudy choked.

Laine tightened her hold on Trudy's shoulders, reason setting in. She spoke calmly. "We'll all miss him."

Trudy frowned and tried again. Leaning forward, she whispered, "He's not here."

"I know," Laine murmured in sympathy. "The difference between someone alive and someone dead *is* frightening." The reality of Sid's death probably hadn't hit Trudy until she had seen him lying in the casket. Sid wasn't at the store, or at work, or on a vacation. His body was here and yet his essence, his soul, whatever spark that had made Sid-*Sid,* was gone. Only a shell of a body remained. Even though she'd been only nine at the time, Laine remembered seeing her mother, pale, still, *dead* at the viewing at the funeral home. The reality of her mother's death hadn't reached her until that moment and she still carried the memory with her. It defined her as plainly as any other form of identification such as a passport or driver's license. Laine took a deep breath and tried to speak the language of adult reasoning. She was no longer that frightened little girl. Even though her stepmother was twelve years her senior, Laine sometimes felt that in Trudy's case it helped to speak as simply as possible. "Sid is gone."

Trudy shook her head, struggling to hold her voice steady. "And someone has taken his place— "

Laine looked up and met Ian's eyes as he moved toward her. She twisted the handkerchief in her hands. "No. No one else can take his place," she said, her voice confident and steady.

"What she means is, there's been some confusion," Ian said.

Confusion? She understood confusion. Confusion had been her bedfellow for the past six weeks. She looked from Trudy to Ian and saw horror and compassion, respectively. Ian touched her elbow and his heat radiated up her arm. He always had this effect on her, and it disturbed her that despite anger, despite disappointment, his touch still caused a physical and emotional reaction.

"Sid's not here," Trudy wailed.

"Shhh," Ian breathed, softly, almost inaudibly and Trudy gulped in response.

"What do you mean?" Laine shook her head, trying to clear it.

Trudy pointed a shaking finger at the casket and whispered, "That's not Sid! It's someone else."

Ian tightened his grip on Laine's arm as she swayed in the high heels. What Trudy's words just didn't register. This couldn't happen. "That can't be," she said.

Ian nodded and then after giving her a look as if to gauge her ability to not fall to pieces, he led her down the hall and into the living room, past the huddled groups of mourners.

Laine felt their curiosity. She wondered— if she stood still and quiet long enough, would she be able to read their thoughts and questions? Holding her head high, she stepped in front of the casket, squared her shoulders, and looked down at the remains of her grandfather. A sob welled in her throat. Pressing her fist to her lips, she struggled to keep from crying out.

Probably *someone's* grandfather. Gray hair swept off

his forehead, the Roman nose, prominent cheekbones covered with nearly translucent skin. "It *looks* like him," she whispered.

"But it's not," Ian said, flatly.

Laine touched the fake Sid's hand. Cold. Blue cold. Her grandfather had large hands, beefy and broad, but this man had long, knobby fingers. "The resemblance is…" Laine stuttered and wavered on her tall high heels.

"Close," Ian said as took her elbow, glanced around the room. "No one else has noticed."

Trudy began to sob and Ian put his arm around her and whispered in her ear. "We need to keep this contained. We'll have total chaos if we don't."

"Reporters?" Trudy gulped. She sounded a little hopeful.

"Stock holders," Ian said. "There's already enough speculation about the company's future." His voice sounded hard and he cut Laine a sideways glance.

Laine spoke up and the steadiness of her voice surprised her. "Sid's been a recluse for a long time. We're lucky that almost everyone won't recognize him and those who can are people we trust." She looked around the room, and her gaze met and held with Sid's doctor. He knew.

"How many old Italians could they have floating

around? How could they screw this up?" Trudy's question, even though whispered, ended on a high octave.

"Who do you think is to blame?" Laine asked. "The hospital, the mortuary?"

Ian shrugged. He dropped her elbow and her arm suddenly chilled. He stood just behind her—his warmth seeping through the thin lacy dress. She couldn't think about Ian. She had to focus on her grandfather. Or rather, this look-a-like grandfather.

Trudy began, "So, we're just going to pretend—"

"Well, where is he?" a voice demanded.

The blonde who had thrown a dirt clot at her blouse stood beside the casket with her arms folded across her chest. "You said he'd be here." The woman opened her hands wide, palms up, and asked again, "Where is he?"

Obviously, more than one person had noticed the fake Sid. In mere seconds the count had risen to from no one to two. Laine's gaze went from guest to guest. Maybe everyone else knew and they were all too polite to say anything.

Except for the blonde.

Laine *hated* the blonde. Generally, she was much too nice to hate anyone or anything, but right now, at this instant, she loathed that woman. "I don't understand how this could happen," Laine said slowly, taking Ian's cue and ignoring the woman. Amazingly, everyone in the room did the same.

Trudy's cry started like a kitten mewing, but steadily grew in volume. Ian shot Laine a worried glance before taking Trudy's elbow and leading her out of the room. He motioned for Laine to follow.

Laine, tired of following Ian, did it anyway.

"Let me get you something to drink," Ian said, steering Trudy to Sid's office. Trudy let him propel her through the door. He set her down on the leather sofa. Over Trudy's head, Ian sent Laine a look that said, *watch her.*

She was tired of following Ian, but she was especially tired of following his instructions. She hated how he didn't have to say a word and she still knew what he meant and intended. She could read him and he could read her. She'd have to work on being less transparent, but she really didn't know how. How could she undo a relationship that had been nearly thirty years in the making?

Trudy's mewing, a high-pitched nasal tone hurt Laine's ears and she moved to the window, opened it and took a deep breath. Leaning against the big desk, taking the weight off her feet, her hands gripped the desk to keep her upright. She wanted to fall, to sink to the floor and somehow disappear, melt away. She didn't want to cause any stir, worry, or commotion; she simply didn't want to be here—or anywhere, for that matter. If she could fade into the wallpaper, she would.

The hot wind blew in, carrying the smell of distant fires and apples. Voices also drifted in. They were barely discernable over Trudy's cries.

"You saw him with Miss Laine," a female said.

Why did they all call her that? Maybe it'd been cute when she was little, a dark- haired Shirley Temple hanging around her grandfather's office surrounded by much older employees, but now that she was older, it made her feel like a preschool teacher. It also isolated her. They called Ian by his first name. Why did she deserve a moniker?

"Well yes, but Jane assured me they've separated," another voice said.

The voices drew closer and Laine eased off the desk. She didn't know if Trudy knew Ian had left her. *Trudy* had left. Why? Where? How had she done that without Laine noticing? There were so many questions without answers. Should she go after Trudy? Or listen to voices outside the window?

"Jane would know—she watches him like a mother bear protects a cub."

Of course, Jane would know Ian had moved out. Jane knew everything. She never had a swarm of unanswered questions buzzing around, immobilizing her. Jane probably knew the hour and minute of Ian's last hiccough. Jane had her eye not only on Ian's contracting diaphragm, but all his body parts. She spent more time with Ian than any other living creature, but Laine hadn't ever given Jane much thought other than making sure that Ian sent flowers on Secretary's Day and a fruit basket on her birthday. Lately, Laine's thoughts had focused on Carly, the project manager, the manager who managed to project herself into Ian's arms.

"Lindy said that since he's now officially president of Leon Homes he can leave her."

Lindy who? Laine wondered. *Know-it-all Lindy obviously doesn't know everything – he left before the transfer of power of attorney.* Her father had told her when the papers had been signed and she knew, as if she could forget, the day Ian had left. Six weeks ago, a Thursday, eight p.m. It had seemed much later because a heavy fog had hidden the stars and moon. A dark night.

Laine wondered if Lindy worked for Leon Land and if she could have Lindy fired. After a moment, when the rage flickered instead of burned, she chastised herself. *No. Not really.* She wouldn't have Lindy fired. It'd be wrong to punish her for saying out loud something that everyone else thought. Still, she'd find out who this Lindy person was and what her performance record looked like…just to satisfy curiosity… not wounded pride.

"He's not that shallow—"

"I hope not." The voice laughed. "For your sake, if you really want to take him on."

Take him on? Who says that? Laine fought back the urge to look out the window and see. *And what does that even mean?* If she, the invisible voice, took him on, would that mean Laine had already taken him off? Could he be flipped on or off like a switch? Could he really be an object to be on or off, willy-nilly, without his say so? She hated him and she hated Lindy what's-her-bucket the soon-to-be-unemployed.

"You forgot someone," the invisible voice said.

"Carly? Do you believe those rumors?"

Laine slipped off the desk and crept back to the couch. A sick feeling settled in her belly. It bubbled there, ready to revolt if forced to revisit the Carly-Ian rumors. *I need to find Trudy,* she told herself, but she stayed on the couch.

Ian pushed through the door holding a goblet of red wine in his hand. She watched him as if she'd never really seen him before. She tried to see him objectively, as if he was a stranger. She tried to not remember how he'd looked the day they first met.

She'd seen Ian weeks before she'd met him. Tall, lanky, dark hair, fair skin and blue eyes. He wore narrow-cut jeans, a button-down shirt, and a pullover sweater, and he'd looked out of place in a school of lumberjack wannabes in plaid shirts, steel-toed boots, and suspenders. The only class they shared was PE. He spent fourth period running while Mr. Teller, track coach, cheered him on. Since Laine spent fourth period avoiding Mr. Teller, hanging out, pretending to exercise, on whatever side of the field was opposite him, it seemed unlikely that she and Ian would ever meet, especially since there were fifty people in the class.

And they didn't meet—then.

But sometime in between the jumping jacks and free choice, Clyde Perkins, Kyle Evans, and Jess Leonard met up with Myles Ackerman. They pinned him beneath the bleachers and tried to suck out his eyeball. Pinning him probably wasn't too hard. Clyde and friends played football and were used to tackling much bigger players than scrawny chess captain Myles, but sucking out an eyeball proved impossible. People talked about it for almost as long as the hickey around Myles' eye lasted.

Ian hadn't interfered with the eye sucking. Like Laine, he probably didn't even know about it until after the black eye had appeared. Unlike Laine, he'd probably been running around the track, oblivious to the kicking, screaming and sucking beneath the bleachers.

What caught Laine's attention happened later, the next day, when Myles sat alone, a bruised and lonely outcast in the school auditorium, target of jokes and spit wads, and Ian, the new guy with his Boston accent and his big city flash, the star of every Thurston Middle School girl's fantasy, sat down on the chair beside Myles, talked to him, and casually draped his arm across the back of Myles' chair.

Laine knew right then and there that Ian was not only kind, but incredibly brave.

And maybe not that smart.

She discovered his intelligence later during a science competition. He had won and she had lost. But today, right here and right now, Laine determined that she was through pitting herself against Ian. Tired of losing. She stood on her ridiculous high heels and pushed past him.

"Laine?" Ian asked, the wine slopping over the rim. He passed the goblet to his other hand and vigorously shook off the wine. Of course, he wouldn't wipe his hand on his suit. He frowned at the drops splattered on the wooden floor. "Where's Trudy?"

"I don't know."

He offered her the wine.

"I gave up alcohol ten years ago." The words choked her. She tossed him the handkerchief she'd been balling in her hand and watched him use it to wipe up the spill. How could he have forgotten? She hadn't been the only participant, although, it seemed to her, that her efforts had greatly outweighed his. She'd endured temperature readings, bloodletting, peeing in a variety of receptacles and meds that made her fat and hormonally crazy; all he had to do was show up without his boxers. After the years of teetotalism and thinking that she may be pregnant or was on the verge of pregnancy, alcohol had lost its appeal. Not that it had ever had very much.

Ian turned to her, the goblet extended, but she walked away, furious with too many things to mention. She stood in the foyer, scanning the crowded room. Bette had finally begun to play. Laine saw the top of her friend's head bent over the piano keys. Trudy had disappeared. The guests mingled around the open casket on one end of the room and the table of hors d'oeuvres at the other. Flowers sat on the mantel and on every spare inch of flat, unoccupied space. It was a picture-perfect viewing. Sid would have been pleased, had he been there.

Laine went through the room, receiving condolences, accepting the kind words, murmuring politely in return. Frustration and anger mounted. As she sat down beside Bette her legs shook.

Bette's gaze flicked over Laine, concern showing. "How are you?" Bette asked her voice barely audible over the music.

Laine shrugged and blinked back tears. She wasn't supposed to get emotional. She'd brought the handkerchief to give to Ian and she realized with a start that that was exactly what had happened, although—not at all how she'd envisioned. He was supposed to be the shaking and crying person.

"Thanks again for playing," Laine whispered. "And for being here."

Bette smiled at Laine, her fingers never faltering over the keyboard. "Anything for you."

Laine patted Bette's thigh and slipped off the bench, the claustrophobic sensation returning. She needed air. Slipping through the kitchen, she moved past the caterers and stopped in the back doorway. If she drank, she would have taken a bottle. If she smoked, she'd have lit one cigarette after another, but since she did neither, she stood on the porch, watching the distant ships on the horizon. Where were they going? Could she go with them? She walked toward them. Her feet scrunched on the dead leaves lying on the cement patio. She liked the quiet echo of being alone, but then realized she wasn't alone after all.

The blonde stood beneath an apple tree in the backyard, and Laine's feeble grasp on her emotions tipped. She tried to march over to the blonde, but her heels poked into the lawn with every step. Step, sink, step sink—this didn't improve her mood. She pointed a finger at the blonde. She wanted to yell, but didn't want to be overheard, so her questions had to wait until she crossed the grass. "No one else in that room recognized the fake Sid, but you. I want to know why."

The blonde folded her arms across her chest and leaned against the tree. "How do I know him? Or, why is it his closest friends and family don't?" She laughed and it sounded cruel.

Laine pushed her curls off her face. She wasn't used to having her hair down and she didn't like the way the wind blew it into her eyes, blocking her vision. "They haven't seen him in years."

The woman sneered. "His close, personal friends—"

"Are mostly dead," Laine put in, tucking her hair behind her ears.

"Yes." She sighed and looked out over the lawn with a sad, wistful expression. The grass sloped toward the Pacific and she stared at where the ocean met the sky.

"Who are you? How did you know him?" Laine took a deep breath. "Have you seen him recently?" For most of her life her grandfather had been a womanizer, but he'd spent the last few years in quiet, solitary decline. "I don't remember seeing you around."

The blonde didn't answer, but stared out at the distant ships. Laine stepped closer, accusation lacing her voice, "He hadn't left the house for almost a decade, and then one day, he decides to *drive* downtown."

"Where he had the gall to die."

"Yes." Laine stepped around the blonde, blocking the ocean view, standing close so that they were face-to-face. "Did you have something to do with that?"

"So inconsiderate," the blonde said, lifting her gaze to meet Laine's. "Why couldn't he have just stayed at home where you could mother him to death?"

Laine opened her mouth to protest and then closed it, pinching her lips. After a beat of silence, she asked,

"What's your name?"

"The same as yours. Madeleine." She took a deep breath and blew it out, like another sigh. "Although I'd never let anyone call me Laine. It's too close to 'lame.'"

A not so unusual name, although more common in Laine's generation, or even her grandmother's generation, than this woman's, who looked to be in her mid-twenties. "Madeleine what?"

"As I said," she spoke slowly, as if Laine was a child or a foreigner and needed time to process and understand. "The same as yours-Madeleine Leon."

The eastern wind picked up and a chill crawled over Laine. "I don't believe you."

"Why not? We could be distant cousins."

"We could be, but we're not." The woman didn't flinch when Laine called her on the lie. "I know you're not who you say you are."

The blonde laughed. "How can you be so sure of that when you're unsure about everything else?"

CHAPTER 3

Ian stepped out the door and it banged behind him. He held a water bottle and wore a dark expression as he crossed the wide lawn in long strides uncompromised by grass stabbing heels. "You no longer drink, you've never taken drugs, and yet I find you out here talking to yourself."

Laine twisted to look behind her, but saw that Ian was right. The blonde had left. Laine cocked her head, listening, pretty sure that she could hear chuckling coming from behind the gate.

"I brought you a water," Ian said when he'd reached her elbow.

"Thank you." Laine took it from him, feeling irresolute. In Aunt Claire's room she'd had a surge of confidence, but it had deflated when she'd seen the Sid imposter. She had thought she could hover in the living room, near enough to Ian to not cause speculation, but distant enough to prevent communication. She'd imagined murmuring a few sentimentalities to the guests and then escaping to her home at the end of the evening. Sid's disappearance had changed some things, but it definitely did not change her desire to stay as far away from Ian as possible. She twisted off the cap and studied him as she lifted the bottle to her lips. The water stung the back of her throat.

Ian ran his fingers through his hair, a tell-tale sign she'd learned to read during their long marriage. "I've wanted to talk—"

She swallowed. "I don't think this is the time or place."

"I've been trying to call for days."

The wind kicked up and toyed with the hem of the dress, lifting it up her thighs. She tried to hold her skirt down and she saw Ian watching, his expression unreadable. "I've been busy. Sid's death—" she began.

"I know. I'm sorry," Ian interrupted. "I loved him, too."

Laine's heart wrenched. Sid had loved Ian. They'd spent hours together, poring over the company's latest project designs, their shared excitement escalating. Even at the end, Ian had been careful to share the tiniest details of the company with Sid and to be very considerate of his opinions, even though Laine suspected Sid hadn't a clue as to what was really happening in the boardroom. All his information had been filtered through Ian. She raised the water bottle to her lips and as she did, the wind lifted her dress again.

"But we're both here, right now, so—" Ian continued, reaching for her hand.

Laine stepped away, even though this took some effort because her high heels were rooted in the lawn. "This is my grandfather's viewing. The house is full of guests—"

A door creaked open and Laine turned to see Sean Marks standing on the patio, looking uncertain. He flushed. "I'm sorry, I didn't mean to interrupt. Please, ignore me." He headed for the door.

"No. Wait," Laine called after him.

Sean turned back, his expression open, smiling as he watched her losing battle with the wind and her dress. "I'm not interrupting some touchy-feely marital moment?"

"Heavens, no." She gave Ian a tight smile as she abandoned trying to keep her dress down. "He thinks we have a touchy-feely marriage."

"Touching and feeling can be nice," Ian muttered for her ears only.

Laine ignored him and called out, "Sean, do you know anything about morgues, mortuaries, or how this mix-up could have happened?" She tried to walk across the lawn with an element of grace, despite the fact that her heels kept aerating the lawn.

"Laine, don't go," Ian said under his breath, reaching for her.

"We have to find Sid," Laine told him, shaking his hand off her arm. "That should be our first priority. We can talk later."

"When? Give me a time and place." Ian folded his arms across his chest.

"You've taken enough of my time." She didn't say it loudly, because, she told herself, she didn't want to put Sean in the middle of a marital discussion. She didn't know whether Ian had heard or not.

Sean took her elbow to help her wrangle a trapped high heel out of the clutches of the lawn as she stepped onto the patio beside him.

"I know this is a viewing, not a fashion show," Sean said, nearly quoting her earlier statement. "So, I hope I'm not out of line by complimenting your dress." He cleared his throat.

He was used to seeing her on the beach in the early hours when the joggers took on the sand. "You like the dress better than my running clothes?" Laine asked, hoping Ian heard *that*.

***

"We need to powwow." Her father stood in the back doorway wearing his funeral best and a motley red face. Laine had learned years ago that *powwow* was a code word for *let's discuss the things I want you to do for me.* George generally used powwow when he wanted a one-on-one discussion. He used "council of war" when he needed to involve others, so Laine was surprised when her father propelled her into the study, left her sitting on the sofa and then returned with Ian, Trudy and Sean in tow.

Laine watched Trudy settle beside her, wondering what powwow input her step-mother could provide, other than a level of hysterics. Laine scooted over a fraction, making room for Trudy, but not enough room for Ian.

George settled himself behind Sid's desk and looked up at Ian sitting on the window sill and then over to Sean leaning against the wall. Sean didn't look out of place or ill at ease in this impromptu family gathering, but Laine wondered if he knew why he'd been included, because she didn't.

George sighed. "Okay. First thing. We don't want anyone to know about this mix-up."

Trudy asked, "What did the police say?"

"This isn't a police matter," George said. Laine

wondered if that was a direct quote or something he'd picked up from watching a television police procedural.

"A decedent has merely sentimental value—" he continued.

Yes, clearly he was quoting someone, because "decedent" was a new vocabulary word that he must have picked up at either his visit to the mortuary or his chat with the police.

"We need to sweep this incident under the rug quickly and quietly without causing a stir or embarrassment for the family and firm," George said.

Laine stared at her father, wondering if she'd heard him correctly. He'd never minded stirring up embarrassment for the family or firm before.

"Hopefully, this will all be a bad dream by tomorrow." Trudy sniffed and then began to cry. Ian reached over and pressed Laine's handkerchief into Trudy's hand. She used it to dab her tears.

"What happens tomorrow?" Laine asked.

"After the memorial." Her father nodded.

Laine sat up straight. "Wait. You're not suggesting that we go ahead with cremation, are you?"

George looked out the window and Laine glanced at everyone else in the room, trying to read their expressions.

Trudy sniffled into her handkerchief. Sean studied his shoes. Only Ian met her gaze.

"We can't have him cremated," Laine said, feeling sick. "Whoever he is, he doesn't belong to us. He needs to go back to the mortuary so they can return him to his family."

"That doesn't even make sense," Trudy said. "He can't be returned to his family. He's dead."

"We have to return his body."

"His body is just an empty shell—" Trudy began. "He is not disgraced or diminished by cremation."

When had Trudy become metaphysical? "I'm not arguing against cremation—I'm just saying we can't cremate someone we don't know."

"Now, I've been giving this some thought." George pressed his palms together before folding them and lifting his index fingers. "While it's true that this is an unusual situation, there's no need to blow it out of proportion."

"Blow it out of proportion" was another of George's codes for "let's not do anything that doesn't need doing."

"No, no, no, no!" the blonde huffed. When had she entered the room and who had invited her? She stood just left of Sean, her hands on her hips and her eyebrows lowered in a scowl. "You have to find Sid!"

Laine's gaze swiveled around the room, watching the others for some sort of reaction. No one flinched or even looked in the blonde's direction. Laine put her fingers to her temples and closed her eyes. When she opened them, the blonde was still glaring at her.

You're out here talking to yourself, Ian had said earlier. And then in the driveway, the catering kid hadn't seen the blonde either. Could it be possible that no one else saw her? *Could I be having a breakdown?* Laine wondered, staring at the Madeleine Leon imposter. Laine pressed her fingers to her wrist, feeling her pulse. It raced beneath her touch. Could a racing heart be linked to mental illness? What *were* the signs of mental illness?

"I'm sorry," Sean said, shaking his head.

Laine's mind scrambled. Obviously, so confused at the reaction, or rather the non-reaction of the others in the room to the blonde, she'd missed a beat of the conversation.

"I agree with Laine," Sean said. "I think it'd be morally irresponsible not to try and track down this man's family. Besides, I'm not a mortician."

George stood and pointed his finger at Sean. "But you are his doctor."

Sean lifted his hands and shrugged. "What do you

expect me to do?"

"Have him cremated, of course," George pronounced, looking firm.

"Stop it!" Laine stood up, only slightly wavering on her high heels. "We can't just cremate a stranger!" Her eyes locked with the woman who nodded in agreement.

"I thought the mortuary was taking care of that," Trudy said, her gaze moving between Sean and George.

"They've decided to go in a different direction," George said, using new code words, ones that probably meant that the mortician agreed with Sean and refused to burn a body without the family's written permission. "So, it's up to you." He looked pointedly at Sean.

"We can't be having this conversation," Laine put in. Her father ignored her, but Sean agreed.

He moved to the center of the room, standing slightly behind Laine, as if providing back up. "I cannot cremate that body. For one thing, I don't have access to crematorium—"

George jabbed his finger in Sean's direction. "You were Sid's doctor, he was under your care, you were responsible for his health and wellbeing." The threat of a malpractice suit passed between the two men.

"Oh for heaven's sake," Laine said, folding her arms

across her chest. "Sid was ninety-seven years old and on the day he died he'd suddenly taken a yen to take the Porsche for a spin. We all know downtown traffic can kill much younger, healthier people."

"But he didn't die in a car accident." George scowled, indicating that Sid's untimely death was clearly Sean's fault. "The car was safely parked on the side of the road."

"Why are you so anxious to cremate this unknown man?" Laine asked.

Her father gave her hostile look and Laine knew the answer to her question. If they went ahead with the cremation, life could resume without hiccoughs and complications.

"Where is Grandpa Sid?" Laine asked.

"He's dead, Lainey," Trudy said.

"You have to find Sid!" The blonde paced beside Sean, her shoes clacking on the wooden floor.

"Who *are* you?" Laine demanded, her voice high and loud.

Sean looked as if she'd slapped him. "I'm on your side," he said.

Laine pressed her hand over her eyes, blocking out the vision, the apparition, the hallucination—the whatever she was. When Laine opened her eyes, the blonde was still pacing. She jerked her head at Sean. "We need him to take us to the hospital."

No one else could see her. No one else heard her.

Laine stammered, "I'm sorry, Sean. That didn't come out right. What I meant to say—" she swallowed. "What I meant to ask is *who* should we call?"

Sean didn't look mollified. "About what?"

"About returning the —" she waved her arm in the direction of the casket in the next room. "The person in there to his family."

"And finding Sid!" The blonde added.

"And finding Sid," Laine parroted, deciding that when entertaining angry delusions it would probably be best to just humor them, smile and agree with everything they said.

George consulted his Rolex. "We have about an hour until this charade ends. I suggest we all stiffen our spines and go out there and face the music."

He might say "face the music," but facing music had never been George's forte. He was more of a dancer—a skater, really. He tended to skate through life to a polka tune, like the music played at the roller-rink. Maybe that's why Laine had taken up the organ; she'd been the perfect accompaniment to her father's freewheeling lifestyle. He skated; she planned, organized, and tidied up. She'd even had the sense and decency to marry someone to run the company.

Today her accompaniment stopped.

"When the last of the guests have gone, we'll meet back here." George looked at Ian and Sean.

Laine didn't wait to hear the other's responses, but slipped out the door, took the hall to the back stairs, and ran to Aunt Claire's room. She closed the door and leaned against it, breathing heavily. Her thoughts spun.

The blonde, Madeleine—no one else could see her; no one else heard her. So the question wasn't just *who* was she, but also *what* was she. A ghost? She seemed tangible enough. Tangible enough to throw dirt. Weren't ghosts supposed to float through walls, moaning? Was there a handbook for proper ghostly behavior? Laine hadn't ever read ghost stories, other than the occasional Edgar Allen Poe assigned in a literature class. She didn't like horror films, other than *Buffy the Vampire Slayer*, and that didn't really count. She hadn't even ever watched *The Ghost Whisperer.*

But those were all fiction. Not real.

CHAPTER 4

Laine kicked off her shoes and after tossing the pillows and the Cabbage Patch doll to the floor, she lay down on the bed and closed her eyes. Madeleine also wasn't real. She was as fictional as The Tell-Tale Heart or a character on The X-Files. *I'm having a breakdown,* Laine reasoned, and she couldn't decide whether this thought comforted or frightened her. She tried to take deep, calming breaths. Sweat rolled off her forehead.

Laine bounced off the bed, went to the window, and pushed it open. The hot east wind blew in, circled the room. She lay back down, closed her eyes, and startled when the window banged shut. Peeking one eye open, she debated on whether it was worth the bother of standing, crossing the room, reopening the window, and trying to find some way to prop it open.

Guillotine windows, Ian had called them when, as newlyweds, they had occasionally house-sat for her grandfather. Laine closed her eyes and remained on the bed, blocking the memories of being a newlywed and trying out every possible unoccupied bed, sofa, or swimming pool.

Before sex had become a means to an end. An unfruitful end.

"Whatchya doing in here?"

"You are not real, so I don't have to talk to you," Laine said, without stirring.

"Whatchya mean, I'm not real?"

Laine opened her eyes, groaned, and lifted to her elbows to address Helene, her grandfather's longtime housekeeper. "I'm sorry, Helene. I thought you were someone else." Typically, Helene wore peasant skirts and bright cardigans. Her clothes tended to have a lot of pockets, usually bulging with stuff she picked up as she cleaned. She'd always reminded Laine of a human piece of Velcro, collecting debris as she went from room to room. She'd been her grandfather's housekeeper, cook, and later, his nurse, for nearly thirty years and he had left her an extraordinarily generous pension in his will. Although her blonde hair was now streaked with gray, she still had a Swedish beauty that was set off by her stiff black dress.

"You gonna wish I was make-believe." Helene sniffed, folded her arms across her chest, and looked around the room. "Because I'm real and mad. Real mad."

Laine followed Helene's gaze to the suit lying

crumpled in front of the closet door, the shoes, both the flats and the heels, in the middle of the floor, and the Cabbage Patch doll sitting on the small mountain of pillows. "I'm sorry. I'll clean it up. I promise. I'm just… well, I'm trying to take a nap."

Helene stepped closer, her eyes narrowed into suspicious slits. "You don't take naps. You're the most not-napping person in Seattle—maybe all of Washington. And you also don't talk to fictional folk. And I no ever see you make such a mess."

"Today, I'm a mess, okay? And I didn't say this person was fictional." Laine sighed. "This person isn't *real,* like when you say, 'get real.'" She closed her eyes, shutting out Helene's curiosity.

"What person? Who is this not real person?" When Laine didn't answer, Helene continued. "I never heard you say 'get real.' Not once in your whole lifetime. Other folks might say 'get real,' but not you."

Laine didn't budge. "I already told you I'm not feeling like myself today."

"Well, whose-ever you feeling like, that person better get off her hinny and get downstairs where's everybody's talking." Helene waited a small beat of silence before she added, "If you don't, I'll go and get Ian."

Laine sat up with and narrowed her eyes. Helene had always loved Ian.

Helene lowered her eyebrows and pointed her finger at Laine, "You need to get out there and show those people you're not cowed by him."

"I am not cowed… actually, I'm stressed."

"You're never stressed."

Laine flopped back on to the bed and covered her eyes with her arm. "Well, today I am."

"I don't believe it."

Laine could feel Helene staring at her, but she refused to open her eyes.

"I'm going to bring you some food. You're looking like a dead bird."

"Thank you for the compliment, but please, do *not* bring me food."

"I'm not talking about some nice plump chicken or goose. You're looking like some scrawny, knobby kneed bird." Helene took a deep breath and although Laine couldn't see her, she was quite sure that Helene was frowning, her ample arms folded across her chest. "I'm getting you some soup."

Helene used food medicinally. She thought she could properly diagnose every mood and prescribe the needed caloric remedy. Angry, hot-headed? Helene would serve ice cream. Lazy, unmotivated? Red-hot chili. Anxious? Soup.

Laine had grown up on soup.

"It's a hundred and ten degrees in this room. I don't want soup," Laine didn't open her eyes. She didn't want any more soup. Ever. "Besides, you're not working. You're supposed to be a guest. What made you come up here anyway?"

"I heard the window slam and I didn't like it."

Sid had always said he didn't need a watch dog because he had Helene and she was twice as scary as any Doberman. "Well, you can go back downstairs." Laine tried to sound dismissive and authoritative.

Helene huffed. "I'm bringing you some soup."

"I won't eat it," Laine muttered when Helene walked out the door.

Helene's food prescription failed for the first time after Mrs. Bartlett's seventh grade English class. Laine had returned from school that afternoon shaking in anger. Helene could usually diagnosis the day and prescribe the perfect after-school snack with remarkable accuracy, but the day Ian stole her thesis sentence, no amount of ice cream could calm her down.

They'd been studying American poetry and Laine had fallen in love with the works of Robert Frost. She'd chosen the poem *Choose Something Like a Star* for her paper and had been so in love with the imagery that she'd started work on it, just a few jotted sentences, during math class while Mr. Fergus yammered about lengths, volumes, and spheres.

After class, books tucked under arm, Laine walked with Marlene across the quad. Lindsey Dolan, in an effort to escape the clutches of Clyde Newton, had bumped Laine from behind, making Laine dropped her books. Texts scattered across the lawn. Her notebook landed on its spine and papers fluttered away in the wind. Marlene, Lindsey and even Clyde, in an uncharacteristic stint of chivalry, chased the papers, and most were retrieved and returned to the notebook, but the wind carried a few away. Including her paper on *Choose Something Like a Star.*

Frost is begging the star to speak to him, Laine had written. Sitting at her desk, clutching the returned paper bearing the giant red A, she knew she should be pleased, but all her pleasure faded when Mrs. Bartlette asked Ian to stand and read his *excellent* paper.

"The narrator is asking for the star's response," Ian had read.

Laine had turned to Marlene. "He stole my paper!" she whispered.

"Shh," Marlene waved her hand at Laine, silencing her. Laine seethed, watching Marlene, her traitorous friend, moon over Ian, who might be sexy-cute, but was also, quite clearly, a literary cheat.

No amount of ice cream could calm her down, not even mint chocolate chip, a surefire remedy for most of life's ills. She'd later learn that when it came to Ian, food wasn't the answer. Helene had yet to learn this powerful lesson and thirty years later, Laine suspected that she never would.She squeezed her eyes tightly, holding back tears. She couldn't imagine her life without Helene.

"I brought you cookies."

Cookies? Helene never brought cookies. Laine opened her eyes and propped up onto her elbows. "You."

"Who did you expect?" Madeleine asked.

"I didn't expect you to bring me cookies." Laine dropped back down on the bed and put her arm over her face. "Another dirt clod, maybe, but not cookies."

"Well, I did. I thought if I sweetened you up I might be able to coax you out of this room and to the mortuary."

"Oh yeah, that's solid reasoning. Everyone gets an urge to visit the mortuary after eating a few macaroons."

"Macaroons? Now where you'd get those and how come they're lying on Miss Claire's clean comforter?"

At the sound of Helene's voice, Laine's eyes few open and she bolted upright. Sure enough, lying beside her were the macaroons. Her gaze darted from the cookies, to Helene and then to the blonde.

"She can't hear or see me," Madeleine sighed. "Only you get that privilege."

"Lucky me," Laine said.

"That's right, girl, and you best start believing it and thanking your stars!" Helene placed the tray holding a bowl of soup and a bread roll on the dresser with a solid thunk. "You're one spoiled child."

"You've spoiled me, Helene," Laine said, her voice soft. She lay back down and closed her eyes. "I'm lucky because of you, but that still doesn't mean I'm going to eat that soup."

"That's right," the blonde said, coming over and sitting down on the bed beside Laine. The mattress shifted beneath her weight. "We don't have time for soup. We have to find Sid."

"Helene," Laine said, her voice low. "Do you think I could be having a breakdown?"

Helene padded over. Laine, with her eyes still closed,

heard her and felt the bed depress as Helene sat down beside her and began to rub her foot.

Laine's eyes flew open. Helene sat where Madeleine had been sitting. Had Helene sat on her? No, the blonde had moved to the rocking chair, which rocked silently as if driven by the breeze. Laine wondered if Helene would notice.

"Chicken, no one would blame you if you started screaming and throwing a thousand conniptions in a million directions what with all you going through right now." She stood and pulled Laine's feet to the edge of the bed. "But sometimes, even if you think you're going crazy and belting out loony tunes in your head, you still gotta get up and get out there."

"She's right." The blonde left the rocking chair and began pacing the room. "We've got to get out and look for Sid!"

Laine, despite her feet being hauled around, didn't budge and reclosed her eyes. "Seriously, I think I'm losing it. Hearing voices, seeing things—maybe you should go and get Dr. Marks. He could prescribe me something. Maybe a sleeping pill." She peeked open an eye, and to her horror she saw Madeleine whispering in Helene's ear.

"That's a very bad idea," Helene said, pulling on

Laine's feet.

"What did you just say to her?" Laine sat up.

Helene stopped tugging and frowned at Laine. "Why you talking to yourself in the third person?"

"I'm not right in the head, Helene," Laine stuttered. "Really, I need Dr. Marks."

Helene scowled while the blonde whispered in her ear. "I'll go get him, but I'm not going to let him give you one little pill." She turned toward the door, stiff with indignation.

"That's fine," Laine said to Helene's retreating back, "because what I want, what I need, are several big pills."

She waited for the door to close before she scooted so that her legs hung over the side of the bed. "What did you do to her?"

"What are you talking about?" The blonde folded her arms across her chest and looked innocent.

"Just then. You did something, you said something to her."

The blonde cocked her head. "I thought I wasn't real."

Laine pointed her finger. "You said something to make her forget about the soup. She never would have left without making me eat if you hadn't said something to influence her."

The blonde laughed. "You're giving me too much credit."

Laine shook her head. "No, I don't think so." She studied Madeleine. What was she—ghost, demon, lost soul, or wraith? Should Laine brush up on paranormal activity? Was this Madeleine Leon dangerous, or nonexistent? If she was a figment of imagination, then Laine really didn't have anything to fear. She'd never had a wild imagination before. As a child, she hadn't had an imaginary friend and she hadn't created fantasy worlds, and so it seemed unlikely to her that at this point in her life she'd start with a cookie-bearing, cranky, twenty-something woman.

Of all the Madeleine descriptions that came to mind, Laine preferred nonexistent. No one else could see or hear Madeleine, but Helene *had* seen the cookies. Madeleine had brought them and Helene had seen them. The cookies seemed to be the only concrete evidence of Madeleine's existence. Laine picked up a macaroon and bit into it. It tasted dry and crumbly.

Madeleine watched her. She had her arms folded across her chest and impatience stamped on her face.

Laine glared back at her and took another bite of the cookie. It hurt to swallow the scratchy macaroon but she continued to eat only because she suspected it annoyed

Madeleine.

The door opened and Helene trooped into the room. Sean followed, carrying a bottle of wine and two goblets.

Laine brushed the cookie crumbs off her dress and said, "I want pills. Lots and lots of pills."

Sean laughed as he set the goblets and wine down on the dresser. "You must know I don't carry around an arsenal of drugs." He poured the red wine.

"Pity," Laine murmured, accepting the goblet Sean offered. She stared down into the red wine. Could it help ease her anxiety? She preferred wine to soup. Slowly she raised the glass to her lips. How much would it take for her to be drunk? She'd never been drunk before and she wondered how that complete loss of control would feel. Maybe if she passed out she'd wake and find Madeleine gone.

"She doesn't need drugs—she needs something nourishing," Helene fussed. "Look at her. She's scrawny."

Laine met Sean's eyes over the glass. "Helene is good for my ego. She likes to keep it small and malleable." The alcohol burned. It'd been so long since she'd had anything to drink. The alcohol swam to her head.

Madeleine frowned at her as she took another sip.

Sean came and sat beside her. Gravity slid her toward

him, the wine sloshing in her glass. For a moment, she brushed against him and then she scooted a fraction away.

"What's wrong?" Sean asked, smiling into her eyes. "Tell me why you think you need lots of pills."

Laine took another swallow of wine, because Sean gave a whole new meaning to bedside manner. *Maybe I need hugs, not drugs,* she thought. The wine warmed her belly and softened the edges of everything in the room—Helene's concern, Madeleine's glower and Ian's surprise.

Ian—when had he joined them? Laine pulled away from Sean's warmth.

"Your father wants to go to the mortuary," Ian said, his gaze traveling from her to Sean, to the bottle on the night stand and then to the empty wine glass in her hand.

When Laine met his eyes, he cleared his throat. "He's expecting us to accompany him."

"You have to go," Madeleine said, stepping forward. "We have to find Sid."

Laine shook her head. It felt maybe only a little fuzzy; she was still a long way from being drunk. "No."

Sean put his hand on her knee. "Laine's not feeling well."

A small flush tinged Ian's neck. The deepening red contrasted with his white shirt and dark hair. Laine stood.

She didn't want Sean speaking for her and she didn't want him, or anyone, touching her. "I'm not going," she said, swaying slightly on her feet. She went to the window and lifted it. The sun had disappeared beneath the horizon and the sky had turned to indigo. The cars that had lined the street were mostly gone. The guests had left—only the catering van remained. She'd missed most of her grandfather's viewing. She'd spent it hiding in her aunt's room. What sort of person does that?

Ian frowned and picked up the bottle on the dresser. His gaze went to Sean's untouched glass and then back to the mostly empty bottle. Laine considered telling him that she'd only had one glass, but then decided it wasn't any of his business. She had stopped being his business the moment he'd walked out their door.

"We have to find Sid," Madeleine yelled. Laine decided that if she had to be haunted, she'd rather be haunted by a quiet, "woe is me," moaning sort of ghost and not this demanding, noisy person. Apparition or whatever.

"I'm not going," Laine said, raising her voice and stumbling toward the adjoining bathroom. She closed the door on them all and locked it with a click. Seconds later, she bent over the commode and vomited the wine and macaroons into the toilet. She wasn't drunk—or if she was, this wasn't at all what she'd had in mind. She wanted oblivion and all she got was smelly nausea. Curling on the floor, she laid her head on a fuzzy white bath mat.

"She said she wasn't feeling well." She heard Sean say through the wall.

"Laine, let me in." Helene knocked on the door.

"Go away." She waited for Helene to say something else. When that didn't happen, Laine moaned, wishing that she could melt into the tile and become one with the grout.

***

By the time Laine felt well enough to pull herself away from the comfort of the cold, hard tile, the house was dark and still. Creeping from first the bathroom and then the bedroom, Laine suspected she was alone in the house, except, perhaps, for the Grandpa Sid look-a-like. She turned on the lights in the hall and although the light chased away the darkness, it didn't lighten the gloom. Laine went down the stairs, wondering why she felt so unsure and off-balance. She knew Sid's house as well, if not better, than her own. After her mother died, she'd spent her afternoons and sometimes her evenings here in the company of Helene and a miniature Schnauzer named Kitty. She'd tagged after Helene and Kitty had tagged after her. When her father collected her, as he usually remembered to do, she'd always gone home with him somewhat reluctantly.

Although Kitty had been gone for years, sometimes Laine still missed her, the brush of her fur against her legs, her cold nose pressing against her calf. Laine wished she were here now. Just the jingle of the dog's tags would help ease the oppressive quiet. Laine flipped on the light switch in the kitchen. The caterers had cleaned every surface, and for an indefinable reason, this bothered her.

Laine wandered into the living room. The furniture had been pushed aside to make space for the casket. The mortuary must have retrieved Mr.-Whomever-He-Was, but the furniture gaped around the empty space where his casket had been. Grateful that she'd finally found something useful to do, Laine tried to put the furniture back into its customary positions. The chairs scooted easily enough, but the sofa wouldn't budge. She gripped the sofa's arm, grunted and shoved, but it barely moved. Sitting with her feet braced against the wall and her back against the sofa, she pushed. It threatened to tip over.

She stood up and looked at the mess. Her efforts had only made the room more catawampus. *Like my life,* she thought. No matter how hard she'd tried, things just got messier.

Depressed, she thought about going home to another

empty house, but then an idea struck and she headed for the attic. She hadn't been up there for years, and she wondered if anyone else had—certainly not her grandfather, and probably not Helene. Her footsteps echoed in the tiny stairwell. She pushed open the door.

Moonlight filtered weakly through the dormer windows. Damp and moldy, the attic's mildew aggravated her allergies. As a child, she had been terrified of the roar of the house fan, and leery of the dark, cobwebbed corners, and as an adult she was overwhelmed by the flotsam of a family she had never really known. Someone would have to clean out the attic, and that someone would probably have to be her. She supposed she could hire someone to haul it away, but the thought of relegating it all to the city dump left her feeling hollow and empty. These were things that someone in her family, for whatever reason, had chosen to keep. She didn't know the sentimental value, because there were so many members of her family she didn't know— her mother, her mother's family, her grandmother.

Spider webs draped over the exposed beams and dust, thick and hairy, covered boxes, abandoned toys and her father's athletic trophies. She wondered if she and her father would have been closer if she'd shared his passion for sports.

Dingy sheets covered mounds of what could be furniture. She peeked beneath a sheet and found a couch that had once belonged in the den. It still had Kitty's fur clinging to its cushions. Dust flew as she dropped the sheet back in place and she bit back a sneeze.

Her father wasn't a sentimental man and her memories of her mother were as vague and opaque as the dusty windows. Like herself, both of her parents had been only children. Perhaps that's why Ian and his enormous Catholic family had appealed to her. Maybe that's why she'd wanted, so very badly, a house full of children of her own.

Her eyes watered and she blinked away the dust. Through her tears she spotted a trunk beside a haphazardly stacked pile of boxes. She made her way toward it, maneuvering through towers of books, magazines, and old newspapers. Squatting beside the trunk, she lifted open the lid. The smell of lemon mixed with ammonia whooshed out at her. A blue dress lay on top, its material brittle with age, the lace collar yellowed and tattered. Beneath the dress, a pair of red high heels, a clutch purse made of beads—some broken, some missing—and a photo album of cracked and stained leather. Gingerly, Laine lifted it out and opened it.

The blonde, Madeleine Leon, stared at her over a

wedding bouquet. A very young Grandpa Sid stood beside her, looking flushed and happy in his tuxedo.

CHAPTER 5

A car pulled into the driveway. An engine cut, doors slammed, headlights blinked off and the car alarm beeped. The mortuary posse had returned. Laine clutched the photo album to her chest, stood, and then kicked the trunk shut. If she stayed in the attic, it was possible that they would think she'd gone home. She couldn't face them. Not Ian, not her father, and not even harmless, silly Trudy.

The back door opened and closed. Voices, muted and unintelligible floated up the stairway. Would they see the attic light? Walking as softly as possible so as not to cause the floorboards to creak, she went to the light and pulled the chain. The light disappeared and immediately Laine felt safer in the dark.

Louder voices. The back door opened, and then closed again. Quiet filled the house. Laine stood stock-still in the center of the attic, emotions competing. She'd wanted to be left alone, and yet—why hadn't they looked for her? Why hadn't anyone asked how she was feeling? Wouldn't at least her father offer her a ride home? Not that any of them had known she'd walked, but still.

Stock-still—that's a funny phrase. What does it mean? Still as a corn stock? Or is it stalk, like to hunt? She remembered a favorite fairy tale Helene used to tell her about gnomes that once caught in the daylight would stand stock-still, eyes wide open, unmoving for years until their eventual deaths. She chided herself for being silly. She wasn't a gnome. Just because everyone she'd ever loved had left had her standing in the attic, that didn't mean she had to stay. *Is the wine muddling my thoughts?* she wondered and put her hand on her forehead as if through skin and skull she could determine her mental capacity.

Tucking the photo album under her arm, she padded down the stairs. The Madeleine that she'd met earlier might not be real, but the Madeleine who had married her grandfather had been and Laine determined to get to know her through any means possible. She'd take the album now, but she promised herself she'd come back and scour the attic for anything and everything she could find about the family she didn't know.

The attic door had an outline of light. Someone had left the light on in the hall. Who? Questions tumbled in her head. Had she turned on the lights before going into the attic? No. It'd been early evening, not yet dark. Someone had turned on the lights and had left them on.

Laine opened the door. Ian stood on the other side, holding her shoes.

It wasn't their wedding day, or their first glance, or even their first kiss, although, of course, she remembered those moments as well, that had caught and held in Laine's mind as the moment that she *knew*. The moment that she knew she was standing on the stairs of the humanities building. Snow lay on the ground, and the steel-blue sky matched Ian's eyes. He hadn't known her schedule, but he'd known most of her classes were held in the humanities building, and he'd waited for her.

During her sophomore year in college, she and Ian had drifted apart. She'd immersed herself in literature; he'd pursued a business degree. She was boring—he was money driven. He'd joined the Silver Club, a team of students who oversaw and managed an investment fund endowed by a group of wealthy patrons. He had expected her to attend the social functions thrown by the business faculty and their friends—an endless round of dinners, luncheons, and box-seats at sporting events. She wanted him to go to poetry readings. Not that she actually expected him to discuss Dickinson, but if she had to go to the US Open and chit chat with overweight businessmen who only talked of the bottom dollar, then he could sit in smoke filled rooms and listen to poems about dying cats.

He stopped calling. She didn't call him. She heard he
was dating a blonde with a red Camaro convertible, "a
pretty filly in a pony car," her friend Chase had said. Chase
had made the blonde filly sound petty and insignificant, but
despite her new friends, despite Chase's hot breathy kisses,
Ian's riding around with the girl in the pony car had hurt.

The business building, a cement and glass edifice, sat
on the northwest corner of campus. The humanities
building—old, brick, with crumbling cement steps—was
near the president's house, in the oldest section of campus.
Laine never went to the business building, and as far as she
knew, Ian didn't come to what she considered her side of
the campus.

And then one snowy day near the end of the fall
semester, she'd left the humanities building and found Ian
standing on the steps. He had his hands in his pockets; he
looked unsure. He caught and held her gaze and then
slowly, he began to speak.

"I've written you a poem. It's not long,
Although it's not short on meaning,
Because it's about how you belong
With me-e-e."

Her lips twitched and then so did his.

"That was—" she began.

"Awful?" he finished for her, smiling. "I know. Wait, I'm not done." He cleared his throat, waiting for a group of girls in sweaters and mittens to pass before he started again.

"I miss you in the springtime,

 I miss you in the fall,

I miss you in-between times

And in the—"

A group of boys in their leather jackets stopped to watch and listen, and Laine flushed with embarrassment. Grabbing Ian's hand she pulled him off the steps. "Please, stop," she said.

Ian shook his head. "No, Lainey, there's more. I worked on this a really long time—the least you can do is listen."

Laine put her finger on his lips. "Would you rather kiss?" she asked, knowing his answer. He hadn't really changed in all the years she'd known him. He was still remarkably like the fourteen year old boy she'd fallen in love with, despite his new affair with suits, ties and briefcases.

He nodded and pulled her to the far side of the building where there were fewer spectators or students.

"I'm not good with words," he said after he'd kissed

her and messed up her hair. "I'm good with numbers. You're good with words. That's why I need you. We're better together—or at least, I'm better with than without you."

And at that moment, the moment that she knew, she had a sudden brief and fleeting image of him as an old man and she knew that she would love him, the older Ian, much, much more than she loved him then.

Standing in the hall, the light glaring in her eyes, the smell of vomit on her breath, mildew and must clinging to her aunt's dress, she saw him once again as that college kid with blue eyes that matched a near-winter sky, and something inside her turned icy.

"How are you feeling?" he asked.

So much better without you, she thought, shrugging, struggling to dismiss all those past feelings that so often threatened to overwhelm her. Yes, Ian would grow old and so would she, and yes it would be somewhat simultaneously, but that didn't mean they had to do it together. "What happened at the mortuary?" she asked.

"I'll tell you on the ride home," he said. "I assume you walked."

He knew her so well. He said "home" so easily, as if he still lived there. His familiarity made her clench her teeth. As she walked beside him, she clasped her hands so tightly that they ached by the time they reached his car. He opened the door for her and she was surprised, although she told herself that she shouldn't have been, to find Madeleine sitting in the back seat with her arms folded and her mouth turned into a frown.

"What are you doing here?" Laine asked, settling into the car.

"Looking for you," Ian said, as he handed her the shoes and closed her door.

"Looking for Sid," Madeleine added.

Laine buckled her seat-belt and looked straight ahead when Ian climbed in beside her. His nearness felt familiar, comfortable, and this bothered her. She wanted to hold on to her anger and use it as a weapon against him. Turning the shoes in her hand, she considered the spiky heels and wondered what sort of damage they could cause. Take out an eye? Puncture skin?

"He wasn't there," Madeleine said, looking out the window at the star studded sky.

"What did the mortuary say?" Laine asked, as if the brick and mortar building had the power of speech. Keeping her eyes on the road, Laine refused to look at Madeleine.

"It sounds bizarre," Ian began.

"Lunatics," Madeleine muttered.

"But I guess misplacing a body isn't all that uncommon," Ian continued. "It's just a matter of human error."

"Well, that goes without saying," Madeleine said, sounding sulky.

"Okay, but how?" Laine didn't try to mask her impatience.

"When someone dies at the hospital, they assign identification tags. The body then travels from the hospital, to the morgue and then to the mortuary. At any time, the tags could be misplaced or lost. The mortician said it's not that rare. In fact, there's a mortuary in Vancouver where the mortician doesn't use any paper-work at all."

"Morticians have to be a little insane to do what they do," Madeleine said.

"The bodies don't really have any value, other than sentimental," Ian said.

"The living think they're so clever, but they're clueless," Madeleine said.

Laine put her hand to her temple, feeling crazy, not even a smidgen clever, and very clueless.

"We have to *find* him," Madeleine said.

"What if we don't?" Laine asked.

Ian glanced at her. "Don't what?"

"Don't find him? Would that be so bad?"

Ian shrugged.

Madeleine began to curse. "We have to find him! He must be found! We can't let him wander the earth, unfettered!"

"Unfettered?" Laine repeated.

"Unfettered?" Ian looked over at her as he pulled into the driveway. He touched the remote on the console and the garage door rolled up. It bothered her that he still had such an easy access to their home. Her home.

"I'm feeling unfettered…" Laine said.

"Unfettered," Ian murmured as he cut the engine.

"Yes," Laine said sharply. She'd defend her word choice if she needed to.

Ian nodded. He stared into the dark garage, hesitant. "I told Gemma you'd be taking some time off."

"You did what?" Laine had her hand on the door, ready to leave, but this news stopped her.

"I thought," he sounded sheepish, "you might appreciate some time away from the demands—"

"How could you?" Anger filled Laine. "You know this is the busiest season for the foundation. The masquerade ball is only a few weeks away!"

"Exactly." Ian gripped the steering wheel. "You don't need that right now. You're coming apart, Laine."

"He's exactly right, you know," Madeleine chimed in from the back seat.

She thought about not returning to the office and a knot inside her chest lessened a fraction. The invisible weight pushing her down eased slightly, but she still held onto her anger. She needed to use it as a protective weapon. "How could you be so," she searched for the word, "presumptuous?"

"You work too much," Ian began.

"How would you know? We haven't spoken in weeks."

"Whose fault is that?" Ian's voice turned hard. "And just because you're not talking to me doesn't mean there aren't others talking about you."

She snorted and it sounded ugly and guttural. "That's rich. You tell me not to listen to the office gossip!"

"What you saw with Carly—" Ian said, his voice strangled.

"I know what I saw, Ian."

"No, you don't."

"And I know what I heard."

"What you heard isn't true." He looked at her hard. "It kills me that you'd believe the office gossip and not me."

"There wouldn't be office gossip if there wasn't something to say."

"You know that's not true. You know people will always find something to say."

"You get to listen to the office gossip, but I don't." She raised her eyebrows at him. "I know you could kill the gossip." *You don't have to work with Carly,* she thought, but did not say. There were so many things she kept inside and replayed to over and over. Carly was in love with Ian.

"Her dog had just died!"

And that was why Laine found Carly wrapped up in Ian's arms. That hurt, too. A lot. But the inner light that filled Ian whenever he was around Carly's—that hurt the most.

"How many more poodles have to die before she makes it back into your arms?" Laine climbed from the car and slammed the door.

"My arms have been pretty empty lately, Laine." Ian followed her into the garage. "Lainey, stop."

She paused at the door leading to the house and then hit the alarm. Sirens and the sound of barking dogs filled the air. She yelled at him above the noise. "Security will be here in seven minutes."

"That's very mature, Laine. Type in the code," he called out.

She placed her hand over the flashing light. "Not until you're in the car." Several lights went on in the previously dark, quiet houses across the street.

Ian looked like he wanted to argue, but after a moment of frowning at her, he got into his car.

Madeleine suddenly appeared at her side with sigh. "I thought he'd never leave."

Laine sniffed, turned off the alarm, and went into the house and flipped on lights. The house seemed empty and barren until Madeleine spoke. "Now, how are we going to find Sid?"

Laine scooped up Cheshire, who had come to wrap herself around her ankles. Cheshire nestled against Laine's chest. "*We* are not going to find Sid," Laine said, as she stroked the cat's fur and headed toward the bedroom.

Madeleine trailed after her. "We have to find him."

"No, *we* don't. I do, and I don't need you to help me." Laine went to the closet, set Cheshire down on a slipper chair, stepped out of the dress, and threw on a Calvin and Hobbs T-shirt. She kept her back turned so she didn't have to face Ian's closet doors. There were gaping holes in the line of suits and dress shirts, a testament of what he had chosen to take and what he'd left behind. His best suits and his silk ties, gone. His hiking boots had stayed as had the down jacket and wool overcoat. Had he left his winter gear because he thought he'd be back before the weather turned?

"I don't need anyone." Laine sucked in a ragged breath, although she did wonder why she was the only one upset about Sid's missing body. Other than Madeleine. "Since you're obviously a figment of my deranged imagination, I don't have to listen to you." She emphasized her words by closing the bathroom door and clicking the lock. When she'd finished brushing her teeth, she found Madeleine sitting on the bed with Cheshire on her lap. The traitor purred as Madeleine stroked him.

Laine stopped in the middle of the room. "He sees you."

Madeleine lifted her hand from the cat's fur and Cheshire gave Laine an accusatory look. "Yes, apparently so."

"Why?"

Madeleine shrugged. "I'm not sure."

"You're my grandmother."

"Yes."

"This is very bizarre," Laine said. "I want you to know

I'd be much nicer if I didn't think you are just my own craziness."

Madeleine smiled.

Laine had to remind herself that she couldn't be too friendly or encourage her to stay— Madeleine wasn't real. She *looked* real. "How did you bring the cookies upstairs this afternoon?"

Madeleine bit back a laugh. "I carried them. Of all the questions you could ask about the after life, you choose to discuss cookies?"

"Well, what did everyone think when they saw cookies floating by?"

Madeleine shook her head, her smile growing faint. "Who cares?"

"But don't you think someone would notice and think it weird that there were cookies flying through the room?"

"Is it really important what people notice and think?"

Laine wanted to go to bed but she didn't want to share her bed with Madeleine and Cheshire. The comforter lay flat and smooth and the pillows were plump yet orderly. They tempted her.

Ian rested like an electric mixer with the power turned on high, a constant whirl of motion, burning calories even while he slept. Every morning for fifteen years, she'd had to tuck in every blanket and sheet when she made the bed. Since he'd left, she could slip out of the bed, smooth down the bedding, fluff the pillows, and call it good. Making the bed was definitely easier without Ian.

"Can you tell me about the afterlife?" Laine asked, her voice small.

Madeleine laughed. "Of course not."

Laine sighed. "Then why are you here?"

"To fetch Sid." Madeleine looked up at her. "I thought you understood that."

"But...why you?"

"Because I loved him the most."

Laine sat down on the bed, trying to process this. A thousand questions went through her mind.

"We need to start looking," Madeleine said, gently lifting the cat and placing him on a pillow.

Laine shook her head. "No. We don't know where—"

"But I do."

"I need to go to bed."

Madeleine placed her hands on her hips. "Honestly, you're such a boob." She raised her voice and did a fair Laine imitation. "I need to go to bed."

"What do you want from me?" Laine picked up a pillow and held it to her chest.

"I want you to help me."

"Why should I?"

"Because you're the only one who can."

"Why?"

Madeleine frowned her and gave her a "don't be so stupid" look.

Laine frowned back. "If I help you, will you answer my questions?"

Madeleine's expression turned guarded. She looked up at the ceiling for a long moment and then returned her gaze to Laine's. "I can't."

Laine rolled her eyes, stood and put the pillow down.

Madeleine stood. "Maybe I can answer some."

CHAPTER 6

Laine scowled and pulled back the comforter.

"You have to understand—there are some questions you probably want to ask that you don't want to know the answers to."

"That doesn't even make sense." Laine took off her earrings and wedding ring and placed them in the bowl beside her bed. "Why would I want to ask questions and not want to know the answers?" When she looked up she saw Madeleine standing at the foot of her bed holding her car keys and wallet.

"Why do you wear your wedding ring?"

Laine opened her mouth, closed it and swallowed a gasp of air.

"See, there are some questions with answers so complicated and painful that it's just better not to know." Madeleine jiggled the keys at Laine. "Let's go."

Laine looked down at the bed with its cold sheets. She probably wouldn't be able to sleep anyway. Shrugging, she went into the closet and pulled out Ian's sweat pants from the hamper. She ignored Madeleine's frown as she stepped into the pants and shoved her feet into a pair of flip flops.

"You're not going to wear a bra?" Madeleine asked, as Laine took her keys.

Laine didn't answer but headed for the garage.

"Or comb your hair?"

"I have no intention of even getting out of the car." Laine pushed the button and the garage rolled up. Her Volvo blinked its headlights at her and for a moment she stood in its uncompromising bright beam. "I'm not going to see anyone—other than you, that is—and since you're not real—there's no need for underwear."

Madeleine laughed. "I really think you're going to regret this decision. People are going to see you."

Laine paused with her hand on the door. "Weren't you the one who, just seconds ago, asked if it's really important what people notice and think?"

Madeleine responded with increased laugher and climbed into the car.

***

Forty minutes later the GPS said they were somewhere near a nameless lake. Tall pine trees, dark and silent, lined the road. They'd left behind street lights, houses and all other signs of civilization when they'd left Highway 9.

"I hope you know where we are," Laine said, gripping

the steering wheel.

Madeleine sat looking out the window, her face illuminated by the glow of the controls on the dashboard. "Stop here."

"Here?" Laine slowed down, looking into the black woods. Her headlights caught the eyes of a wild creature lurking in the bushes. Before she could identify it, it scurried out of sight. Raccoon? Fox? Bobcat? All of those animals had a valid excuse for hanging out at the edge of the world, but Laine did not. What if her car broke down and stranded her out here—what would she do? She probably didn't even have cell service and she'd have to walk, but to where?

Madeleine slipped out the door.

"Wait, where are you going?"

Madeleine nodded at the woods before closing the door. A small wave of doubt washed over Laine. She could leave. She could start the car and go home. Crawl into bed and forget about bossy grandmother ghosts. Madeleine was already dead, so it's not like something horrible could happen to her. But how long would it be until Madeleine returned? She seemed to be able to travel in nanoseconds. Laine realized she was gripping the steering wheel so hard it hurt. Sighing, she leaned forward to rest her head on the wheel and then she took a deep breath and opened her door.

This is crazy, she told herself as she climbed out of the car. *Almost as crazy as talking to my grandmother's ghost.*

The Chinook wind teased the trees as the moon inched toward its zenith. One owl swooped out of the woods while another called out. Owls are an omen of death, Laine remembered, as she watched her grandmother's ghost disappear into a black thicket of alders. Laine followed. Madeleine stood at the edge of a small lake. Moonbeams glinted in long wavy strips across the water. The tree's shadows swayed, black against gray. Madeleine stared into the lake as if searching for something in the water or in her elongated reflection. She looked up, her face sad.

"I thought maybe he'd be here," Madeleine said.

Why would he be here? Why would anyone be here? Laine wondered.

"This is where we met," Madeleine said, as if she'd picked up on Laine's thoughts. "Clary and I saw Sid and Leo bathing, naked. They'd put their clothes over there." Madeleine pointed to a fallen tree. "It's still there. That same tree, covered with moss and a little more decayed, but it's still there. Everything here looks the same." She brought her gaze back to Laine. "Except for me, and now Sid, and even you. You weren't anything more than a figment of our imaginations."

A smile tugged Laine's lips. "Did you take his clothes?"

Madeleine laughed. "Of course. It was too good of an opportunity to pass up."

"And you didn't even know him?" Laine tried to imagine her grandfather as a young, naked man and failed.

"I got to know him very well, very fast." She laughed. "Oh laws, he was mad."

"I bet. What did he do?"

"Bellowed like a hell-demon."

"And what did you do?"

"Clary and I spied on them until Sid caught sight of us. We ran for the highway."

"No." Laine started to laugh out loud. It felt good and little strange because once she started she found it hard to stop. It occurred to her that she hadn't laughed in weeks.

"Of course, Highway 9 wasn't much in those days, but it was long before the interstate so anyone coming or going from Seattle to Canada had to pass by."

"Grandpa Sid…. he didn't actually run out onto the highway."

Madeleine shook her head. "No, but I did. I had an armful of his clothes and he looked so mean I thought I'd rather go head to head with a logging truck than face him."

"So, what did he do?"

"Well, he and Leo were weaving in and out of the trees swearing and yelling." She snorted. "They'd taken big maple leaves and were using them like flapping loin cloths, and then Mrs. Rowblinski, her dog and her three children came by. The dog, some sort of giant hound, went insane—almost as noisy as the naked boys."

Laine doubled over with laughter.

"The boys dropped their leaf loin cloths and climbed that cedar." Madeleine nodded at a large tree.

"Oh no!" Laine snorted and wiped laughter tears from her eyes.

"I'd never seen a naked male before. And a sight from that angle is something any fourteen-year-old girl shouldn't have to experience." Madeleine pointed to the giant cedar with branches fanning out toward the ground.

"Yikes."

"Mrs. Rowblinski stood underneath that tree, spouting scripture at those boys for so long that Clary and I got bored and went home."

"That's it? That's the end of the story?"

Madeleine turned and headed toward the car. "Of course not, that was only the beginning. We did marry, although I have to say, after that afternoon, the wedding night wasn't *too* much of a surprise."

Laine followed Madeleine, still laughing. "Why did you think he'd be here?"

"You're right; I guess this was a much better memory for me than for him." She spoke softly as she made her way back to the road. "I really just wanted to see it again."

Laine thought of her cold and lonely bed before inserting the keys in the ignition. "Now where?" she asked when the car roared to life.

Madeleine considered this and then sighed. "Rose Arbor I think. 22 Cob Street, Rose Arbor," she said slowly as Laine punched the address into the GPS.

They left the dark woods and traveled the highway to the small town of Rose Arbor. The mean wind blew down the deserted Main Street, tossing leaves and the occasional bit of trash. Less than a quarter of a mile long, Main had three stoplights that bounced and threatened to abandon their thick cables. The flags of the United States and the state of Washington had been left raised and they floated above the town green. The flags flapped, snapped in the wind; tiny pulleys attached to the cords bearing the flags pinged against their metal pole. Laine knew Rose Arbor well. Bette, her college roommate, lived on French Street.

The GPS directed them up Olympic Hill and over to Cobb. They pulled in front of a brick bungalow.

"It's gone," Madeleine said, her voice flat.

Laine looked over the house and neighborhood. While some of the tiny homes looked newer, as if they'd been given facelifts, most appeared to have been built in the early part of last century. 22 Cobb certainly looked old.

"There was a tiny house behind that one, a converted garage. We lived there until Georgie came along." Madeleine's voice turned soft. "It looks like someone tore it down."

Laine put the car in gear and Madeleine put her hand on Laine's thigh, stopping her. "Do you mind if I just sit here for awhile?"

Moments later, Madeleine climbed from the car and shut the door without a sound.

So much for sitting, Laine thought, but she suddenly realized that she didn't mind. It actually felt good to be doing something other than hiding out at home, alone, brooding over her failed marriage. She wouldn't say that she *liked* Madeleine; Laine still found her bossy and demanding, but she was an interesting, if not sometimes entertaining, distraction. Laine would rather be traipsing around Rose Arbor in the dead of night than lying in a lonely bed.

Madeleine wandered down the front walk, past the house. The neighborhood remained dark. Not even the blue light of a TV or computer screen flickered. Laine guessed that this was a neighborhood of senior citizens who probably wouldn't enjoy being disturbed. She tried to think of a reasonable excuse for parking in front of 22 Cobb after midnight and since she couldn't think of one, she followed Madeleine, worrying about noisy dogs, nosy neighbors and no trespassing signs.

She found Madeleine at the edge of the woods, sitting in a swing that dangled from the branch of a large maple. "It had mold growing on the walls and moss growing on the roof," Madeleine said, her voice low and soft. "Years later, on a trip to Scandinavia, we saw the palaces with flowers growing on the roof and it reminded me of our little house here. The trees blocked out any sunlight," Madeleine motioned with her head toward a stand of pines, "We were always in the shade and the house had a pungent mushroom smell."

Laine knew her grandparents had started off poor, but she really had never given it much thought. In her life, money had always been as plentiful as air. She'd never known what it was like to live in a moldy house. Her grandfather had always been so fastidious, such a connoisseur of the sumptuous that she had a hard time imagining him in any other sort of economic condition.

"The open beams were very low and Sid was forever hitting his head on them," Madeleine said. "I could stand on a chair and hide things on them. More than once when I was desperate to have a baby, I hid Sid's keys on the lowest beam so he'd spend the morning with me." She winked at Laine. "You know all about that."

Laine thought about all her unsuccessful baby-making attempts and eventually sex had become more chore than pleasure. "You obviously had more success."

Madeleine laughed. "Or more sex."

Laine rolled her eyes. It struck her then that she had to be truly insane to be standing in the woods after midnight listening to her dead grandmother talk about reproduction.

Madeleine's eyes looked dreamy. "Georgie was so cute, so fat. He had fingers and toes as round as marbles. He was pink and soft and when he laughed I felt as if I'd burst from the pleasure of him." She sniffed. "It broke my heart to leave him."

"Then why did you?" Laine wondered how life might have been different for her dad, for herself, if Madeleine had lived.

Madeleine leaned her head against her hand holding the swing's rope. "I didn't have a choice, not really. It was my time. *'The dust will return to the earth, and the spirit will return to God.'*"

"What's that from?"

Madeleine stood and brushed off her dress. "It's scripture." She headed back toward the car.

Laine followed. "So, it's one of those otherworldly things you can't tell me."

"I shouldn't have to tell you. After all, it's right there—all you have to do is look for it."

Laine opened her mouth to protest and then closed it because Madeleine was right. Everyone had access to a Bible. She mutely trailed Madeleine back to the car. Thick dew covered the grass which tickled her ankles as she walked. Feeling for her keys, she fought panic.

Madeleine leaned against the car's hood, watching Madeleine frantically patting all her pockets. "What's wrong?"

"I can't find my keys. I know I had them."

Madeleine checked the passenger door while Laine went to the driver's side. *Locked.* Peering through the window, she saw she hadn't left the keys in the ignition, which meant that she'd probably dropped them. Looking out over the lawn to the thick, black woods, discouragement and frustration swept over her.

"You'll have to call your husband."

"No!" Laine spoke too sharply and the porch lights of 22 Cobb flipped on. She edged toward the black woods, away from the porch light's beam.

Madeleine followed. "He has an extra set of keys, doesn't he?"

Laine dropped her voice to a whisper and kept her gaze on 22 Cobb. She thought she saw the curtains twitch. Someone in the house was watching her talk to her imaginary ghostly grandmother. "Of course, but—"

"What other choice do you have?"

She'd rather spend the night on a park bench than call Ian. She'd rather get down on her hands and knees and search the grass and woods than call Ian. She stooped over, feeling the grass with her fingers and then tripped over a tree root. Catching herself on outstretched hands, she kept her face from hitting the dirt. Pain shot through her right pointer finger. *Oh please,* she whispered to the night gods that seemed to be conspiring against her.

Madeleine put her hands on her hips. "What are you doing?"

Laine sat down, cradling her hand. "I'm hurt," she

said. Dirt and small stones clung to her palms and she tried to rub them clean on Ian's sweat pants without causing her finger further pain. Tears welled in her eyes. She ached inside and out.

Looking back at the house, she saw a face staring out at her. What if the window watcher called the police? What if Laine was picked up for trespassing? She limped across the grass and crouched behind her car.

"Now will you call him?"

"Hush!" Laine said, trying to move her finger. It already looked as fat as a hotdog. In a bun.

"You know no one but you can hear me!"

Laine leaned her forehead against the car door and sighed. *I'm going crazy.* She sat back on her heels and battled tears.

"So call him," Madeleine said.

Laine shook her head. "I'd rather die."

"I could arrange that," Madeleine muttered. "*'All flesh shall perish, and man shall turn again unto dust.'*"

Great—more scripture. She looked up at Madeleine and then slowly stood. "Thanks, but not today. Or tonight. Or whenever." The window watcher remained vigilant. Holding her throbbing hand against her chest, Laine walked down Cobb Street.

"You're not seriously considering walking home?" Madeleine trailed behind. "Call your husband!"

Laine turned onto French Street. One street light lit up a Craftsman cottage surrounded by plastic garden gnomes. Bette lived in Rose Arbor—in fact, Bette lived in a craftsman cottage on French Street, but she had a flower garden without gnomes. Famous for her garden, not only did Bette write for local gardening magazines, she'd been featured in *Sunset Magazine*. Laine knew she'd be able to recognize Bette's house even in the dark,

"Where are you going?"

"My friend lives on this street. She'll help me."

"What if she's out?"

Laine lifted her chin as she pressed into the dark night. "She won't be. Her husband died a few months ago and she's always been very quiet. She's into genealogy. You should have chosen to haunt her. She'd love you."

Madeleine folded her arms across her chest. "I'm not haunting you. I'm asking for your help."

"Yes, but that's a problem. You want my help and right now, I can't even help myself. I'm coming apart at the seams." Laine stopped in front of a pretty craftsman with a bright red door. All the lights were on. An Anita Baker tune floated from the window.

A giant Mercedes sat in the driveway.

Laine opened the white picket gate. Most of the flowers had faded, but their fragrance lingered. She paused on the stone path when Bette and a man appeared in the large picture window. *Who was he?*

CHAPTER 7

He looked nothing like Bette's first husband, Greg.
Greg had been built like the football players he coached at
the high school. This guy looked like Errol Flynn. He stood
behind Bette, his arms wrapped around her waist, his lips
pressed against her neck. She had one hand on his that
rested on her waist and the other on his head, holding him
against her.

Somewhere nearby a dog barked. Bette looked up and
caught sight of Laine. Her eyes widened in surprise. Laine
lifted a limp hand to give a halfhearted wave. She wished
the earth would gape open and swallow her whole. Maybe
it wasn't too late to arrange for that returning-to-dust
Madeleine had talked about.

Seconds later Bette stood at the door, holding it open.
"Laine? Oh my gosh, what are you doing here?"

Laine took a deep breath, knowing she'd need to lie.
She already looked crazy, she didn't want to sound crazy,
too. Breath caught in her throat and she hiccoughed.

Mr. Errol Flynn held the door while Bette hurried
down the path. She wrapped her arm around Laine and led

her into the house. "You're *dirty*," Bette couldn't hide her shock. She sat Laine down on the sofa and sat down beside her.

"Errol, will you please bring Laine some tea?"

Laine hiccoughed again and bit back a short laugh. "His name really is Errol? I was just thinking that he looks like Errol Flynn."

"I know, I think so, too." Bette smiled and leaned forward to whisper. "And his middle name is Lee."

"Early?" Laine whispered back. "So, is he always prompt?"

Bette got a dreamy look in her eye and nodded. "He's right on time."

Laine swallowed back more tears. When Greg died of a sudden heart attack more than a year ago, Laine had worried Bette would be lonely for the rest of her life. And now, Mr. Early had come to keep her company. "I'm interrupting."

"Not at all." Mr. Early pushed through the dining room door holding two mugs of steaming peppermint tea. "I was on my way home anyway, now Bette has someone to help keep the boogie men at bay." He placed the mugs on the coffee table and then leaned forward to kiss Bette on the cheek. "Bye," he murmured in her ear. "I'll call you tomorrow."

"Bye," Bette said

"Bye," Laine parroted, feeling awkward, like a third wheel on a bicycle built for two.

When the door closed behind him, Bette turned, her eyes full of concern. "So, did you meet a boogie man? Because, no offense, but you sort of look like you might have tried to fight more than one."

Laine leaned forward and took the tea cup with her good hand. She looked around for Madeleine and wondered where and when she'd gone. She swallowed the tea and a sense of peace flooded her. "When I was going through my grandfather's things I found an old photo album. It had a picture of a house at 22 Cobb Street, the first house my grandparents lived in when they were married." The lie came easily enough and she knew that she'd told it well by the way Bette leaned forward, her interest piqued.

"I couldn't sleep, so I drove out here. I couldn't find the house, so… I know this sounds crazy, but I went in the woods looking for it."

"And then?" Bette urged.

The words came out in a rush. "I tripped over a tree root, hurt my finger when I fell and dropped and lost my keys."

"Oh!" Bette exclaimed.

"My phone and purse are in the locked car."

Bette looked her in the eye. "Do you want to call Ian? He must have keys to your car."

Laine didn't need to lie. Bette was one of the few people who knew Ian had left weeks ago. She shook her head.

"Good!" Bette patted her knee. "We'll have a sleep over. I'd offer to drive you home, but you know my car…"

Laine smiled. Bette drove an ancient, temperamental Jeep. Laine suspected her reluctance to replace the Jeep had more to do with sentimental reasons than financial concerns, because Greg had carried a substantial life insurance policy.

"It does better in the daylight, when it knows there are tow trucks available to help, if needed," Bette said, setting down her tea cup and standing. "Come on—let's find some clean sheets for your bed and a towel." She stopped on the stairs. "Will you be able to play tomorrow at the memorial?"

Laine froze. The memorial. How had she forgotten? She looked at her swollen finger and felt nearly as bad as her finger looked.

Bette put her arm around Laine's shoulder and

shepherded her up the stairs. "We'll worry about that later."

**

The sun beamed through lacy curtains. Birds sang and Laine put a pillow over her head to drown out their noise. She peeked out the window and saw an unfamiliar rhododendron bush. Its clusters of bright pink flowers reminded her that she wasn't on Lily Hill but in Rose Arbor. Last night's events washed over her. She looked at the little pewter clock ticking happily on the night stand. Eight a.m. Two hours until the service.

Sitting up, she brushed her hair from her eyes. She'd fallen asleep with her hair wet minutes after her shower, and as a result, it'd gone wild. Trying to smooth down the curls, she twisted it into a French knot. She had no make-up, no clothes, not even a bra. She'd have to go home, and soon. Being late for her grandfather's service wasn't an option.

There was supposed to be an open casket. The mortuary wouldn't send the fake Sid—of course they wouldn't. She shivered, remembering Madeleine's first appearance at the chapel. It seemed so long ago, but it had only been yesterday morning. As if thinking about her conjured her, Madeleine suddenly appeared in the middle of the room. She looked beautiful in a drop waist black dress covered with pearl seed beads.

"How do you do that?" Laine asked groggily.

"Do what?"

"Suddenly appear, looking all beautiful, first thing in the morning." Laine ran her tongue over her fuzzy teeth. She couldn't remember the last time she'd gone to sleep without brushing and flossing.

"Get up and we'll make you beautiful, too."

Laine flopped back against the pillows. "I don't think that's possible." She held up her hand and inspected her yellow and purple finger. It looked like a moldy sausage. She wouldn't be able to play the organ.

"Oh, ye of little faith." Madeleine stood over her, fists on hips, frowning.

"You know, for being sort of a cranky, unpleasant person, you seem to know a lot of Bible verses."

Madeleine's frown disappeared and she laughed, as if Laine had said something amusing and surprising. "*I'm* cranky and unpleasant?"

"Well, I'm just saying that maybe if you were more… I don't know, angelic, you wouldn't have to hang out here with me. On earth."

"Where the truly cranky people are."

The door opened a crack and Bette stuck her head in.

"Good morning! You'll never guess what Errol brought over!"

Not everyone's cranky, Laine thought.

"He's here already? I guess he really is early." Laine propped herself up on her elbows, lifted her eyebrows at Madeleine and then looked back at Bette. "Let me guess, a black dress."

Bette stepped into the room, closed the door and leaned against it. "How did you know?"

"And there are matching shoes, too, right?" Laine sat up and tried to smooth down her wayward hair.

"Yes!" Bette's eyes went wide.

"He brought those for you, silly."

Bette shook her head and sat down on the bed beside Laine. Picking up Laine's hand, she studied the discolored finger. "He knows they won't fit me."

"Then where did he get them? He couldn't have gone to the mall. Just because he's early doesn't mean everyone else is."

Bette touched Laine's fat, swollen finger. "They belonged to his wife."

"He's a widower?"

Bette scrunched her nose and gently placed Laine's hand back on the bed. "I guess he's sort of more like an exwidower. They'd been separated for years before she died."

Laine climbed from the bed and one handedly helped Bette strip the sheets. She thought about Ian dying. It'd be awful. They had unresolved issues and if he died, she would carry around anger and hurt indefinitely. Knowing that she needed to forgive and forget Ian, she sat down on the bare mattress and thought about his death.

Her father rarely talked about her mother. For years, Laine had assumed it was because talking of her caused him so much pain, but then as she got older and understood her father better, she realized that her dad couldn't handle any sort of emotional discussions. Emotions were best shoved into a very small bottle and secured with a tight lid—not a cork, because corks pop. And, in her father's world, messy emotions were best bottled up.

If Ian died, would she be able to talk about him? Or would she be like her dad? Mentally, Laine shrugged. It was a moot point. She and Ian didn't have a child, so she wouldn't have to talk about his death.

Not that she wanted him to die.

Bette prattled on about the clothes while gathering the sheets into a bundle and Laine tried to give her friend her attention and stop planning Ian's memorial service.

"His wife, Dot, was very Hollywood and collected

vintage clothing. Fortunately for you, his daughter saved her favorite bits." Bette paused for air. "Come and see."

"He's down stairs? Now?"

"*And* he brought muffins."

"Oh, I like him," Laine said, glancing at Madeleine, who had suddenly appeared in the corner rocking chair. "He seems too good to be true… much too good to be faced so early in the morning."

"Let's go." Bette reached for her good hand and tugged her off the bed. "Stop being so vain. You look gorgeous."

Gorgeous? "I don't even have a bra."

Bette's eyes lit up and she held up her hands like she was stopping traffic. "Wait right there!"

After she dashed out the door, Laine turned to Madeleine. "How did you do that?"

"Do what?" Madeleine laughed and the chair squeaked as she rocked.

"You know—get Mr. Punctuality to bring me clothes."

Madeleine shook her head, still smiling. "Honestly, you must think me all powerful and I assure you, I'm not."

Bette burst back into the room carrying a pink and white striped Victoria's Secret bag. "Okay, this is weird, but I really think they'll fit you." She pulled out a leopard spotted bra. "Wait!" she giggled. "There's more."

Laine looked at the tiny pair of panties dangling from Bette's fingers and shook her head, laughing. "I love you, but I cannot wear your underwear." She glanced at Madeleine and saw amusement on her face. The chair rocked, but Bette didn't notice.

"Well, they're not mine, obviously." Bette held them up so Laine could see the generous cup size. "See, they still have the tags. Some kids put them in Gregg's locker as a gag. He brought them home for me." She looked at the underwear sadly. "I guess I could have worn the panties, but after Gregg died... well, no one sees my underwear anymore. Besides, I'm more of a training bra sort of gal and the panties without the bra just aren't fun." She looked at Laine's chest. "I bet you could fill this out."

The rocking chair squeaked and Laine knew without looking that Madeleine was laughing.

"Is it wrong to wear fun undies to my grandfather's funeral?" Laine took the underwear and fingered the silky fabric.

"Your grandfather loved irreverence."

"Well, that's true," Laine said.

"Put them on," Bette said. "I'll go get the dress and shoes."

***

They took Errol's car to the service. Laine sat in the back with Madeleine, subject to all her whisperings. "Now that your friend is playing the organ, you'll have to sit with Ian."

At least I'm wearing sexy underwear, Laine thought.

"Everyone will be watching the two of you," Madeleine whispered, leaning back against the seat.

Smoothing down the dress and liking the feel of silk on her skin, Laine wondered why Madeleine bothered to whisper, since no one but herself could hear her.

"Did you bring tissues?" Madeleine asked.

"I'm not going to cry," Laine said and then blushed when she realized she'd spoken out loud. Bette looked over the seat at her, and Errol glanced in the rearview mirror.

"I mean, after all your efforts with my make-up, it'd be a silly thing to do," Laine floundered. She'd left her hair down and curly, and in some way, she felt that her hair in its wild state matched the animal print underwear.

"Sweetie, everyone cries at funerals. It's expected," Bette said. She motioned to Errol. "Errol even cried at his ex-wife's funeral."

Errol shot her quick, suspicious look. "You were buried behind the piano, so how would you know?"

Bette shrugged, grinning. "I was watching."

Errol looked back at the road, smiling. Bette settled back against the seat and Laine suddenly felt isolated and alone. The pair in the front seat belonged to a closed society, an exclusive club of two.

"We met at his wife's funeral," Bette explained, talking to Laine by way of the rearview mirror.

"She stole a book from my library," Errol added, smiling at Bette.

Bette reached over and smacked his arm. "I returned it." She looked over the seat at Laine. "And I didn't have to—he would never have known it even existed if I hadn't told him."

"What sort of book?" Laine asked. She really didn't care, but it seemed a polite thing to ask and she'd rather have a conversation with Bette and Errol than with Madeleine. Laine didn't want to hear anything Madeleine had to say. "And why would you need to steal a book—you work with thousands at the library. It's hard to imagine you stealing anything other than loaves of bread for starving children. It must have been a humdinger of a book."

"It was the diary of my great-great grandmother," Errol said.

"A romance I'd absolutely fallen in love with," Bette

said, her eyes shining.

"I didn't know it, but Dot, my wife, had hired Bette to write the history of my ancestors, survivors of the Great Seattle Fire," Errol said.

"I thought everyone survived that fire," Laine said.

Errol laughed. "But no one survives burning love," he said in a deep, seductive voice.

"That is not a line in the book!" Bette turned to Laine, eyes bright with laughter. "I promise you, I did not write such a cheese-ball line."

Laine smiled and tried to be engaged in the conversation, but failed. She looked out the window. They were crossing the Lake Union Bridge. The Space Needle pointed into a mass of dark clouds. Today Lake Union matched the slate gray sky. Laine thought about her own family, her own ancestors, while Bette talked about mercy. When had the conversation shifted? Mercy bordered too closely on topics like forgiveness and compassion, subject matters Laine shied from.

"Trent and Mercy had seven children," Bette said.

Seven children? And then Laine understood that Mercy, in this case, was a proper noun and not just a good idea. Laine slid her gaze over to Madeleine. "I'm interested in researching my family history," Laine said. "I found some trunks and photo albums in my grandfather's attic and I…well—" Okay, the truth was she really hadn't been thinking of researching her family, but at the moment, it seemed like a perfect plan.

"Oh, I'd love to help you," Bette volunteered.

"I don't really know where to start," Laine said.

"You should read the book Bette wrote. She called it *Stealing Mercy*," Errol said.

Mercy—that word again. Laine hoped she could get Errol and Bette to stop using it.

"Ian's already here," Madeleine said when Errol pulled his car into the chapel's parking lot.

"Thanks again for playing for me," Laine said, trying to keep her eyes off Ian's car parked beside the mortuary's limousine. If Sid hadn't been misplaced, there would have been a hearse, a casket, and Sid.

"I'm playing for Sid, too," Bette said.

"Where ever he may be," Madeleine muttered.

"He always loved you," Laine said to Bette. She caught sight of Ian, dressed in black, talking to the pastor. He had his back turned to her and at the sight of his straight shoulders, Laine's nerves faltered. Apprehension curled in her belly. Suddenly, the leopard spotted bra pinched.

"Once I might have believed you," Madeleine said.

"I'm sure he loved you," Laine said out loud to Madeleine. Her grandfather had been a kind and loving man. It seemed impossible that he wouldn't have loved his first wife. Some long- ago learned scripture came to Laine's memory. *Love the wife of thy youth. Where had that come from?* She wondered, but then decided that she'd been spending way too much time with Madeleine.

Ian stood beneath a tree, a hundred feet away. Weeks and months and years away from where they'd once been. The life they'd once shared long passed. She took a deep breath. She could do this. She could face the world, standing beside Ian.

Just not yet.

"The music!" Laine blurted. "I left the music at home."

"I know some pieces," Bette began, "the standard hymns."

"No, you'll need this music." Laine brushed her curls away from her face, feeling the heat of her lies. "Do you know *In the Garden* by Austin Miles?" She began to sing.

"I come to the garden alone
While the dew is still on the roses
And the voice I hear falling on my ear
The Son of God discloses."

Bette scowled. "That doesn't sound like something your grandfather would have liked."

"I don't know if he liked it, but he wanted it played at his funeral," Laine said. Seriously, her lies were falling so fast and thick now, if they didn't stop, she'd have to speak with the pastor. Not that she believed he could do anything to help her. Her thoughts on repentance, confessions and absolution laid somewhere in that murky mercy category she avoided.

Laine had played *In the Garden* at the funeral of one of the ladies who served with her on the foundation—Gabbie Lewis, a tiny Scottish woman with flaming red hair. Her elderly sisters had sung. Closing her eyes, Laine pictured the trio of women, sharing the sheet music, the words almost unrecognizable because of their thick brogue.

And He walks with me, and He talks with me,
And He tells me I am His own;
And the joy we share as we tarry there,
None other has ever known.

"Laine!"

She started out of the memory and realized that Errol had parked the car beneath the shade of a maple tree. The morning sun flicked through the autumn leaves and cast a warm light into the car.

"Are you alright?" Bette asked.

"No. I mean yes," Laine stammered. "You should go in and start the prelude. I'll just walk home and get the music. It won't take long." She started to open the door.

"Don't be silly," Errol said. "I'll drive you."

"You can't walk three blocks in those heels," Bette said.

Bette and Errol both looked at Laine as if she'd lost her mind and maybe she had. She took a deep, steadying breath. "Okay, good plan. Bette, you go in and start the prelude. Errol will drive me to get the music."

And then I'll have to sit with Ian.

CHAPTER 8

Sharing a pew with Ian, feeling the solid hulk of his warmth, it felt so right it made her angry. He avoided her eye, which suited her just fine, thank you very much, because she avoided his as well. She'd seen the look on his face when she'd walked in with Errol—the flash of hurt in his wide eyes. The satisfaction she'd expected hadn't been there, which made her feel like nothing was where it belonged. Sid was missing. No casket. Madeleine had disappeared. Her parents were late. And a man named Errol Lee, Mr. Punctuality who was the complete opposite of Greg, sat on the back pew, waiting for Bette

She didn't have anything against Mr. P., but he wasn't Greg and if anyone was to be waiting for Bette, it should have been Greg. It just wasn't right for him to be gone, to be replaced by a man who had the bad form to look like a devastatingly handsome Errol Flynn.

Ian held his shoulders stiff. He didn't know about Mr. P and Bette. All Ian knew was that Laine had arrived in Mr. P.'s car. Bette sat on the organ bench, relaxed and happy as she pounded out that ridiculous song. The words sang in

Laine's head.

He speaks, and the sound of His voice,
Is so sweet the birds hush their singing,
And the melody that He gave to me
Within my heart is ringing.

"I got a call from Tucker Towing this morning," Ian said. He didn't look at her, but had his eyes focused on the stained glass window behind the pulpit. Following his gaze, Laine remembered the first time she'd met Madeleine. It'd been here, in this chapel. She'd thought Madeleine was a child. Even now, a day later, a whole day and a night of Madeleine's almost constant company, she didn't know how to categorize her. A ghost? A spook? A hallucination?

Laine touched her forehead with her fingers. "Tucker Towing?"

Ian radiated with some sort of pent up emotion Laine couldn't define or read. This surprised her. She thought she knew how to read all Ian's signs.

"Your car. You left it in Rose Arbor." He sounded hurt and angry and she heard the question behind the statement.

Telling herself that she didn't owe Ian anything, not one drop of information, she frowned. Why impound her car? "Is Tucker Towing expensive?" she asked, knowing that the cost wasn't the issue. Ian wasn't fuming over the bill. "I didn't know I'd parked illegally." A dark street sprinkled with potholes. No sidewalks or curbs. She'd bet dollars and doughnuts that Rose Arbor didn't have street sweepers. Had she parked in front of someone's driveway?

"We'll find out this afternoon."

The implication hit and settled in her belly like a brick. "I can pick up the car," she said, just as her father and Trudy slipped in the pew beside her. George sat down, put his arm around Laine's shoulders and gave her a squeeze. Laine momentarily laid her head on her father's shoulder. She wanted to cry, but she was too mad at Ian. Too angry with herself.

George wore a dark suit and flashy gold cufflinks. Trudy wore a hat that would have made the queen mother envious. It looked like a flying saucer had perched on her head. And yet, from beneath a curtain of black lace, Trudy shot Laine's dress a surprised look.

Laine smoothed the silky fabric. It really was beautiful. She crossed her legs and saw Ian watching. "Did you hurt your finger in Rose Arbor? Is it broken?"

Lifting her chin, Laine watched as Pastor Clark took his place behind the podium. She didn't have to answer any of Ian's questions. Not now. Not ever.

"Let us pray," the pastor said.

Laine bowed her head but snuck a glance at Ian and saw that he still had his eyes on her legs.

"Dear Father, today we thy children gather before thee to commend the life of Sidney Leon," Pastor Clark began.

"Have you seen a doctor?" Ian whispered.

Laine shushed him and tried to focus on her grandfather. The image of him racing through the woods, naked, yelling for his clothes made Laine smile. Of course, she'd never known him young. She'd never known Madeleine. What she didn't know about her grandparents suddenly seemed huge, immense and important. More important than anything else.

She snuck a glance at Ian. A vein throbbed in his neck. She wondered what he'd do if she reached out and touched it. He reminded her of a volcano, simmering, waiting to erupt.

Pastor Clark gripped the podium. "On mornings such as this, while the birds sing and flowers grow, we who are left behind have to ask, where has he gone? Is he happy there? Have his health and youth returned? And if so, how is it done? Are these questions that someday, somehow we'll find the answers? Are we travelers in mortality? Is earth a foreign land? Or, is it all we'll ever know? The poet William Wordsworth wrote:

Our birth is but a sleep and a forgetting:
The Soul that rises with us, our life's Star,
Hath had elsewhere its setting,
And cometh from afar:
Not in entire forgetfulness,
And not in utter nakedness,
But trailing clouds of glory do we come
From God, who is our home."

Where's my home? Laine wondered. *If I don't belong with Ian, where do I belong?* She leaned forward, her elbows on her knees, and put her head in her hands. George rubbed her back, an uncharacteristic physical display of affection.

"Life moves ever forward," Pastor Clark said. "The child grows from youth to adult and maturity comes one life lesson at a time. We may question the purpose and problems of life and ask if they bring us closer to God, but our return is inevitable. Together, age and experience draw us closer to His heaven. Job of old centuries ago asked, 'If a man die, shall he live again?'"

A better question: If a grandmother dies, will she live again to haunt her granddaughter? And if so, why? It was so much easier not to believe in Madeleine when she wasn't around. Without her, the world made sense. With her, Laine felt confused. What if Madeleine didn't exist? *Of course, she doesn't exist,* Laine told herself. *I don't believe in ghosts. I'm not sure what I believe about the afterlife, although I hope that question is the only similarity I share with Job.* If she had to pick a Bible character to emulate, she wouldn't pick him. She thought about boils and shuddered.

Madeleine had arrived at a weak moment. The death of her grandfather and the end of her marriage had made her vulnerable. Madeleine was a projection of her imagination. True, until this point in her life, she'd been remarkably unimaginative, but still, Madeleine was nothing more or less that her mind's way of talking to herself, making her ask difficult questions, helping her to work out issues that were too painful to face any other way.

22 Cobb Street? She'd gone there after looking through the photo album. Okay, so maybe she didn't remember actually seeing anything about 22 Cobb in the album, but that didn't mean something hadn't somehow registered. Sitting up and straightening her shoulders, she thought, *the mind is a powerful thing.* And then she noticed Madeleine sitting on the organ bench beside Bette and added, *I'm losing mine.*

***

"What are you doing up there?" Helene's voice carried up the attic stairs.

"I'm collecting family stuff," Laine said. She'd left the funeral as quickly as possible, changed her clothes into something ratty, and hurried back to Sid's house. She'd managed to avoid Ian and his questions and had thought herself safe in the attic, but evidently, she'd been discovered by Helene. She sighed, rocked back onto her heels and pushed her hair off her sweaty forehead, grateful Helene wasn't Ian. While carrying one box, she scooted the trunk across the dusty floor with her foot. She placed the trunk and box in her "memorabilia of interest" pile. Looking over the railing, she saw Helene standing at the foot of the stairs, frowning and holding a fruit smoothie.

"Oh, is that for me?" Laine bit back a smile. At nearly forty years old, she still loved being babied by Helene.

"Well, there isn't anyone else here but ghosts." Helene held out the smoothie, tempting her.

No, the ghost, thank goodness, is missing, Laine thought. She glanced at her collection, wondering where she should start. Mindful of her wounded finger, she picked up the trunk and headed down the stairs.

"Now where you going with that?" Helene asked, trailing after Laine, holding the smoothie up like a beacon.

"It's hot and sweaty in the attic." Laine deposited the trunk in the center of her aunt's room. The Cabbage Patch doll watched from her position on the bed. Helene must have tidied the room after Laine's breakdown yesterday. The thought made Laine uncomfortable.

"Did you—" she motioned to the bed.

Helene nodded. "I told Ian I'd stay and help get the house ready for sale."

Laine put her hands on her hips. Why would Ian be selling the house? Did he inherit it? That didn't make sense. "Ian's selling the house?"

"George thought it a good idea." Helene would never criticize Ian, but she didn't mind giving her say so about George. Her father had inherited and Ian was taking care of its sale. Why hadn't anyone asked her opinion? What was her opinion? She didn't know. Ever practical, selling made sense. But still. Someone should have at least told her.

Laine took the smoothie from Helene, feeling cross. It tasted sweet and tropical like pineapple and something she couldn't define. The ice melted down her throat and she almost moaned with pleasure—her frustration melted like the ice. "I'm glad you're staying." *Even if it's to help Ian.* "What about the Florida condo?"

Helene shrugged, smiling, watching Laine drink the

smoothie. "Florida's been there for centuries. It can wait."

"You're an angel." Laine drained the glass and licked the edge with her tongue. "And that was heaven. What was it? It was different."

Helene smirked. "Passion fruit."

That meant Ian was somewhere nearby. Laine knew how Helene worked. She turned her back on her grandfather's housekeeper and set the glass down on the night stand with unnecessary force.

The front door opened. "Laine?" Ian's voice called up from the foyer.

She'd thought she'd lost him after the service by slipping out of the chapel immediately and hitching a ride home with Bette and Mr. Punctuality.

"Up here," Helene called out. "Honey, you're a mess," she whispered, stepping over and running her hand over Laine's curls. Laine had changed back into Ian's sweat pants and a t-shirt once she'd reached her grandfather's house because she didn't want to ruin the borrowed dress. She regretted her decision because now Ian would know that she wore the clothes he'd left behind. Embarrassment increased her anger.

"Thank you. And you're a demon." She swatted Helene's hand away.

"Two seconds ago I was an angel." Helene folded her arms and frowned.

"Angel, demon, same thing." Laine picked up the trunk.

"All I'm saying is you look like you climbed from the swamp." Helene followed Laine out into the hall. "Now, where you going with that?"

"Well, it's obvious I'm not going to be able to work here in peace," Laine said over her shoulder, lugging the trunk through the hall.

"Work? What work?"

"I told you—I'm going to try to do some genealogical research." Standing at the top of the stairs, she saw Ian and her heart did the same fluttering thing it'd been doing since junior high. Well, enough of that. The fluttering had officially ended. It should have stopped years ago. In fact, it should have never started.

"Hey," he said softly, climbing the stairs. His glance took in her/his clothes and the corners of his lips lifted in an almost smile.

"You're right," Laine said to Ian, lifting her chin.

"I'm what?" He couldn't have more surprised if she'd announced he had broccoli sprouting from his ears.

"I've decided you're right. I need some time off work."

Laine shifted the trunk for a tighter grip. Ian took it from her. She considered wrestling him for it, and then thought better of it. Let him carry the trunk. Why not? Why not make him carry all the boxes? She'd been planning on walking home, taking them one at a time, but that was dumb. "And I need your help."

"I'm right *and* you need my help?"

She folded her arms and scowled at him. "Is that so amazing?"

"Coming from anyone else, no, coming from you, yes." Ian held the trunk easily, as if it weighed nothing. She hated that.

"Should I ask Helene to help carry boxes from the attic?"

"You would never ask Helene to carry boxes from the attic, but then, I would have guessed you'd never ask *anyone* to help you carry boxes. Unless they were very heavy boxes."

Laine looked at Ian's dark suit, pristine white shirt and silk tie. "They're not heavy, but they're dirty."

"Is that why you're wearing my sweat pants?"

Laine didn't know how to answer that, so she said, "There are cob webs, and maybe rat poop."

"Rat poop," Ian muttered. "I can't imagine you within

fifty feet of rat poop."

Knowing there hadn't been any signs of rodents, Laine pulled open the door and walked outside. The Chinooks had stopped blowing but the warm air remained, lingering. It wouldn't be long before the trees, so vibrant in their fall colors, would become bare. The flowers were already looking tired and droopy. "I can get the others later."

Ian stopped beside his car. "Is the rat poop why you changed your clothes?"

Oh, I've changed more than my clothes. She tried the door, but it was locked.

"I looked for you after the service. It's like you disappeared." Ian nodded toward the car. "The key is in my pocket."

She sent him a stern look and he shook his head. "Fine, hold this." He handed her back the trunk.

It weighed a ton and it made her neck, shoulders and arms ache to hold it while Ian unlocked the car. He took the trunk from her and placed it beside his golf clubs.

"You were going to carry that home, weren't you?"

"No, of course not."

"And the other boxes as well, the ones covered with cob webs and rat poop."

She shook her head.

"Laine, I know when you lie."

Facing him, she folded her arms across her chest. "I don't lie."

He smiled. "Not often, but I can tell when you do."

Instinctively, she put her finger on her fluttering eyelid. *I'm a twitch,* she thought, willing her eye to hold still. No more twitching. No more fluttering.

"Where are the other boxes?" Ian asked. "In the attic?"

"Do you mind getting them?"

"Anything for you." Ian caught and held her gaze.

"I don't believe you."

"I wish you would."

When Laine didn't respond, Ian sighed and said, "I'll go get your boxes. How many are there?"

She told him and then watched his retreating back. Helene, carrying another passion fruit smoothie, came out after Ian went in.

"I want to go to the cottage," Madeleine announced, suddenly appearing in the back seat. "Ask him to take us to the cottage."

Cottage? She didn't know anything about a cottage, but it didn't seem like a place she wanted to go to with Ian. Still, after a few minutes of heckling from Madeleine, Laine sighed and asked Helene, "Do you know anything about a cottage Sid owned?"

Helene looked surprised and then sheepish.

Ian reappeared before she responded.

"Do you need a ride to your car?"

"Tell him yes." Madeleine said.

Helene handed Ian the smoothie. Laine bit the desire to tell him not to drink it. She felt out numbered. Ian, Madeleine and Helene had joined ranks. But why? Why were they conspiring against her? What did Ian want? Why would Madeleine and Helene take his side? Especially when no one knew what side he was on?

After giving Helene a brief tight hug, she climbed into his car. Why was it Ian's car? Why would she call it Ian's car when her name, as well as his, was on the title?

"I need to stop by *my* house for the keys and my wallet." If he noticed the inflection in her voice, he didn't comment.

He climbed in beside her. "How did you know about the cottage?"

"Were you keeping it from me?"

"I can't keep it from you. Legally, it's yours. I just found out about it when Harry brought over the will."

He started the car and gave her the extra patient look that always made her feel about six. "Remember, I told you when Harry was reading the will. You chose not to come."

Yes. That had been stupid. "The cottage is mine?"

Ian backed out of the drive and headed home. "Everything is yours, except for the house. That belongs to George."

Laine remembered her conversation with Sid where he told her that she'd receive the bulk of his inheritance with Ian as executor, so she wasn't surprised by the news. And she understood Sid's reasoning. If George and Trudy had been left the business, they would have sucked it dry and left its carcass to bleach in the sun. "He doesn't seem upset."

"He's not. As a shareholder, he still gets a generous salary from the company, although it's not as generous as yours."

Laine sniffed, thinking of how all her earnings went to her foundation. "It's not really a salary."

"Mine is." Ian tightened his fingers around the steering wheel.

"I can't fire you, can I?"

Ian barked a short, harsh laugh as he pulled onto Lily Hill. "Would you really, if you could?" he asked.

What would it mean to cut Ian completely from her life? To never see him, never hear of him, no more rumors or innuendos? If they didn't share the company or a marriage, they'd share nothing. If they'd had children there would have been a tie and they'd still have to navigate around each other because of their shared interest in a child. Soccer games, dance recitals, school plays, graduations and weddings. Laine blinked away sudden tears. No children. She could walk away from Ian and never see him again.

Except for the company. She trusted him to run the company. Thinking of anyone else in that position was impossible.

As Ian drove down their street, Laine took a deep breath, steadied her voice and prayed he hadn't seen her tears. "Tell me about the cottage."

"It's on the Sound," Madeleine said. "You can watch the sun set into the water in the evening and hear the gulls and birds call in the morning."

"I don't know very much about it," Ian said as he pulled into the drive, pressed a button and her garage whirled open. Killing the engine, he gave her all of his attention.

"Are there tenants?"

"Not unless you count rodents." Ian shook his head before opening the door and climbing from the car. "It's west of Rose Arbor." Popping open the trunk, he reached inside.

"There was an owl in the tree outside the window. Sid used to throw apples at it because it kept him awake," Madeleine said.

"Is it pretty?" Laine asked, watching Ian's back muscles move as he pulled the trunk from the car.

"Pretty remote." He motioned to the boxes. "Where would you like all this?"

"Remote sounds good." Laine pointed at the garage floor. "Just put it down. I think I'll take it to the cottage with me. Did Harry give you the keys?"

Ian froze. "You want to go there?"

"It's mine, right?"

"By yourself?"

She nodded.

"This isn't like you, Laine."

"I just want to see it."

"It's probably *condemne*d, Laine. I'm not sure if there's even running water or electricity."

"I want to see it, not take up residence." Although that was exactly what she planned on doing. Maybe not for long, maybe not at all. *I'll have to see,* she thought, turning toward the house so that Ian couldn't see her twitching eyelid.

She left Ian standing in the center of the garage, frowning. When she came back with her keys and wallet he still hadn't moved. His suspicions were stamped all over his face.

"You don't have to drive me to Rose Arbor," she told him. "I called a taxi."

"You found a taxi to take you to Rose Arbor?" The suspicions hardened into a stony expression.

"Tucker the Tow Guy has a brother named Riker the Driver."

"You'd rather ride with Riker the Driver than with me?"

She let his question hang in the air of the empty garage.

"Fine." He got into his car.

Fine, she thought as she watched him pull away. *Fine and dandy.*

CHAPTER 9

"I don't like it." Helene placed her hands on her hips and frowned at Riker as he piled Laine's collection in the trunk of his Chevette. Riker, a man of many tattoos and not very many words, didn't seem to care about Helene and what she did or did not like.

"I'm just going to get my car," Laine said, handing another box to Riker.

A multicolored snake ran up his arms and across his shoulders and as he lifted and bent, the snake writhed. Watching the tattoo was strangely hypnotic and it almost made her sad when he stood upright, brushed a hand across his face and grunted, "Ready?"

"If you're just getting your car, then why is there a suit case in the back seat?" Helene fussed and went to look in the taxi's window. "You can't tell me that Louis Vuitton bag belongs to Riker."

"It's mine," Riker said, folding his arms across his chest and glowering.

Helene shot him a surprised look, as if she hadn't thought him capable of stringing together two whole words.

"Oh, yeah? Well, then why does it have a tag saying Madeleine Collins, Lily Hill?"

When Riker didn't answer, Helene shook her finger at Laine. "People who lie have something to fear. What are you scared of?"

What she thought was, *Of losing my old life, of starting one new, of finding where I do or do not belong,* but she said, "That I'll hide behind Ian for the rest of my life and never really know what it's like to be me."

"What does that mean? I don't even know what you're trying to say and I don't think you know either." Helene sagged, as if suddenly defeated and deflated. She turned to Riker. "Just come inside for a glass of ice tea."

"No!" Laine said. Heaven only knew what the tea could hold, what it had the power to do.

"The man is hot," Helene said. "Look, he's sweating. It's a miracle that snake doesn't just slide right off his arm and slither away."

"He doesn't need a tea." Although, at the moment, he did look as if he thought a tea was a good idea. "We have to go before Tucker Towing closes shop."

"We don't have to worry about that," Riker put in, proving that he could speak in complete sentences. "I got a key to the gate."

"But he's expecting us," Laine argued.

"It is awfully hot—" Riker whined, sounding like six year old.

"Just tea," Laine warned Helene.

Laine opened the door of the Chevette and the smell of cigarettes mixed with a pine scented air freshener rolled out. It was going to be a long ride to Rose Arbor.

***

After retrieving the Volvo from Tucker Towing, Laine and Madeleine headed west on Pioneer Highway and then turned off near a sign advertising free firewood and homemade ostrich jerky. At that point, her GPS screen turned blank and the Volvo was just a little animated car driving off into nowhere, or so it seemed, as the two-lane highway dissolved into a narrow road scarred with potholes.

"Are you sure you know where you're going?" Laine asked Madeleine.

Madeleine rolled her eyes. "I've been dead for thirty years. For all I know someone's plowed this forest and turned it into a tire factory."

What am I doing here? Laine wondered for the hundredth time.

"But it's not as if you were doing anything else,"

Madeleine said.

Laine started to say that she had a life, she had important things to do, but that didn't really seem true anymore. She glanced over her shoulder at the boxes of memorabilia and told herself this would be fun. An adventure. She'd never really been open to an adventure before and right now seemed a perfect time to start.

Since she'd already lost her mind.

And her way.

The trees formed a thick vibrant canopy and splotches of sunlight landed on the blacktop. A row of four mailboxes sat on a wooden structure beneath the dead-end sign. The dirt road branched into three directions and Laine got out to investigate. Mailboxes meant neighbors—that was a good sign—but after peering down each of the dirt roads she felt less encouraged. She didn't see any houses. Squirrels raced around and up trees. A robin darted through the branches. A crow watched her from a perch in an aspen.

"There's nobody here," she said to Madeleine.

"Well, it seems unlikely that the wildlife would have need of the postal service," Madeleine said through the open window.

Laine got back in her car. "Now where?"

Madeleine pointed west and they started down the hill.

A wooden sign had CAUTION spelled out in big red letters.

"That's just there for scaredy-cats," Madeleine said.

"Or for scaredy car owners," Laine said, wincing as her Volvo bumped and pitched down the slope. A small stream ran across the road at the bottom of the hill and Laine stopped the car at its edge.

"Well, what are you waiting for?" Madeleine asked.

Laine stared at the stream trickling through rocks.

"Honestly, it's two inches deep."

Laine took a deep breath and plowed through, listening to the mud splatter her car. She turned a sharp corner and suddenly emerged from the trees. Before her, a long stretch of the gray Sound. To her right, a three story stone house complete with bay windows and a widow's walk.

"This is a cottage?"

Madeleine shrugged.

"What made you think Sid would be here?"

"Oh, I don't think Sid will be here."

"Then why did we come?"

"I wanted to see it again."

Flabbergasted, Laine leaned back against the seat. "I thought we were looking for Sid."

"We are. Just not here."

"I don't get you." Laine bit her lip and followed the rutted drive to a barn that had been converted into a garage. She parked the car and got out. Madeleine followed.

"What does that mean?" Madeleine asked. "How can you *get* someone?"

Laine slammed the door and the sound seemed astoundingly loud in the quiet. She followed the cracked stone path, then climbed the wide cement steps to the front door. "I don't understand you," she clarified.

"Well, obviously you do, because we're communicating—"

"Not very well."

She looked around the deserted property. This was hers. All this belonged to her and just this morning she didn't even know it existed. Weeds everywhere, broken flagstone, peeling paint, shattered windows, rusted gutters. She loved it.

As if she could read Laine's mind Madeleine said, "We have what we have so we can bless others." Madeleine's voice turned soft and sad. "This place hasn't been a blessing to anyone for a long time."

This looks like it could use a blessing or an exorcism, Laine thought as she tried the door. It didn't budge. Of course it would be locked.

"Try again," Madeleine said. "It sticks."

Laine leaned into it and the door gave way. Tumbling, she caught herself in the entry. "I thought the most important thing, the reason you're here on earth, is to find Sid so he doesn't have to spend eternity 'unfettered.'"

A young girl's voice asked, "Who are you talking to?"

CHAPTER 10

Laine stopped short. The door, heavy walnut with beveled glass panels swung back and the knob hit near her spine, sending tingling vibrations down her legs and arms. "Ow!" she said, swallowing back words inappropriate for young girl ears.

"Who are you?" The girl tilted her head at Laine and pinned her with a blue eyed stare.

Laine stared back. She looked ethereal, blonde, wispy and insubstantial. If not for her Lucky Charms t-shirt, cut off jeans and sparkly pink flip-flops, Laine would have thought her a fairy. *I see ghosts—why not fairies? Why not Jaberwocks?*

Laine stopped rubbing the sore spot on her back and drew herself to her full height. "I'm Laine and this is my house." Why did she feel as if she was trespassing or interrupting? She had every right to be here. She owned this property. Being intimidated by a child of eight made her feel cowardly and embarrassed.

"This is your house?" The girl stepped closer and ran her gaze up Laine. "Are you the crazy lady?"

"What? No!" *Maybe.* "Why would you ask that? And who are you? Why are you here by yourself?"

"My brother's watching me." The girl's stare didn't flinch; she seemed to be looking for signs of lunacy. Unsure, she inched away.

"Well, he's not doing a very good job."

"He never does. When he's with his friends he likes to ditch me. He told me to wait here while they look for Charlotte."

"Charlotte?" Laine looked around the cavernous room. Dusty wood floors, twelve foot ceilings, fading wall paper, dingy white molding framing tall, thin windows and a massive fireplace. Gray sheets draped over lumps of furniture. Why hadn't she brought cleaning supplies?

"Charlotte Rhyme, the crazy lady."

Laine's attention snapped away from the dining room's web covered chandelier. "You mean Charlotte Rhyme the artist?"

The girl nodded solemnly. "She's missing. Again."

Laine had heard that Ms. Rhyme lived in Snohomish County. Brilliant yet reclusive, Ms. Rhyme hadn't been seen in public in years. Laine didn't really follow the art scene, but her work on the foundation often put her in contact with people who did. She'd heard the rumors.

"Miss Claris, the librarian, she's offered a reward."
The girl leaned forward, her eyes wide. "Fifty dollars."

Fifty dollars? Laine suspected that a few zeros had
been conveniently forgotten.

"If I find her, Max said he'd buy me a butterfly
garden."

"A butterfly garden?"

The girl nodded solemnly.

Laine stepped into the living room and bumping into a
cloth covered sofa. Dust curled in the air, making Laine
sneeze. She wiped her nose and turned to face the girl.
"What's your name?"

"Missy Clements."

Laine stuck out her hand and the girl took it in a tiny,
yet wiry strong grip. "Missy, my name is Laine Collins and
I don't know how to find Ms. Rhyme."

"The crazy lady," Missy piped in.

"I bet she doesn't like to be called that." *Crazy people
probably don't think they're crazy,* Laine thought. *They're
probably much too busy doing other things, like having
conversations with their grandmother's ghost and looking
for their dead grandfathers.* Where was Madeleine? When
had she disappeared? "Anyway, I can't help you find Ms.
Rhyme, but I can help you build a butterfly garden."

Missy's eyes went wide. "You can?"

"Sure. You help me clean this place up and I'll help you get the butterflies."

"There's more to a butterfly garden than just butterflies, you know. You need the right flowers and plants."

Laine nodded, understandingly and then motioned around the house. "And there's really a lot of needed cleaning around here." She squinted at Missy. "But I don't know… maybe you're not very good at cleaning. I should probably find someone who has experience with mops." Laine walked through the dining room and ran her finger along the cherry wood table, leaving a trail in the dust.

"I can mop. I'm good at cleaning." Missy followed her.

Laine began a mental list: ammonia, vinegar, rags, buckets, mops, brooms. "You would have to ask your mom first."

Missy bobbed her head in agreement. Laine stopped in the kitchen. Twelve by twelve white and black checkerboard tiles on the floor. Kelly green cabinetry, white tile backsplash, and a giant ceramic sink. An archaic looking oven stove combination and a gaping hole where, she guessed, a refrigerator used to be. How long would it take to make this habitable?

She stopped herself. *I'm just visiting. Consider this a holiday. A break and a breather before the breakdown. To prevent the breakdown. Or recover from a breakdown.*

"Maybe we need to start by finding Max." And ammonia.

A strange scratching noise followed by the thunk of a window slamming shut came from a room down the hall. The scratching sounded like frantic little footsteps. *Madeleine?* Laine watched to see if Missy could also hear the noise. She did. Or, at least her head swiveled in that direction.

"I think I know where Max is," Missy said, her voice low and full of dread. She headed down the hall.

Laine followed. The corridor had a row of closed doors. Missy stopped in front of the one with noise behind it and put her finger to her lips for silence. Laine wasn't used to taking directions from children. All the children she interacted with she met through the foundation. In general, they were an extremely grateful, well-coached lot under careful adult supervision. Laine rarely met children in the wild, or in their natural habitat—except for Ian's vast array of nieces and nephews. She didn't see them often enough to know them well. Now, she wondered why not. She put her hand on the doorknob.

"Don't open that," Missy warned, too late.

A squirrel darted out. Missy squealed as it scampered over her toes, then hurried after the creature. Laine ran after Missy, thinking of rabies, infections, and Lyme disease—or was that from deer? Rats? Rats, deer, squirrels—all the same thing.

The creature ran down the hall to the living room and quickly disappeared beneath a dust covered cloth chair. Missy dropped to her knees on the floor, lifted the cloth, and peeked—and screamed as the squirrel crawled onto her head.

"Get it off! Get it off!" Missy jumped around, swatting at her head.

Laine, trying desperately not to think of other animal spread diseases, like the plague, grabbed a mop from the kitchen and ran back to use it to knock the creature off of Missy's head. The squirrel climbed onto the mop, ran up Laine's outstretched arm, scampered across her shoulders and then jumped to the piano. It skittered across the closed lid before falling to the floor. It lay there stunned, its chest rising and falling in tiny huffs. Laine's accelerated breath matched the animal's. She grabbed a nearby empty cleaning bucket and slammed it over the squirrel.

"Way to go, Dumbo—you killed it." A kid about ten years old stood in the doorway, his arms folded across this chest. He had an uncanny resemblance to his sister—lanky limbs, wispy blond hair, light green eyes. Laine wondered what it would be like to have a sibling and share not only noses, but most everything else. Even traumatized squirrels.

"My brother—Max." Missy sighed the introduction.

***

After purchasing cleaning supplies, Laine headed to the library where she'd agreed to meet Mrs. Clements, Missy's mom. She sat on a big comfy sofa with a stack of books at her feet. *Poltergeists at the Picnic, The Big Bad Book of Spooks, Science Probes the Afterlife, Mental Illness for Dummies*—for a tiny library, Rose Arbor actually had a decent collection of books—just not a lot of what she was looking for. She wanted something that would tell her she wasn't crazy. The books weren't helping. She read from the book written by the Ghost Guru.

"Mental projection is a form of consciousness/spirit/intelligence projection from the emotional/astral plane to the mental plane. Adepts say they are able to project first to the emotional/astral plane (or directly from it after death) and then onward to the mental plane by completely calming their emotional processes and

withdrawing their emotional senses."

What? Adepts? Adept at what? Projecting their soul into another dimension? Laine leaned her head back on the sofa and considered the portraits on the opposite wall. A Mr. and Mrs. Rhyme stared back at her. They both had poofy hair—pompadours, popular in the 1940s. According to the plaque beneath their pictures, the library had originally been their home. Were they still here, but in another dimension? On some sort of emotional/spiritual/astral plane? The thought that they might be watching made Laine uncomfortable. She returned to the book.

"Like astral projection, mental projection is performed during sleep, between lives, during meditation-contemplation, or through 'psychic' (soulful) separation of the mental body from the emotional/astral body via the silver cord. Planes beyond the mental are accessible through use of the 'gold cord'. According to many esoteric philosophers, when projecting in these higher planes one has no humanoid shape and is just a lotus- or egg-shaped 'auric body' of consciousness."

So, according to the Ghost Guru, if Mr. and Mrs. Rhyme were here, they wouldn't have bodies or even poofy hair. She wouldn't be able to see them. So, why could she see Madeleine? Why wasn't Madeleine some phantasmagoric blob? Laine looked over at the circulation desk and watched Claris Rhyme, the librarian. Maybe Claris could see her grandparents. They had bequeathed the mansion to the town and Claris had converted it into a library. Maybe they wanted her to keep their home so they could stay here and not move onto the next plane. Maybe that's why the artist Charlotte Rhyme went crazy.

Laine couldn't blame them for wanting to stay. Tapestry rugs, down filled sofa, wing back chairs, and hard wood floors—take away the rows of books and the circulation desk and it would still feel like a home. Laine wondered if the cottage could ever feel as cozy and warm. It was a limestone mansion—she really had to stop calling it a cottage.

What had Claris thought when she'd checked out Laine's books. Did she have an opinion on the Ghost Guru? The bells on the door jingled and a breeze blew in. Laine looked up to see Missy and a solidly built woman heading toward her. Quickly, Laine gathered her books and placed them on the sofa with their spines facing the cushion. She draped her sweater over the back cover photo of the Ghost Guru.

She didn't want Missy's mother to think her crazy

***

Laine walked down Olympic Hill to the town green. She hugged her books against chest, her arm covering the Ghost Guru's intense face. All around her the townspeople bustled in and out of shops. Most of the store fronts had preserved a turn of the century feel and according to the marker in front of the large white gazebo in the middle of the green, Rose Arbor had been incorporated in 1903. A number of the people on the street looked nearly as old as the town, but not Bette. She emerged from Bernadette's Bakery holding a small white bag. Even from here, despite the blowing mower and the swirl of cut grass, Laine thought she could smell apple fritters. The scent took her back to her days at the university. She loved Bette and she loved apple fritters. At that moment, she couldn't say which she loved more.

Bette adjusted her sunglasses, looked across the green, spotted Laine and waved. Laine sat down on a park bench and waited for her friend. Other than the silver streaks in her fly away hair, Bette looked remarkably like the college co-ed in constant search of a pencil. Laine had at first found Bette annoying and then had grown to love her. Personality wise, they were as different as a pair of comfy well worn jeans and a pair of Prada shoes. Laine's prim and tidy dorm room had curtains that matched pillows on the bed that coordinated with the rug on the floor that were the same color as her bath towels that matched the bedspread. Bette's pillow often had chocolate on it because there were candy wrappers on her bed. Laine had a calendar on the wall with all of her upcoming school assignments marked in red, tests marked in yellow and social events marked in blue. Bette had a calendar, but she often didn't know where it was, and her meager budget couldn't keep up with her frequent loss of pens and pencils. Back then their relationship had been symbiotic—Bette needed pencils and Laine needed friends. Bette had a plethora of friends and Laine learned how to share her writing utensils. Now, Laine hoped that Bette had brought apple fritters to share.

Bette dropped onto the bench and opened the bag. The pastries warm smell wafted out. Laine looked in the bag. Two fritters. Bette smiled as she lifted one out.

"This," she said, "is a bribe."

Laine waited.

"I'll give it to you, if you'll answer all my questions." Bette bit into her fritter, and Laine scowled. "Oh, there's one for you. No worries."

"How did you know I was here?"

Bette laughed. "This is a small town, remember? Lots

of people know you're here."

"But no one knows me."

"They know you're the new owner of the Leon mansion." Bette nodded at the grocery bags at Laine's feet holding bottles of cleansers, lemon oil, rubber gloves and a bundle of cleaning clothes. "And that you've offered to build Missy Clements a butterfly garden if she'll help you clean it up. But it was the broken finger that cinched it." Bette took another bite and smiled like she'd tasted manna. "How many rich, clean freaky, broken fingered tall, dark curly haired women can there be in Rose Arbor?" Bette licked her fingers. "I've answered two of your questions and you've answered none of mine."

"But other people must have answered some of them," Laine said. "You know about the cottage."

Bette lifted her eyebrow.

"Although, it's more mansion than cottage." Laine corrected herself.

"What are you doing here, Laine?"

"Remember—I told you about my grandmother's photos and journals. I'm going to try to write her personal history." Laine paused. "Can I have my fritter now?"

Bette shifted the bag to the other side of the bench. "Have you left Ian?"

"How can I leave him when he left me six weeks ago?"

"Does he know you're here?"

"I don't know—does it matter?" Laine held out her hand for the fritter.

Bette narrowed her eyes.

"He left me! Six weeks ago!"

Bette scowled. "There's something you're not telling me. Is there someone else?"

"Not for me, no."

"And Ian?" Bette's voice turned soft.

Laine's shoulders slumped. "I don't know."

Bette's gaze held Laine's for a moment, and then she relinquished the fritter.

"Thank you," Laine said.

"You're welcome." Bette took a breath. "You know, I left Greg once."

Laine choked on her fritter and fumbled for a napkin. Bette pressed one into her hands. Laine used it to wipe up the crumbs that had escaped her mouth.

"You never told me that."

Bette shrugged. "It was only for five days. Now that he's gone, I'd do anything to recapture that lost time." She folded the now empty bag into a square. "It was this time of year, early autumn. Central Park was gorgeous—the changing leaves, the cold, crisp air."

"You went to New York?" That must have been expensive. Bette and Greg had always lived very modestly on Greg's school salary. Laine found it hard to believe Bette would pay for a trip to New York as a lark.

Bette nodded. "To Julliard. I just hung around campus, snuck into the practice rooms. I found a harpsichord in one...." Her voice drifted off. "I think of that week whenever I hear Bach."

"What made you go?"

"What made you kick Ian out?"

"I didn't—"

"Oh, please Laine. Don't lie."

"Why did you go to New York?" Laine pressed.

Bette sighed. "Because I was young and stupid and I thought I was old and world-wise. Greg and I grew up together." She looked around. "We grew up, here together, and it became clear to me that we were going to grow old, here, together. Same guy. Same town. If I didn't do something, *anything,* this was going to be all I'd ever know." She took a deep breath. "I thought I wanted something else."

Laine put her arm around Bette's shoulder and squeezed her tight. They shared this commonality, the love

of boys they'd known most of their lives. Laine knew that
Bette still loved Greg, and yet, here she was, in the middle
of her life with a new man. The knowledge fluttered in
Laine's stomach.

Bette leaned her head on Laine's shoulder. "I miss
him. I miss him every morning and every night. It's
football season, you know?"

"Do you go to the games?"

Bette shook her head no. "Errol likes plays. He takes
me to restaurants and tiny community theaters on Friday
nights." She paused. "I love it, but it's different." She
looked sharply at Laine. "Are you sure you want something
different?"

"I don't want someone different, if that's what you
mean." Laine answered quickly, thinking of Sean Marks
and his lingering touch on her skin.

"Does Ian?"

Laine shrugged. "Carly," she burst out, "this woman
Ian works with. She's always at his elbow. Everyone at the
office talks about them—treats them like they're a couple.
They work together—eat breakfast, lunch, dinner and
probably snacks in between. Carly maneuvers herself into
ready and willing position whenever Ian entered the room.
She laughs the longest and loudest at his jokes and he acts

differently around her—more confident, wittier, smarter."
And that was what hurt the most.

"Do you think he's—"

Laine shook her head. "I don't know. Maybe not, but he certainly hasn't been sleeping with me."

"That's hard to do when you're not speaking to him." Bette laughed. "Although you could try some cave woman pantomime."

Laine tried to smile. "The infertility—"

Bette nodded and squeezed her hand. Bette knew. She understood the horrors of hormones and infertility treatments. She also understood and sympathized with Ian's reluctance to adopt, much better than Laine did. It was something Bette and Laine had discussed relentlessly. Laine turned her thoughts away from babies. Those thoughts only led to dark, unhappy places.

"Don't you think an emotional affair can be just as painful as a physical one?" Laine asked. "Isn't it just as much of a betrayal? Back to the cave man—that whole pounding on-chest- me-man-and-must-have-woman thing—isn't that more forgivable and understandable than an affair of the heart and mind?"

"No." Bette snorted.

"Sex is more elemental—it's easier to control than

your mind."

"Says you," Bette said, licking her fingers. "I really don't think you would make this argument if you thought for even one tiny moment that Ian had slept with Carly."

"Maybe he has. You don't know."

"Do you?" Bette asked.

"No."

"Have you asked him?"

Laine gave her head a small shake. "I can't. We're not—"

"You're avoiding him." Bette made it sound like she was bludgeoning dogs and skinning cats.

"I can't talk to him. Every time I see him I clam up. I literally start to shake. My heart beats fast and then it's like the real me disappears and a phantom witchy me takes over." She took a long breath. "I wish I could disappear. Just fade away like I don't exist...right now the cottage seems like the perfect way to make that happen." She took another deep breath, desperate to change the subject. "Your trip to New York—it was just five days."

"I knew in three I wanted to go to home. Home, for me, was Greg."

And now he's gone, Laine thought.

"Yes, now he's gone," Bette said, as if she'd read

Laine's thoughts. "And I'm still here. But unfortunately, the fritters are gone too." She glanced at her watch, a pretty silver and sea shell thing that sparkled in the sun. It looked expensive and fragile, the sort of thing that practical Bette would love but would never buy. Laine wondered if it had been a gift from Mr. Prompt.

Laine used the napkin to wipe her sticky fingers. "Do you want to come see the cottage?"

"I'd love to, Lainey, but Errol is picking me up." She looked at her watch again. "Oh, I've got to go. I'll come out tomorrow." She cocked her head at Laine. "Do you think you'll still be there?"

Laine nodded. She wasn't very sure of most things, but she was quite sure she'd be at the cottage tomorrow. *I'll stay as long as I have Madeleine with me*, she told herself. Together, they'd look for Sid, work on her grandparent's life stories, and try to restore the cottage to its former glory.

With those decisions made, Laine pulled out her phone. She needed someone to take care of her cat.

***

"Oh my gosh, Laine, where are you?" Gemma breathed into the phone. Every phrase came out in a huff, accompanied by a small rhythm of clicks. Laine imagined Gemma sitting at her desk, taping out a tiny staccato with her bright red fingernails—Gemma's preferred form of fidgeting.

Laine swallowed. "I'm visiting an old friend." Did she really consider Madeleine a friend? She certainly could be classified as old.

The fingernail staccato grew louder and Laine knew Gemma wasn't satisfied with the vague answer.

"Where are you?" The tapping stopped. "No, wait. It'd probably be better if you don't tell me."

Why would Gemma say that? Laine rubbed her sore neck and looked around the town green. She felt the breeze on her skin, smelled the fresh cut grass and saw children running through the gazebo, but in her mind, she was back in the office with Gemma.

"Are you hiding from Ian?"

Laine snorted. "Of course not, I just want some time away and I need someone to take care of Cheshire."

The fingernail tapping resumed and Laine imagined she heard Gemma's unasked questions. "If Ian asks if I've heard from you, what should I say?"

"The truth of course."

"Really?"

"Yes. I'm not hiding from Ian or anyone else."

Gemma breathed out a sigh. "Okay, if you're sure,

because here he comes."

Laine's breath caught. "What?"

"Oh laws," Gemma whispered. "He's wearing his 'I'm the man face.' You're so lucky you're not here. He looks really, really angry."

"Gemma," Ian said, loud enough for Laine to hear him through the phone. "Any word?"

Laine held her breath while Gemma paused. After two beats of silence, Gemma answered, "No, Ian. I'm sorry."

Laine shoulders slumped in relief and she sent Gemma silent prayers of gratitude.

Ian said something Laine couldn't hear.

"Totally not like her," Gemma agreed.

Gemma paused and then said, "Okay, will do. Any idea who I should call?"

The sound of a pencil scratching on paper came through. After a moment, Gemma said into the phone, "I'm supposed to call your friends Bette and Marlene. Should I?"

"No. Thanks for lying for me."

"That's what good friends do," Gemma said.

"Even when I told you not to."

"A really good friend knows that what you mean isn't always what you say."

"I owe you."

"Yes, you do. Are you coming home soon?"

"I'm not sure—"

"What are you doing?"

Laine couldn't very well tell Gemma she was hanging out with her grandmother's ghost, so she said, "I'm building a butterfly garden and writing my grandparents' life stories."

"That sounds lovely." Gemma dropped her voice to a whisper. "He's back and he looks furious. Laine, Ian is out of his head, you need to talk to him."

"Gemma!" Laine heard Ian bark.

"I've got to go," Gemma whispered. "Come home soon."

"Love you," Laine said into the phone, unsure if Gemma heard her or not.

***

"I know it all looks rather grim," Madeleine said, as she helped Laine pull the sheets off the bed.

The sun, a pink blur on the Sound's horizon, cast a fading light into the room and threw long shadows along the wall. The open windows let in the breeze, replacing the musty and mildew smells with the odors of autumn—dry leaves and apples—mixed with Sound's brine.

"I wouldn't call it grim," Laine said, looking around

the white paneled room at the hodgepodge of circa 1930's furniture. The ceiling, swirled plaster, soared above them. "It just needs some love."

She gathered up the sheets and bedding and placed them on the chaise in front of the window and imagined sitting there herself, watching the wind tossing the waves on the Sound.

Madeleine ripped into the package of new sheets and began to make the bed.

"Why did you want to come here?" Laine asked her. "If you knew Sid wouldn't be here, why are we?"

"This is where I died, you know," Madeleine said, her voice soft. Bending over the large four poster bed, she pulled the sheets and blanket tight. "It has, for me, happy memories."

Laine stopped unzipping the plastic surrounding the down comforter. "Your death was a happy memory?"

"I was talking about the memories created *before* my death. Although it was terribly sad to leave Sid and Georgie, my death wasn't so very tragic."

"No?"

"Not for me," Madeleine said, seconds before she faded into nothing.

"I hate it when you do that," Laine said into the empty

air. *When she doesn't want to finish a conversation, she pulls away and hides.* The thought rang a familiar bell and Laine dismissed it and stuffed each fat pillow into a case with more violence than the pillows deserved. Tiny feathers escaped the casing and floated around her. The bedding, white and puffy, looked incongruously new in the antique room.

The sun dissolved into a pink and orangey puddle and to keep the darkness at bay, Laine turned on the bedside lamp, grateful the cottage had electricity. The lacy shade made flowery shadows on the walls.

The wood floors, still slightly damp from her spin with the mop, squeaked as she walked to the wardrobe. A few wire hangers dangled from the rod. Laine ignored them and placed her overnight bag on a shelf still shiny with lemon oil soap. "I'm only staying the night," she said to no one as she pulled out her pajamas.

The room was sleep ready, but Laine was not. Her body ached from the hours of cleaning, but her mind was wide awake. She considered cleaning the kitchen, a project she knew would take hours, even with Missy's help, but dismissed it. Her arms and shoulders hurt just thinking about more mop time. She padded down the stairs, stopping at the landing to look at the results of her hard work. The wood furniture and floors gleamed. The mirrors sparkled. Sure, she still had lots to do, but the house looked fabulous and she felt great.

She hadn't felt this good in weeks. Maybe months.

Outside, the cool air blowing off the Sound hit her, reminding her that even though the Chinooks burned warm, it was autumn. Soon, the Indian summer, as well as the leaves and so many other things, would die. The grass had already been killed by a dandelion overdose. Laine thought about the yard and garden, wondered what they would look like if she covered them with flowers like Bette's yard. *Maybe Bette could help,* she thought, but then she remembered Errol, Mr. Prompt, and wondered if Bette had the time.

She carried in the boxes of photos and memorabilia and put them in the dining room. The library would be a better place for them, but she hadn't yet cleaned that room and the books smelled of mold. Spreading the photos and albums across the table, she decided to see if she could find Madeleine's happy memories. Someone had labeled each photograph with a date and an occasional comment. Madeleine, Fort Casey, 1959. Sid's Chevrolet, 1957. Madeleine and Sid at the cottage, 1948.

Laine fell asleep with her head cradled in her arms on

the dining room table. The moment she realized where her dreams took her, she struggled to wake up, but she stayed asleep, transported back in time to a long ago camping trip. *Wake up! Wake up!* she urged her sleepy mind, but it stayed firmly on the shores of Shasta Lake.

They were with Ian's sister and her family. The kids ignited marshmallows in the campfire. Nelson, age three, liked to whip his lit marshmallow through the air and send sticky marshmallow strings flying. Pre-teen Jen had become painfully aware of the boys in the neighboring campsite, and the antics of her little brother made her sigh and occasionally grunt in frustration.

"Mom! Make him stop!" She'd say without looking up from her Cosmo-Girl Magazine. "He's getting marshmallow in my hair!" Which was true, but since they were on day three of camping and she hadn't showered or shampooed since leaving Seattle, who cared? Laine glanced at the boys sprouting acne and peach fuzz at the neighboring site. They seemed more interested in Harrison's neon boomerang than in Jen.

Harrison, age five, sent his boomerang sailing into the woods before running after it. Laine watched his red sweat shirt and shocking white hair disappear into a thatch of bushes. The sun had settled beneath the water and the moon hadn't yet the strength to penetrate the dark woods. She waited for his return and listened to the snapping of twigs where he'd gone.

Ian had once said that he tried not to worry about his sister's kids. If she lost one it could be easily replaced. Plenty more where that came from, he said with a tight smile, as if infertility hadn't wounded their marriage.

In the flickering firelight Jason and Ian loaded the wooden picnic table with their hiking treasures. Each appropriately admired the other's prize sleeping bag, or camp stove. Posturing, really. Together the men had climbed Whitney and descended to the floor of the Grand Canyon.

Harrison returned with his boomerang. With a Tarzan yell he sent it flying into the lake.

"Way to go, Dumbo," Nelson laughed, suddenly looking and sounding like Max.

Wake up, Laine commanded, but she stayed seated on a camp chair beside a roaring fire.

Harrison stood perplexed, watching his toy sink into the black water. He shot his mother a furtive look and took off after it.

Laine uncurled from her place beside the fire. "Wait, Harrison! I'll get it!"

"No, I will," Ian said, and he vaulted over a camp chair and ran toward the beach. He quickly overtook Harrison and dove into the lake. He stood for a moment, ferreted in the water and then held the boomerang up like a prize.

Harrison let out another jungle call before plunging in after him. Ian grunted like a gorilla and sprinted through the water to the shore where he wildly shook the water from his hair and body.

Her love for him was tangible. She could taste it, feel it, and she lived in it every day, usually giving it as little thought as the sun, and yet knowing, like the sun, that her world revolved around him.

But occasional moments, like that early evening on the shore of Lake Shasta, stood out in her memory as still frames. If she had a photograph of that moment, its caption would read, here is love.

***

Laine woke with a start and peeled her face off the dining room table. A photograph stuck to her cheek. Prying it loose, she saw a picture of a 1950's Sid holding a fish in his arms. *Camping.* She hated camping. Slowly, she pulled away from the table and all the memories of someone else's marriage. Her legs felt wobbly when she stood, and every inch of her body screamed with complaints. Up the stairs, into the bedroom, she crawled between the new, cold sheets and prayed she'd sleep without anymore dreams.

But lying back against the pillows, her mind returned to another camping trip. Day three of ovulation. A blanket in the woods, far away from nieces and nephews, a peep show for squirrels and chipmunks.

CHAPTER 11

Laine woke the next morning to deathly quiet. Slowly, the world came into focus. Sunlight through dirty windows, birds' songs in the neighboring trees, the gentle whoosh of the Sound and the call of gulls.

I'm at the cottage, she reminded herself, pushing onto her elbows and surveying the bright bedroom. *And I like it here.* She began a mental list of all the things that needed to be done. *Clean kitchen, wash windows, check to see if the washing machine works....*

A door banged closed and the noise echoed through the empty house. Laine sat up and brushed hair out of her eyes. Madeleine stood in the doorway holding a steaming cup of tea.

"That wasn't me," she said, lifting the teacup to her lips.

"You can eat?" Laine watched Madeleine blow on the tea.

"At a time like this? Sure."

"Not just now, but anytime?"

Madeleine shrugged. "If I want. I don't have to. It's a

choice."

Laine really wanted to pursue this conversation, but footsteps on the stairs stopped her. She caught a glimpse of herself in the wardrobe's mirror. In the wavy, silvering glass, she didn't look like herself. Her loose wild curls and white cotton nightgown, her skin pale in contrast to her dark hair—she looked as Victorian as the mirror.

The footsteps approached. Laine pulled a wrap over the nightgown for modesty. The crunch of tires on the gravel and the sound of a bumper scraping the ground drew Laine to the window. A police car idled in the drive-way. Laine turned back into the room and lifted her eyebrows at Madeleine.

"I wanted to file a missing persons report…" Madeleine said, smiling.

"For Sid? No, you didn't." Laine tugged the nightgown over her head, jumped into her jeans, and searched for her bra. At home, everything had a place. She'd yet to find her place here. What had she done with her bra?

Madeleine nodded. "Sid has lost his soul."

"Don't even say that. It sounds creepy." Laine found the bra beneath the bed. That was so unlike her—she must have been so tired that she tossed off her clothes. She threw on a white t-shirt.

"If we don't find him, it'll be true." Madeleine frowned at her. "Sweetie—"

"Who's to say what's true and what's not." Laine yanked open the door and saw Missy and Max on the stairs.

Missy waved in greeting, and then said to Max in a loud whisper. "She talks to herself, but she's very nice. So, I don't think she's the crazy lady...even though, she does talk to herself."

Max nodded, but didn't take his eyes off Laine. He stared at her chest. How old was he? Ten? Twelve? He seemed far too young to be ogling.

"Laine," Madeleine called after her.

Laine ignored her and greeted the children.

Missy focused her eyes on her toes. "My mom said I could help as long as Max came, too. I hope that's okay." It didn't sound okay to Missy, but Laine could understand Cheryl's concern.

Max glared at her boobs. It definitely didn't look okay to Max, either.

"Are you going to help clean?" She'd already offered Missy a butterfly garden; she really didn't want to have to pay Max. He seemed to have a weird fascination with her chest.

"Yeah," Max grumbled, finally looking away. "For a

stinking butterfly garden."

"Mom said Max and his scout troop could help build it."

"Really?" Laine bit her lip. Build what? She'd thought she contracted to buying a few butterflies and their favored plants. She didn't want to oversee Boy Scouts with hammers, nails and saws. And power tools? Boys liked power tools, electronic toys capable of removing fingers.

A knock rapped on the front door. "Hello?" a male voice called out.

"Laine, wait!" Madeleine called out as Laine headed down the stairs.

Neither of the children heard Madeleine and Laine pretended she didn't either.

A heavy-set man sporting a crew-cut stood in the open doorway. He wore a green police uniform and introduced himself as Floyd. "I followed the Clements kids over. Their mom told me about you."

Laine thought over yesterday's brief encounter with Cheryl. Had she done anything to warrant a police visit? Other than being seen with a pile of books about ghosts? She extended her hand and Floyd took it in a brief handshake. "Laine Collins."

Floyd ran his hand over his hair stubble and took a

quick look at her chest. His eyes flinched back to her face. "Just thought I'd introduce myself. Let you know I'm around, should there be trouble."

"Trouble?"

Floyd looked in the house with obvious curiosity. With the subtraction of the dust clothes and the addition of lemon oil, the furniture, despite its age, looked pretty good. Yesterday she'd cut a bunch of Scotch Broom, and put it in a pickle jar of water and placed it on the dining room table. Her grandparents' photos were still scattered across the table, giving the room a lived in, cheerful appearance.

"No one's been out here for years," Floyd said, his voice dripping with questions.

"I know. It belonged to my grandparents."

Floyd nodded, looking only slightly less curious. "You all alone out here?"

"Yes." She didn't mean for her tone to sound so defensive, but really, what was this impromptu visit all about? Was this how all newcomers were greeted to Rose Arbor? Because, it wasn't very friendly or welcoming.

"Well, if you see anything odd, or hear anything—just give me a call."

"He means if you see the crazy lady," Missy clarified.

"Oh." *Maybe Floyd wasn't so weird.* She caught him

staring at her chest. *Maybe...* Laine followed his gaze and saw what everyone else had already seen—her leopard spotted bra, clearly visible through her white t-shirt. *Argh.* Laine folded her arms across her chest.

Floyd frowned at Missy. "Ms. Rhyme, a local resident of Harmony Manor, is missing."

Missy nodded. "She painted Tonto green."

"Tonto?" Laine asked.

Missy nodded and Floyd looked at his shoes. "The Neilson's horse," Missy explained.

"Really?" Laine glanced at Missy in surprise.

"Tonto is a Palomino, so the green really stood out," Missy said.

"She's an artist," Floyd said, as if all artists use equine as a medium.

"Tonto got sick," Missy continued. "Almost died. Mr. Neilson was really, really mad."

Floyd sighed. "It's upsetting for everyone, especially her niece, and the director of Harmony House—"

"And Tonto—" Missy chimed in.

"Well, if I see her, I'll let you know," Laine said. "Although, this place is pretty remote. She probably wouldn't get this far."

Floyd lifted his eyebrows. "You'd be surprised. She

gets around."

***

Three days later, Laine turned to Missy and said, "I could use an ice cream."

Missy nodded solemnly over her feather duster. "An ice cream would be awesome."

Laine put down her wash rag. What she really wanted to do was look for Sid, but since she hadn't seen hide nor hair—did ghosts have hides or hairs?—of Madeleine since she and Missy had started cleaning, she didn't have a clue how to look for him on her own. So, she looked down at her sweaty shirt and said, "How about if you go and ask your mom for ice cream recommendations while I take a quick shower?"

Maybe Madeleine would reappear if Missy left. Maybe Madeleine had already found Sid and they'd moved onto the other side without saying goodbye. Although Laine knew that was what she should want, the thought bothered her like an unreachable itch.

Missy's expression turned sour as she helped Laine gather up the cleaning supplies. "Then we'll have to take Max."

"Not if we can't find him." Laine packed the supplies into the mudroom closet.

Missy handed her a broom. "If ice cream's involved, he'll find us."

"We'll be fast and sneaky," Laine said.

Missy put her hands on her hips. "You don't have an older brother, do you?"

Laine and Missy scowled at each other for a moment, both thinking of ways to ditch Max. "I know," Laine began, "we'll tell him we're going to the library. I want to go there anyway."

"Can I get some books on butterflies?"

"Of course. You get some butterfly books, I have some things I want to look up on the computer, and then we'll stop for ice cream on our way home."

"So it won't really be a lie," Missy said, happily. Her face fell as she considered the plan. "The only problem is there aren't any computers at the library."

"What?" Laine lifted her heavy hair off her forehead.

"Our library... my mom says it's sad. It's really just the old house where the crazy lady used to live."

Laine considered the library charming. Honey oak floors, tapestry throw rugs, heavy molding, and a smattering of antique furniture, but no computers?

"I guess you'll have to go to a bigger library," Missy said.

"No worries." Laine wiped her hands on her jeans and left smears of dirt on her legs. "If there are butterfly books and ice cream nearby, nothing can stop us. Not even Max."

"Especially not Max." Missy looked firm.

After a Rocky-Road chocolate/mint chip double ice cream cone, Laine dropped Missy off at her house and then pointed her car toward Seattle. As she passed over the bridges that led to the university district, her thoughts went back to Madeleine. Why had she disappeared? *Because there was work to be done?* Or was it because Laine had been focused on real things? Cleaning and laughing with Missy hadn't left her with any spare time for her mind to conjure up grandmother-type ghosts.

She reflected on her earlier reading and the questions it had raised. What is truth? What is reality? Can reality be distorted by perception and personal experience? If so, can reality be altered by experience? Can desires be realized through thoughts? Can ghosts?

By entertaining ghostly thoughts, she allowed herself to be haunted, not by ghosts, but by her own deficiencies. She knew she wanted a family. Losing first the prospect of having children, then Ian and then Sid…maybe it had all been too much for her. All that loss had sent her into a tailspin—or a head-spin—and suddenly a grandmother ghost. A cranky, bossy and obnoxious ghost, but still her grandmother.

Laine gripped the steering wheel as she pulled up at a light and stared at the building in front of her. She had driven to 44 East Elm on auto-pilot. There, in front of her, stood the offices of Leon Land Development. Her eyes traveled to the top floor. Ian's office. Mentally, she saw him sitting at his big desk. She could go in and talk to him. Tell him about the cottage outside of Rose Arbor, tell him it wasn't a cottage at all, and how after some spit and polish, it really was a beautiful house. In the spring, she could redo the landscaping; maybe Bette would help. She could tell him about Missy and Max, butterfly gardens…and maybe Madeleine.

No. She couldn't tell him about Madeleine and she wouldn't walk through those doors. Not now. Maybe not ever again. Thinking about her work at the foundation, she gripped the steering wheel tighter. He'd been right in having her take a leave of absence, although not for the reasons he thought.

A Volkswagen behind her bleeped its horn. The light had turned green. When? How long had she been parked there—not really coming or going, stuck in neutral?

The Volkswagen bleeped louder and longer. Raising

her hand in apology, Laine turned onto High Street, away from Ian. Irrationally upset, angry with herself for being overly emotional, she headed the car toward the university district and answers.

***

Of course, being on campus brought more memories than answers. She tried to fight off the angst-tinged nostalgia, but sadness dogged her as she tried to meld with the flow of students. Jeans, a t-shirt, a cardigan—she didn't dress so differently. Why did she feel so ancient? When had the school started admitting twelve-year-olds? Catching snippets of conversations, she eavesdropped on the students hurrying past. Class schedules, exams, professor woes, parties—a different world. A different life. She climbed the steps to the library and stopped near the top, her hand resting on the balustrade.

She resisted the memory, but went there anyway. It'd been a late summer night. School hadn't started yet, but she and Ian had already moved into their prospective dorms. She lived in Heath Hall. He was in Norman Hall. They met at night to run. *I'll race you to the library steps.* Ian tore away from her and she chased after him. When his first place position was secure, he turned toward her, running backwards, grinning, his knees kicking high into the air.

She smiled at him, picking up speed, watching while Ian back-stepped into a massive lilac bush. Sprinting past him, she laughed while Ian slipped in the fallen flowers. Seconds later, he caught up to her, but she pushed him on to the lawn and he skidded in a muddy patch. A girl stopped to help him up. Laine stumbled to a stop at the stairs, watching the girl flirt with him.

After a moment, she had that uncomfortable, skin-pricking sensation of not being alone. Looking down, she saw a couple making out at her feet. They lay on the lawn, legs entwined, totally engrossed in their own private biological studies. Embarrassed, Laine stepped away.

Ian jogged toward her, flushed. He stopped where Laine had stood moments before. Unaware of the couple at his feet, he doubled over, feigning exhaustion, placed his hands on his knees and pretended to gasp. Laine had to cover her mouth to stop from laughing, but she also had to pull Ian away. She grabbed his arm. He outweighed her by sixty pounds and he didn't want to move. They struggled and the couple on the ground lifted their heads to watch Ian pretending to have a heart attack.

"You beat me," he wheezed.

Laine, giggling, reached for his hand. He pulled her to him, but then he stopped, suddenly realizing they had an audience.

"Oh, hello," he addressed the couple on the ground. "Is your dorm room occupied?"

"Are you talking to me or them?" Laine asked as she led him down the path, away from the flirty-girl, away from the couple on the grass.

"Who do you think?" Ian asked, kissing her beneath a street lamp that shone down on them and lit drops of dew like a million sparkling diamonds on the sidewalk.

The diamonds weren't sparkling, and Ian was gone. Laine pushed up the library steps, away from the memories. Like an automaton without feelings or emotions, she made her way to the computers.

Settling into the carrel, pushing away all memories, she booted up the computer and found articles on ghosts written by believers and nonbelievers—mediums, ghost-hunters, professors of paranormal activity and skeptics. She copied down the name and contact information of a philosophy professor who specialized in metaphysics with an office in North Hall. For an inexplicable reason, her heart sped.

"What are you looking at?" Madeleine spoke in her ear, making her jump.

Laine sighed, and although she couldn't say why, she

was glad for Madeleine's company. Glancing around at the studious adolescents hunkered in the surrounding carrels, Laine lifted her finger, motioning for Madeleine to wait. She fished her phone out of her bag. It told her that she had fifty-eight missed calls. Fifty-eight, really? Laine pushed the ignore button and lifted the phone to her ear.

Laine's gaze swept over her grandmother. Today she wore vintage red lace and matching shoes with ribbons that tied around the ankles. *Where did she find her clothes?* "Where have you been?"

Madeleine rolled her eyes and smoothed down the front of her dress as she perched on the carrel. "You really didn't think I wanted to stay and clean, did you?"

Laine shrugged.

"Why didn't you hire someone? You didn't have to do all that yourself. Now your hands are chapped because you didn't wear gloves."

Laine looked at her hands and broken nails. Her finger had turned an interesting blue purple color tinged with yellow. "I did hire someone."

"And now you both need manicures," Madeleine sighed. "That little girl couldn't possibly have helped."

Laine disagreed. Missy had helped, and not just with the cleaning. "You didn't tell me where you've been."

"Looking for Sid, of course." Madeleine sighed again, deeper.

"No luck?" Laine asked. She thought about asking why Madeleine involved her, since she obviously could look for Sid on her own, but she bit back the words.

Madeleine shook her head. "I hate to return without him...I've waited so long."

Pointing at the computer screen, Laine said, "It says here that we need to embrace whatever we're feeling and not resist. Trying to suppress or ignore our emotions will cause them to grow. Give them power." Which actually seemed contradictory. If she ignored Madeleine, would she go away? Wouldn't indulging her give her power? Laine rested her head in her hand while she held the phone to her ear with the other. She was so confused. According to this professor, she needed to acknowledge the negative emotion, aka Madeleine, and not fight the emotions she caused, but rather focus on something pleasing. Supposedly, without negative emotion Madeleine would melt away. Sort of like the Wicked Witch of the West. Is that what she wanted? Did she want Madeleine to fade away?

"Maybe you need to accept that Sid is lost," Laine said.

A guy with acne and an untrimmed beard from a neighboring carrel turned to give her a dirty look. Laine held the phone to her lips and turned her attention to the computer screen. "It says here that when you take control of what you are creating with your thoughts and are able to attract to you what you desire, you will begin to experience the true meaning of power, peace, fulfillment, abundance, and happiness."

"Nonsense."

"He's a philosophy professor and he's actually won a host of awards."

"That doesn't mean that he's ever lost someone he loves." Madeleine's voice sounded sad, and she glanced out the window at the yellowing leaves.

Laine fought the temptation to reach out to Madeleine. As of yet, she'd shied away from touching her, not knowing what she'd find. The thought of hugging thin air scared her. *Maybe I don't want to believe she doesn't exist, because if she doesn't exist, then there's a part of me that's also make-believe, empty fantasy. Maybe I want to believe she is real. Maybe this is my way of coping with Sid's death. It's certainly easier to accept it if I know he has a place to go with someone who loves him.*

"Okay, where do you want to look next?"

Madeleine's face lit up. "You mean you'll help me?"

"I've been helping you," Laine spoke so sharply that several of the students lifted their heads above the walls of their carrels to look at her.

"Not really."

"I drove around in the middle of the night!"

"Yes, but you didn't want to."

Who wants to drive around in the middle of the night? Laine sighed, remembering Professor Abbot's advice to embrace the emotion, don't try to suppress it. "What do you think we should do now?"

"To look for Sid?"

Laine nodded.

Madeleine looked out the window. "We need to go to the Leon Land offices."

Laine groaned. "We can't."

"We have to. You know he loved his work!"

Just then her phone chimed. Surprised, Laine pulled it away. Her ear rang painfully. When the acne guy turned to give her a slant-eyed look, she hit the ignore button just after catching Gemma's name. She really wanted to talk to Gemma, but right now she needed to help her grandmother. *Acknowledge and embrace the emotion.*

Still. "I can't go there. Ask me anything else."

"What happened to embracing and succumbing?"

She whispered, "Why do you need me? You can go anywhere you'd like without me."

"But I can't ask questions."

Laine considered this. She could be her grandmother's spokesman because she also needed to know what had happened to Sid. She didn't think she'd ever be at peace if she didn't know where he was. It was possible, of course, that another family had mistakenly cremated or buried him. Laine didn't know why that should be any different, and yet it was.

Acne guy grunted and hunched his shoulders. Laine wondered why he wasn't wearing an iPod like ninety-nine percent of all the other students. She turned her back on him and began to gather up her books and notes. Laine decided that she'd spend one day humoring her ghost and then after that she'd go the crazy route. She'd have Madeleine exorcised. Whatever that meant.

Following Madeleine through the library, Laine considered renting the movie *The Exorcist.* She'd tried to watch it as a kid, but had spent most of the movie with her hands covering her eyes. Ian had laughed at all the neck-twisting and ventriloquism, but it had terrified her. For weeks, whenever he had wanted to tease her, he'd talk in what he called his Satan voice. That was before he could shave.

Once they were outside on the steps, Laine said into her phone, "Let's wait until after the office closes."

"You're such a chicken."

Laine nodded, thinking of her experience with *The Exorcist.* She really didn't want to call a ghost expert— someone like that could have all sorts of connections to the Otherworld. Not that Laine believed in the Otherworld, but she really preferred to keep all of her connections firmly attached to *this* world—the only world she had any intention of ever knowing…unless, of course, Madeleine was real. And there really was a life after death.

Maybe instead of talking to a ghost expert she should talk to a priest. Her family had never been particularly religious, but she could talk to the pastor who'd conducted Sid's funeral. The thought comforted her and yet made her nervous. Just thinking of confessing to someone that she saw and talked with her grandmother's ghost made her sweat. She tripped on the last step and bumped into a girl sucking a smoothie.

"So sorry," Laine said as green goo plastered her shirt and trickled down her jeans.

The girl still had her straw between her teeth and the

now smashed cup in her hand. "Thanks," she said.

Laine blinked, trying to decide if the girl was a master of sarcasm.

"Seriously, you've done me a giant favor." The girl dropped the cup in a nearby trash can and wiped her hands on her oversized psychedelic t-shirt. "My boyfriend is gaga over green smoothies and well, I'm not. Thanks for finishing that off for me."

"You shouldn't try to like something just because he does," Laine blurted. *Where did that come from? Suddenly she was Dr. Laura, spouting advice to random strangers?* She tried to correct her bad behavior. "I've ruined your shirt. You should let me get you a new one."

"Yeah, this goop doesn't come out for anybody's business. My boyfriend's sofa is covered in green spots. Looks like it has a bad case of mold. Kind of smells like it, too, but then, he lives with a bunch of guys. But I can't let you buy me a shirt—after all, it's not as if your shirt is in any better shape."

"But I bumped into you."

"Maybe I drew you to me, knowing that you'd make me spill my drink. Maybe I even stood in your way."

Laine laughed, wondering if this girl could have possibly been looking over Laine's shoulder and reading her research on the power of the mind. "You wouldn't have done that."

"How do you know? You just met me. There you were, distracted, talking to yourself—you were an easy target."

The phone ploy—was it fooling no one? Did she really look like the sort of person who went around having long, fruitless conversations with dead people? "Okay, I won't buy you a shirt and I won't buy a smoothie. Is there something I can do to make up for the mess?"

The girl cocked her head, thinking. "Yes...."

***

At five-thirty, Laine stood in front of the Leon Land offices in her brand new t-shirt dress. "Are you sure you didn't have anything to do with this?" she whispered to Madeleine.

Madeleine laughed. "You bumped into her."

"And you didn't know she was a fashion design major with a boatload of summer clothes to unload?"

"How would I know that?" Madeleine looked wide-eyed and innocent. "Besides, you're gorgeous."

Laine looked down at the color-splattered dress. "I look like I'm wearing a Pollock painting."

"I really like the shoes, and the bag is a nice touch."

"You don't think it's too much?" She hitched the bag over her shoulder and then tugged on the dress so it hit a little lower on her thigh.

Madeleine laughed and pulled open the door. "Remember, we're coming after hours, so he won't even be here."

Laine followed Madeleine into the cool, marble foyer. "Then why are we here?"

"To look for Sid, of course."

"But you just said he wouldn't be here."

"I wasn't talking about Sid."

"Fine, you look for Sid. I'm going to get my extra set of car keys from my desk. "

"And what happens when you see Ian?"

Laine opened her mouth to say something and then closed it when Leroy, the security guard, suddenly appeared. "Evening, Miss Laine."

"Oh, good evening Leroy. How are you?"

"It's a fine night." He looked at her oddly. "You want me to ring Mr. Ian for you?"

"No. No. I just came to get something from my office." She practically ran to the elevator and then sighed in relief when the doors closed shut. After a quick glance at the security camera, she turned her back to it and whispered to

Madeleine, "He's here."

Madeleine looked bored. "You knew he'd be here. He's always here."

"Not always." Laine sank to the floor, sitting with her knees pointing up in the air. The guards in the security office could probably see up her dress, but she didn't care.

"Pull yourself together. This isn't about you or Ian. It's about finding Sid."

Laine rested her forehead on her knees. "Fine, where do you want to look? I'll go anywhere but the sixth floor." In her mind, she saw that floor, home to the head offices. Lush green plants in shiny brass pots, low pile carpet a tapestry of jewel tones, picture windows with views across the Sound. Since she'd been a child, she'd been a frequent visitor to her grandfather's office. Sitting on his lap as he sat behind the giant desk, she had often amused herself with his multicolored tacks and sticky notes. When Ian had taken over the office, she'd sat on his lap, too, but she'd found better entertainment than tacks and sticky notes.

"You shouldn't let him dominate you."

"How can he dominate me when I'm not even going to see him?"

The elevator dinged and the doors slid open to the fifth floor, where Ian stood, waiting.

CHAPTER 12

Laine scrambled to her feet while Ian placed his hands on the doors, preventing closure.

"Where have you been?" His white lips and the vein pulsing in his neck told her that he held his anger by a thin string.

Laine brushed down her dress and looked at her shoes. Pink shoes without laces, Ian followed her gaze, but then placed a finger beneath her chin lifting her face to his. "Three days, Laine. Nobody knew where you were."

Laine bit her lip. She was a breath away from forty. Coming and going without permission should be allowed, but then she saw the worry and hurt in Ian's eyes. She had to do something about that, but she didn't know what.

"I've been staying at the cottage in Rose Arbor."

He dropped her chin. "I went there." His tone sounded accusatory. "It looked like its only inhabitants are vermin."

She gave him a tight smile. "That's me, vermin. Actually, I've been cleaning and it looks great…" her voice trailed away.

"You've been cleaning. Why?"

"Well, I own it, right? I might as well make use of it. I really like it out there."

"It doesn't even have cell service!"

"Maybe that's one of the things I like."

He looked at her as if she'd said she liked sporting with dragons.

"Wait, why did you come out? Did you need something?"

Ian opened his mouth to say something and then closed it. He rubbed his eyes and looked tired. "Three days, Laine."

She touched his arm. "You've been gone for six weeks, Ian."

"If you needed me, you knew where to find me."

She let his words hover between them, not knowing how to respond. After a long beat of silence, she asked, "What did you need?"

"They've found Sid."

Laine's heart sped. "Where?"

"Soap Lake. I want you to come with me."

"Soap Lake?"

"It's north of Ellensburg."

"I didn't know there was anything north of Ellensburg."

"We can go through Wenatchee."

"Wait. What? We both don't need to go."

Ian pursed his lips, something he did when he had to say something he didn't want to say. "I'd like us to go together."

"Why?"

"Because you're next of kin. Besides George."

She didn't even consider asking her dad to go. Glancing at Madeleine, Laine knew she had to go. But not *with* Ian.

"I'd love to go."

Ian looked at his watch. "Good. I'll throw together an overnight bag and then swing by to pick you up."

"An overnight bag?"

Ian looked at a spot on the wall behind her, not meeting her gaze. "Well, it's a three-hour drive."

Laine folded her arms across her chest. "You won't need an overnight bag, and you certainly won't need to pick me up. I can drive my own car." She narrowed her eyes at him, trying to read him. He wanted something, something he didn't want to tell her.

Ian shuffled his feet. "It's three hours, six round trip—"

"Which is exactly why we should take separate cars."

Laine moved past him toward her office. The empty desks around her made her sad and a little lonely for Gemma, Marcia, Kelsey and Bob. How were they managing without her? Why hadn't they called? Then she remembered the fifty-eight telephone messages, and a wave of guilt washed over her. How many days until the masquerade ball?

"We could use the time to talk." Ian followed her.

"For six hours?" She shook her head as she pushed open her office door. The dying sun lingered on the horizon of the dark Sound. She loved this view. Other, larger offices had been available and she could have had any of them, but she'd chosen this one. Ian had wanted her on the sixth floor near his office, but she'd said that she wanted to be near her staff. Her real reason was that she loved the west facing view. And now, she was glad she didn't have a daily performance of the Carly-Ian drama. She was grateful to be away from Jane's ever watching eyes.

Ian's office, as well as most of the sixth floor, had rich cherry paneled walls, maroon carpet and a heavy solid walnut desk. Laine flushed, remembering that more than work had been completed on Ian's desk. It hadn't even creaked beneath their combined weight. She shoved the memories to the back of her mind, suddenly grateful for her own insubstantial chrome and glass desk. Taking a deep breath, she glanced at the photos lining the walls. Most were from her fund raising galas and many featured the women and children for whom she'd worked so very hard, but many were also of Ian. Not just Ian, of course, but now, looking around, she noticed that he was in almost every photo. If she tried to cut him out, she'd leave great, gaping holes.

She could take more photos. But could she still work in the same building? And how could she possibly ride in the car with him for *six* hours?

He stood in the center of the bright floral throw rug, his arms folded. A quilt made by the children from Lindsey's House hung on the wall behind him. Each child in the shelter had dipped their hands in primary colored paint and left their handprints and splatters of paint on the white cotton. Laine glanced down at her Jackson Pollock dress and realized that she fit perfectly in this charming office. Ian did not. Especially not when he wore that expression.

"Granny Ivy's sick," he said.

And suddenly, Laine understood.

"She loves you," he said simply.

Laine bowed her head and opened her desk drawer, looking for her keys and hiding her emotions. She loved

Ivy, and she loved visiting Ivy's ranch in the tiny mountain town of Glen Louise. "And you don't want her to know you left me."

Ian's scowl deepened, something she hadn't thought possible. "I don't want her to know you threw me out."

Laine returned her attention to the desk drawer. Yellow plastic paper clips, hot pink sticky notes, a purple stapler— *a place for everything and everything in its place.* She picked up her extra car keys and dropped them into her bag. If she hadn't lost her keys on Cobb Street, she could have avoided this conversation. She hated confrontations.

But she loved Grandma Ivy. If Ivy died, which, given her age, had to happen sooner rather than later, and Laine had missed an opportunity to say goodbye, she'd feel terrible. Even more terrible than she already felt. Ian's accusation sat on her shoulders until the weight of it made her ask, "What's wrong with her?"

Ian shrugged and looked out the window. "She wants to see you."

Laine laughed and leaned back in her chair. "That's what's wrong with her? Are you saying she must be delusional to want to spend time with me?"

Ian gave her a hard look. "That's not what I meant, but if you're feeling guilty—"

"I'm not feeling guilty! I'm not the one who should have any guilt!"

"Oh, and I am?"

"Stop it. If this is how you think you're going to convince me to visit your sick grandmother—"

"You're right. I'm sorry, Lainey." Ian ran his fingers through his hair. "It's hard to think of her being sick—she's always been such a pistol."

"A very young ninety-four pistol."

"Ninety-four isn't young in anyone's book." Ian turned the full impact of his blue eyes on her. "Will you come?"

"I'm not staying the night at the ranch."

"It'll be nine before we get to the church where they have Sid."

"I'll sleep in my car before I spend the night at Ivy's."

"That's a possibility." Ian shrugged and laughed, probably because he knew that she would never stay the night somewhere without someplace clean to brush her teeth and shower. "There isn't a Marriott for miles around there."

"Then we can leave tomorrow."

"NO! NO! NO!" Madeleine. When had she shown up?

"Actually, there's a wedding at the church where Sid is…staying. They'd like to move him as soon as possible."

"But it'll be late already when we get there. How can we make arrangements—"

"If we get there tonight we can have him moved tomorrow morning."

Laine sniffed and looked out the window at the sinking sun. "We'll take two cars. Meet at the church in Soap Lake, stay the night in Ellensburg, and I'll leave my car at Ed's Superette."

Noticing Ian's frown, she smiled. "You're afraid one of your precious cousins will see us and tell your grandmother we came in two cars."

Ian shrugged and sat down the red wing chair. "Two cars, two tanks of gas, two hotel rooms…"

"It's the price we pay." For years she'd teased Ian about his poverty complex, his guilt over his wealth when most of his family was so poor, his constant frugality, his birddog watchfulness over all his pennies. She no longer found it even remotely funny.

"Are you really willing to pay such a high price?"

And she knew he wasn't talking about the cost of a trip to Central Washington.

***

Armed with a small overnight bag, a GPS, reservations for a hotel in Ellensburg and a full tank of gas, Laine pulled onto the east bound I-90. Madeleine fidgeted beside her. Laine glanced over at her and realized she was nervous. "How long has it been since you've seen him?"

"Oh, I've seen him plenty, but he hasn't seen me."

"You've visited him before?"

"Many times. He just hasn't known it."

Laine cleared her throat and gripped the steering wheel. "So, you know about Jennifer, Laurel and the others?"

Madeleine looked out the window. "So many others."

"And you don't mind?"

"Of course I mind! But what could I do about it? I'm dead."

Laine chewed on the inside of her lip as a semi-truck pulled in front of her. "How did you visit him?"

"I lurked," Madeleine said without a tinge of embarrassment.

"That must not have been easy for you."

"Oh, it was very easy. The chances of him noticing me were nil."

"That's not what I meant, although that raises another very good question. What I meant was—it must have been difficult for you to see him with other women."

Madeleine raised her eyebrows. "It was at first. In the

beginning, I thought his behavior negated the one true love and soul-mate fairy tale, but after some time I realized that he was sad, lonely and looking to recapture what he thought we'd lost." She was quiet for a beat of silence. "I had compassion for him. He didn't understand that our separation was temporary."

Laine flipped on her headlights as she headed up the pass. A cloud shrouded the mountain top and drizzle gathered on the windshield. "I admire you," Laine said suddenly, surprised by her own outburst. She glanced over at Madeleine and saw that she'd surprised her, too. "I really do. You were able to look past Grandpa Sid's behavior and see his real motivation. I think that's remarkable."

"You know what's really remarkable?" Madeleine asked.

"That I'm having a conversation with my grandmother's ghost?"

Madeleine laughed. "That's not remarkable at all."

"It's not?"

"No. The dead visit the mortal world all the time."

"All the time?"

"You probably meet the dead countless times a day and not even realize it."

A chill passed up Laine's spine. "But why? How?"

"The same way you meet anyone. We cross paths. Our agenda's collide."

"You have an agenda?"

"Of course. You know that. We've certainly been talking about it for long enough. I'm here to take Sid to his next life."

"But the dead you said I've met—are they here for the same reason?"

"Maybe, maybe not. There are many reasons for the dead to visit the living."

"Is it like a door you pass through?"

"You do know I can't tell you everything."

Laine sniffed and tried a different tactic. "Tonight, Sid will see you, even though he never could before."

Madeleine nodded.

"Because you're both dead?"

Madeleine nodded.

"How do you know he'll be there?"

"I don't, but it's typical for the newly departed not to want to leave their bodies."

"What if he doesn't want to leave now?"

Madeleine sighed and shook her head.

They drove in silence over the crest of the mountain. The road cut a path through the thick forest. Laine looked into the woods, wondering what it would be like to navigate into a dark, unforeseeable unknown. She completely understood why her grandfather, as well as anyone else who had just recently died, would be hesitant to leave their bodies, leave the only life they've ever known, or could remember. Was there more to remember? Should she ask her grandmother about a pre-earth existence? Would she even know? Maybe there were things she didn't know, or couldn't remember.

How comforting it would be to be met by a loved one on the other side of life. So much better than trying to make that transition alone. Who would meet her? Ian flashed in her mind and Laine tried to dismiss him and replace him with an image of her mother—Ian's face wouldn't leave.

Laine clenched the steering wheel as the drizzle dissipated. Heading down the mountain, into a valley of pastures and farms, the wet pavement gleamed and reflected the setting sun. Typically, Laine loved this time of day. Blue light, her mother had called it. Not quite day and not quite night, a brief time hovering between—not one or the other. She loved the soft, diffused sun, the glow below the trees, slipping into the horizon from sunset to nightfall, but today she wished for more light, less gloom. "How long has it been since he's seen you?" Laine asked, her attention drifting from the road and backlit trees.

Madeleine answered by pointing her finger at the side of the road. "Let's go down there."

Laine squinted at the dirt road lined with blackberry bushes taller than her car. "What?"

"There used to be a fishing cabin," Madeleine insisted. "I want to see if it's still here."

Is she stalling? Laine wondered. *After all her fuss and impatience to find Sid, is she now nervous?* Laine considered ignoring her grandmother, but since they'd made good time thus far and they had more than an hour until they were to meet Ian at the church and less than twenty miles to go, and since scoping out an old fishing cabin seemed way more preferable than hanging around a church waiting for Ian, Laine turned her Volvo down the dirt road. "Whose cabin are we visiting?" *Will we be arrested for trespassing?*

"It belonged to John Rhyme, Sid's friend." Madeleine looked at her. "You don't know him?"

Laine didn't remember her grandfather having *any* male friends; he'd been much more interested in the opposite sex. She didn't tell her grandmother this, although she suspected that her grandmother already knew.

"Charlotte Rhyme now owns this land."

Laine gripped the steering wheel as the Volvo bounced over the rutted dirt road. Pot holes as big as crab-cookers pitted the road and Laine tried to avoid hitting them, worrying that if she happened to land in one, she might not ever be able to get out. "The crazy lady?"

Madeleine laughed. "I wouldn't call her that."

"That's what everyone I've met in Rose Arbor calls her." In an effort to avoid a pothole, Laine ran over a fallen branch. They bounced over it; Madeleine's head almost hit the Volvo's roof.

"And what would they call you if they knew that you hold long conversations and take directions from your grandmother's ghost?" Madeleine asked, as she clenched her seatbelt, hanging on for life.

But she was dead. Laine asked, "Why are you wearing a seatbelt?"

Madeleine looked at her as if she was as crazy as all of Rose Arbor would most assuredly think if they knew about her—her *what*? Relationship? Interaction? with Madeleine.

Laine pressed on. "I mean, what can happen to you? Can you get hurt? Is your body even real?"

Madeleine answered with a scream.

Laine turned her attention back to the road in time to come bumper-to-nose with a giant deer. He lowered his antlers at her as she laid on the horn and swerved sharply to the left. The buck dashed into the thicket of alders as the Volvo careened off the road. Blackberry bushes and a substantial maple flew past her windshield. The spinning green tangled around her, giving her the sense of being swallowed and sucked into nature's belly. Things bumped and thwacked against the car. Seconds later, although it seemed like hours, the car broke free from the foliage and hurtled into a stream. They lurched to a stop and the airbags burst out, pushing Laine back against her seat.

Laine leaned forward and rested her head on the airbag. The seatbelt cut into her skin, but she didn't care. She was alive, unhurt. She wondered if she could say the same for the Volvo. Looking over at where Madeleine had been sitting, Laine fought waves of queasy hysteria.

"This is all your fault!" Laine said, her voice rising with every word. She looked wildly around for Madeleine, didn't see her, but continued to yell anyway. "Let's go see a fishing cabin! Whatever for? Why are you taking me on your trip down a muddy, pothole-laced, deer-infested memory lane?"

Laine struggled with the door, and after a few moments she managed to push it open. The creek, shallow and slow-moving, poured in. Laine continued to curse her grandmother as the cold water hit her legs and filled her shoes. *It could have been worse,* she told herself. She could have been hurt, or killed. She could have hit the deer. She abandoned the car in the ditch and picked her way out of the stream to follow a trail into the woods. Hurt and confused, she didn't know which way to go. Mosquitoes teased her. She repeatedly waved them away, and slapped at the ones that lit on her neck and face. Her shoes sloshed with water as she walked. The soaked hem of the Jackson Pollock dress dripped like the edge of an umbrella.

Under a thick canopy of pine trees the trail disappeared at the clearing that surrounded the cabin. The small wooden structure, hardly bigger than a tent, appeared to be on the edge of collapse. *I must be going the wrong way,* Laine thought. She needed help, professional mental health help. She stepped onto the wood porch and peered through a dirty window, and saw one room dominated by a brick fireplace. A three-quarter width bed and a trestle table with three ladder back chairs seemed to be the only furniture. She considered lying down on the bed, but turned away.

Laine sat on a low rock wall overrun with moss, lichen, and fungus, nearly hidden by an outcropping of ferns. She gazed at the creek tumbling through a bed of rocks and around the hood of the Volvo. She kicked at a mushroom growing near her foot and felt overwhelmed with rioting emotions. She felt cold and stupid.

The trees rustled, and a bunny jumped out of the thicket. She had been quiet so long that the animals were no longer nervous and resumed their activity. Crows wheeled over her head; a bobcat slunk through the huckleberry bushes and Laine urged the bunny to run.

She couldn't run, but she couldn't stay, either. She had to find her way back to the main road. Slowly, she stood. Dark had fallen around the thick trees. The shadows had grown with the last of the sun. Wind, cold and sharp, whistled through the woods and stung her damp legs. Laine listened to the wind, the rustling trees, movement in more than the air. She heard a footfall. She froze, held her breath, but heard nothing more than her own heart. She glanced back at the cabin and then at the path, but if there was someone—something there—she couldn't see. Perhaps the deer had returned. She felt its eyes on her. Telling herself that wild animals wouldn't bother her if she didn't bother them—was that true for animals? Or just bees? She took faltering steps in what she hoped was the direction of the highway.

More footsteps. Whirling, she saw a tall form emerge from the trees. She tried to run, but the wet shoes slid from her feet, slowing her. A hand on her arm stopped her.

"Lainey, it's me!"

Ian? How had he found her?

He held her tightly against his chest. "You're not hurt?" he murmured into her hair. Pushing her away from him, he ran his hands over her arms. Satisfied, he pulled her against him again. She tried to pull away, but he had her pinned. He lifted her chin and kissed her.

She willed herself to fight. Sanity told her to step away. But she couldn't and as his kiss deepened, she realized that she'd lost sanity a long time ago and if she didn't do something, *anything,* she'd be right back where she'd been before Ian stepped out the door. No. She sank deeper into his comfort. Had it always been this way? Kissing Ian—why did such a small meeting of lips make her knees buckle? Placing both her hands on his chest, she pushed him away. She stumbled back, out of his embrace. Frustration marked his face and he raked his fingers through his hair. He looked at her and his gaze lingered on her legs. Puzzlement overtook the frustration and then he grinned.

"You have no right—"

Ian fought his smile, but it still lingered around his lips. "Actually, I do. I'm your husband, remember? Marital rights."

"That's barbaric."

Ian folded his arms across his chest. "I'm a barbarian? If I were truly a barbarian, I'd carry you into that shack and strip off your clothes."

Laine threw the cabin a worried glance and stepped away from it, which brought her one step closer to Ian. She shuffled to the side, closer to the road.

"Don't think I haven't thought about it. I'm considering it now."

"How did you find me?"

"Delicious."

Laine flushed. "That's not what I meant, and you know it."

"No one would hear you if you screamed." Ian looked around. "I think we're very much alone."

"Were you following me?"

Ian walked to the cabin and looked in the window.

Laine watched his retreating back. The wind whistled around her and the shadows deepened. Suddenly, thunder cracked. She knew she should be glad he'd come. With the Volvo firmly mired in the creek she'd have a long wet walk to the next town. Not that she was glad for his company... her fingers traveled to her bruised lips. When was the last time he'd kissed her like that? She couldn't remember. His seduction style was generally much more subtle. In his custom-made suits and silk ties, he never played the Tarzan role. Of course, since they'd started the infertility treatments, kissing, as well as a good many other once-enjoyable past-times, had become much more perfunctory.

Lightning flashed. Fat, cold raindrops fell. She could join Ian on the porch or go and find the Mercedes. Watching him, debating, she realized for the first time that his jeans were soaked.

He turned back to her. "You're going to get wet."

"You're already wet," she said, pointing at his jeans.

"The Volvo," he answered. "I think it may be ruined. It doesn't have a hull."

"I know. I'm sorry. I swerved to hit a deer and lost control."

Ian nodded. The wind picked up volume and speed and Ian raised his voice. "I hit that deer."

"You what?" Laine pushed her wet hair off her face. The rain stung her arms and legs.

Ian called out over the howling wind. "I hit the deer. Its antlers are tangled beneath the car."

"What?"

Ian shrugged. "It'll have to be towed." He turned his

back to her and opened the cabin door.

Laine knew what he was thinking and she didn't like it at all. She started walking in what she hoped was the direction of the road.

"Lainey!" Ian called.

She ignored him. Spending the night in that cabin alone with Ian was not debatable. It was not going to happen. Come heaven or hell or high water... of course, all of those seemed to be conspiring against her. She stood at the edge of the creek, watching the water bubble inside the Volvo's cab. Heaven was sending rain, the water was drowning her car, and hell...well, hell was spending the night alone with Ian. She glanced back at the cabin and trudged through the mud and pelting rain, repeating like a mantra all the reasons she hated Ian. *Overbearing, dictating, charming and double-handed.*

She stopped in the middle of the road, staring at the hooves of the deer protruding from underneath the Mercedes. It looked like the car was being held aloft by the antlers. Blood mingled with mud, and to climb into the car she'd have to wade through the muck. And then what? Try to drive away with a dead deer attached to the car's underbelly? The right front tire wasn't even touching the ground.

Thunder crashed and the wind whipped the tree's branches. They creaked and moaned under the assault. Laine considered going to the highway. How many miles until the next town? Twenty? Alone, dark, cold, a storm—this was the stuff of nightmares. She tried to imagine climbing into a trucker's cab and couldn't do it. With slumped shoulders she headed back to the cabin. Smoke rose from the chimney, welcoming her.

Her teeth chattered and her arms shook from cold. Folding them tightly across her chest, she pulled open the door to face her husband.

"We're trespassing." She stood in the doorway, watching Ian fan a small fire in the grate. He had taken off his shirt, but oddly, enough, not his drenched, mud splattered jeans. She'd seen him naked countless times, but somehow, this time was different. His hair was longer; it curled along his neck. Watching his back muscles work as he poked at the smoldering fire, she wondered if he'd been working out more.

"I'd rather be trespassing than wet." He didn't turn to answer her.

Laine looked down at her soaked dress and noticed for the first time the streaks of pink and green running down her legs. "Oh!" The paint on the dress—who would be stupid enough to make a dress with water-soluble paint? Who would be stupid enough to buy one? Laine sat down hard on a wooden chair and slipped off her muddy canvas shoes. Just as she had thought. Her feet were now purple. They looked like egg plants.

Ian turned to her, smiling. "You should take it off."

"You wish."

He turned back to the fire. "Yes, I do. But my feelings aside, you really should hang it up to dry. You must be cold."

She ignored him and looked around the cabin. A large bed dominated the single room. She sat at the lone table; one other chair sat on the other side. A stack of firewood was piled near the hearth and a jar of matches sat on the mantle. The kitchen consisted of some wooden shelves stocked with canned foods and a few utensils. Glancing at the bed she saw that it was as clean as the rest of the room. A large quilt, fat pillows… she looked away quickly and met Ian's eyes.

She shifted her gaze to the fireplace. He'd coaxed the tiny flame into a roaring fire. A pot hung from a hook. "Soup?"

"I'm not hungry."

Ian shrugged. "Me neither, but I thought maybe you'd

be."

Laine cleared her throat. "This all belongs to someone."

"We'll leave money and a thank-you note on the table."

She didn't doubt that Ian would be generous. "What if they find us here?"

Ian looked out the window at the raging storm. "They'd have to move the Mercedes deer combo blocking the road first…"

Lightning lit up the small room, momentarily blinding Laine. After a moment, the room returned to the cozy glow.

"Your pants are wet," she said.

Ian turned his back to her, shrugging, his shoulder's shaking with suppressed laughter. "Your legs are purple."

"My bag is the car," she told him. "It's probably as ruined as the upholstery."

"Do you want to wear my shirt?"

She looked at the shirt he'd hung on the chair to dry, but then realized that he meant a shirt from his overnight bag. Frustration rippled through her. It seemed unfair that Ian had everything he needed while her things were all sopping wet.

Ian turned from the fire, riffled through his bag, and

pulled out a large t-shirt, the sort of thing he slept in when they stayed at hotels. He tossed it to her and she caught it. It smelled of his cologne. At home, he slept in his boxers. The memory made her flush and she turned away so he wouldn't see.

She quickly stepped out of her dress and pulled the t-shirt over her head, hypersensitive to him, wondering if he watched her. Her skin tingled. She heard him moving behind her and turned to see that he'd pulled back the covers on the bed.

She folded her arms across her chest. "If you think—"

Ian sighed. "Lainey, as much as I'd like to, I'm tired and cold. You're swaying on your feet. Tonight I think you'll find sharing my toothbrush to be as much intimacy as you'll be able to stand. Besides," his eyes twinkled, "you've always been a morning girl."

He knew her too well.

He gestured at the bed. "Would you like the right or the left side?"

***

Laine shifted. She couldn't find a comfortable place. The bed, much smaller than their king sized one at home, groaned every time she moved. Staring at the embers burning in the fireplace, she willed herself to sleep. The colors in the grate shifted and she turned her attention to the much more boring and static ceiling.

Beside her, Ian lay on his side, his back to her. She knew he wasn't sleeping by his breath. It'd taken her weeks to get used to sleeping alone and now she couldn't sleep because he lay beside her. Ian didn't seem bothered at all where as she suddenly seemed a collection of protruding, restless bones. She tucked her knees into her chest, lying on her side, her arm pinned beneath her, cutting off her circulation, slowly growing numb. She eased onto her back and the bed groaned.

The sheets smelled musty, but they seemed clean enough. No obvious stains. She didn't think she could have tolerated that. As far as beds went, this one wasn't so terribly uncomfortable. Just noisy.

She considered the mound in the blanket beside her. He'd slept by her side for nearly twenty years—why was she so ridiculously aware of his breath, his smell, the warmth of his body? Laine tried to make herself as small and as still as she could. Huddling in the fetal position, she wondered how they'd get out tomorrow. No cell service— they'd have to walk to the main highway and then hitch a ride into town. Of course, being with Ian would be much better than being alone. Safer. That's all.

Her neck hurt. She rolled over and punched her pillow. She had down pillows at home. This pillow had been made from shredded cardboard. It smelled like oatmeal. Maybe it'd been made from a recycled cereal box. Why wasn't she asleep?

"Lainey?"

She went still. Played dead.

The blankets rustled as Ian rolled over. Laine scooted to the far side of the bed.

"Why are you awake?" he asked.

"How could anyone sleep?" she asked. "This bed is noisy. The pillow is made of gravel." She didn't like the sound of her voice. She knew she sounded spoiled and petulant, and she hated being the spoiled princess. "I'm cold."

Ian hitched himself onto his elbow. "Here," he said, enveloping her in his arms and pulling her against him.

She nestled against him. He was warm.

His arm draped across her, holding her against his chest. She settled between his arm and above his ribs. Ian adjusted so his chin rested on her head. He smelled of cologne and of the fire, a mixture of the familiar and of the primitive.

"Lainey," Ian murmured into her hair.

CHAPTER 13

Laine woke with the sun on her face and quilts tangled around her legs. She watched Ian sleep, an activity of long ago. She'd forgotten what this was like, watching him in his unguarded moments. He looked different. Older. He hadn't shaved and his hair had been mussed. Stirring, he flung his arm over her. In his sleep, he pulled her close and she let him draw her to him.

She had so many questions. A night in a cabin didn't answer any of them. In fact, their night together just seemed to highlight all her questions in red. *How had he found her? How had he known that she needed him?* His hold on her tightened and his breath fanned her cheek.

At this moment, did she turn away? Sanity told her that she should, but she closed her eyes, seduced by the warmth, quiet, and comfort.

She had so many questions, but they could wait.

***

Cold. A breeze smelling of doused fire blew from somewhere. Instinctively, she reached for Ian's warmth, but found only icy sheets. Realization washed over her and she sat up, brushed her curls from her face. Her eyes felt gritty, her teeth fuzzy. She needed a bathroom. A real one. One with white porcelain and running, flushing water. She wanted bath salts, body gel and a loofa. Lying down, she pulled the quilt over her head.

She'd spent the night with Ian.

Nothing had happened.

That, at least, was good. Right? Sex would only have complicated things.

She'd cuddled up to him. For warmth.

Peeking out from under the quilt, she wondered where he'd gone. And why.

Outside the window, a bleak sun shone in a steel gray sky. Laine sat up and looked at all the damage the storm had caused—downed branches, bent trees and thousands of pinecones scattered on the ground. Just yesterday, it'd been warm. Or was it two days ago? She couldn't remember.

Where had Ian gone? She knew he wouldn't leave her alone. Laine climbed from the bed, but she took the quilt with her. Wrapping it around her shoulders, she went to inspect her dress. It'd dried stiff. The paint had turned from splatters to streaks and the colors had melded to a smear of puce. She didn't want to wear it, but what choice did she have? Sighing, she sat down on the bed. Where was

Madeleine when she needed clothes? She spotted Ian's bag in the corner.

He'd left the bag, but taken his wallet and phone. Twinges of guilt pricked her as she went through Ian's things. She told herself he wouldn't mind—after all, it wasn't so long ago when they would have shared an overnight bag.

Like they'd shared everything.

She gathered what she needed—toothbrush, toothpaste, and comb. Her hair, a snarled curly mess, resisted her efforts, and she twisted it up into a bun. She went outside in search of a privacy tree or make-shift potty. Lots of trees, but no Ian.

She returned to the cabin and put Ian's toiletries back in his bag. A small book hid beneath his clothes. *I'm not snooping,* she told herself, although, of course, she was. Turning the book over in her hands, she admired the leather-tooled cover and embossed lettering. A collection of poetry by someone who had an unfortunate name without vowels. Welsh, maybe? Inside the back cover, she found a photograph of the poet, a shaggy-haired, morose-looking man. Ian didn't read poetry. He snored through poetry.

Laine tightened the quilt around her shoulders, hugging it close as a chill swept over her. Flipping open the front of the book, she read a handwritten inscription, *For Ian, in celebration of Free Thought Day, October 12th, the annual observance by freethinkers and secularists of the anniversary of the end of the Salem Witch Trials. May your thoughts always be free, Love, Carly*

Witch trials? What did that mean? *May your thoughts always be free?* Free from what? The bonds of marriage? She turned to a poem.

Ruins of remembrances
Tumbled stones of doubt
Dark musty corners of tears
Ghost of spiders
With their telltale webs catching the glimpses of memories left behind.

Whatever tiny bit of her anger toward Ian had melted during the night, it returned with a surge. After placing the book in the bottom of his bag, she threw on her dress, slipped into her shoes and marched out into the bleak sunshine.

Up the road, she saw Ian talking to a man in baggy pants standing beside a giant tow truck. The Volvo dangled from the truck's massive hook. In the distance, the dead deer lay on the side of the road beside the parked Mercedes.

She stopped in a patch of sunlight shining through the

boughs of trees. She marshaled all her anger and self-righteousness and tried to wrap them around her like a shield, but she felt her emotions draining. She worried they would bleed completely away. After all, she had told Ian to leave. *Get out*—her actual words. And she'd been nothing but prickly ever since. Weeks and weeks of prickliness. And if she wanted to count backwards, how many proceeding months of bad behavior had there been?

How many nights spent pressed together, body to body? Not enough. If Carly sent him poetry, how could Laine blame her when, if she could be gut-wrenchingly honest, she'd admit that she wanted do the same? Laine wasn't good at gut-wrenching honesty. She didn't know how to combat jealousy. The feelings of contrition sparked with suspicion only darkened her mood. Carly had sent Ian the book of poetry, not the other way around. Ian would never have asked for one, so his having it couldn't be his fault. But why keep it? Why bring it?

The poem haunted her. *With their telltale webs catching the glimpses of memories left behind.* What did that mean?

Ian saw her and waved. Laine slowly walked toward him, pulled as if by an invisible, unbreakable thread. She didn't want to be a memory left behind.

"Wait!" she called.

The man with the baggy pants gave her paint-splattered legs a quizzical look before climbing into the truck.

"My purse!" Laine waved for the tow truck guy to stop. Ian retrieved her purse and handed it to her.

"Thank you," she said, her voice small.

The engine roared to life, and after a few moments of mud spraying and beeping, the truck and Volvo climbed the hill and then disappeared.

Ian's eyes swept over her and lingered on her legs. He turned away, smiling. "Are you ready to go?"

She nodded.

"Let me grab my stuff," he said, going back into the cabin. Through the window, Laine watched him put some money on the table, fold the quilt into a fat square, and sweep out the ashes from the fireplace. Remorse filled her. Ian was a good person. Careful. Responsible. No wonder Carly loved him.

Laine settled into the Mercedes and tried to pull the rain-ruined dress down over her knees. Moments later, Ian tossed his overnight bag in the back and climbed behind the wheel. Locked together in the closed confines of the car, Laine didn't know what to say. Should she tell him she found the book of poetry? A part of her wanted to tell him she was sorry, but she didn't know exactly what for, and she didn't know if he would misconstrue her apology into something she didn't mean. She didn't know what she meant.She didn't know what she wanted. Did she want to be married, or not? For years and years she'd wanted a baby. She'd thought a baby would make them a family, seal or bind them together in a way that the marriage had failed to do.

A baby, she now decided, would be a very bad idea. How could they love a baby when they couldn't even love each other? How had she not seen that?

Ian swore.

Laine looked at him in surprise. He almost never swore.

"The battery's dead," he told her.

"Oh. Well, you should have asked the tow guy to jump the car," Laine said.

"I would have—*if* I had known the battery was dead."

Laine raised her eyebrows and almost laughed.

"This isn't funny."

He looked like he wanted to hit her, so she climbed from the car. Ian followed her. "Where are you going?"

She slammed her door and headed for the highway. "I

guess we'll have to walk."

Ian slammed his door twice as hard. "We can't walk. The next town is more than twenty miles."

Laine turned on her heel and headed for the highway. "Maybe someone will stop. How did you get the tow truck?"

Ian caught up to her in two strides. "He happened by."

"That was lucky."

"No one has been lucky on this trip."

She sent him a sharp glance. "We're going to reclaim my grandfather's dead body. It wasn't meant to be a pleasure trip."

Ian mumbled something that sounded like, *being with you is never a pleasure trip.*

Laine ignored him and turned onto the highway, walking on the gravel shoulder. Ian hitched his bag and trudged beside her.

"Hungry?" he asked.

How could he think about sleep and food? He was so *elemental.* His needs so basic. She worried about their relationship and he fretted over breakfast. Fallen tree branches, strewn leaves and bracken littered the highway. Ian walked over all the debris while Laine avoided the bigger branches.

He pointed at a distant red barn with a large sign. "There's a farmer's market. Would you like anything?"

Laine sighed. This was what was wrong with them.

"Lainey—are you hungry?" He frowned at her.

She shook her head. "But you should get something. Besides, I'm sure they have a phone we can use." The barn sat at the edge of the road, surrounded by corn fields. The corn stalks had been mowed, leaving only brown stubble. Pumpkins ranging from baseball to watermelon sizes dotted the adjoining field. A split-rail fence surrounded wooden bins filled with produce. A tiny woman in a red-checked apron fussed over a container filled with sunflowers. Laine nodded at her. "Maybe she'll let us borrow a phone and we can call a taxi."

"This isn't New York. They don't have taxis here."

Laine folded her arms across her chest. "I *know* this isn't New York and you don't *know* there isn't someone who will give us a ride."

Ian's frown wavered. "You don't want anything?"

Laine shook her head. The thought of food made her ill. Ian always did that. He never apologized, but if he was rude or unkind he tried to make it up by offering her something. She wouldn't be bought.

Laine sat on the fence, crossed her painted legs, and

hugged her arms across her chest. Everything looked green and wet. Puddles sprinkled the parking area, and Ian sloshed through mud to get to the barn. Raindrops sparkled on the trees. The sun, although bright, had only a lackluster heat. A motorcycle and a heavyset woman dressed in black leather roared up beside her. A tiny dog in the woman's backpack yapped at Laine. The poodle's fur matched the woman's curls.

"Goodness, I almost didn't see him hiding beneath your hair," Laine laughed. The dog growled at her and the woman gave her an appraising stare as she straddled her bike.

"He's not friendly," the biker said in a deep voice, and Laine realized that the poodle owner was male, not female as she'd originally thought.

Laine glanced at Ian's stiff shoulders and thought, *he's not the only one.*

"Would you mind watching him for me for two ticks of a second?"

"Um, sure. What's his name?"

The biker slipped off the backpack and handed it to Laine. The poodle squirmed in the backpack, but didn't try to run away. "Disco," he said. Then he turned his attention to the poodle. "Now baby, you be good while Daddy gets us some jerky."

Disco eyed Laine with a curled lip and Laine tried to smile in return, holding on to the backpack with both hands. Why had she agreed to hold this dog? What is that they say at the airport—never hold anyone's belongings? But of course, this wasn't an airport and a terrorist attack seemed highly unlikely, and what harm could a poodle named Disco do?

Seconds later, the biker returned with a bag full of fruit in his arms and a strip of jerky in his mouth. "Thanks," he mumbled around the jerky, taking the backpack with his free hand. But the backpack slipped and in his effort to catch it and prevent Disco from being ejected into the mud, he dropped the bag, and apples rolled in several directions.

The biker groaned in frustration, handed Disco back to Laine and bent to retrieve his rolling fruit. Laine held Disco with one hand and gathered loose apples with the other.

"Thanks a lot," the biker smirked after securing the bag in his side saddle. He swung the Disco-laden backpack over his shoulder and then drove away, his hair blowing out over the dog's head.

Ian returned moments later with a bag of nuts and dried fruit and a basket of blueberries. The blueberries were for her. She loved them and he hated them. "Thank you," she said, her voice catching in her throat.

"You're welcome," Ian said with stilted formality.

"That does not look fun," Ian said, nodding at the retreating motorcycle.

"For him or for the dog?"

"Either. Do you have any change? They have a payphone."

Laine nodded and reached for her purse.

It was gone.

The dog, the rolling apples, the backpack—the biker must have picked up her purse and stuffed it in the backpack when she wasn't looking. Laine sat down, frowning. "There was a biker and a dog named Disco."

"Disco?" Ian asked.

"Of all the impossible things to believe you're focusing on the dog's name?" She looked up at him and he glared down at her. "That biker took my purse."

"You lost your purse? You never lose anything!"

"I didn't lose my purse. Someone with a dog name Disco stole it." She pointed at the distant black spot eating up the highway.

Ian shoved his hands into his pockets, looking as if he wanted to secure them to keep from strangling her. He turned on his heel and stomped through the mud. Laine watched his back and read the frustration in the set of his shoulders. He was right. She never lost anything. She still had the charm bracelet he'd given her their freshman year of high school.

If she followed him she'd get her shoes muddy. They were already ruined, of course—their paint wasn't anymore waterproof than her dress—but she hated the thought of sloshing through muck. Take the road and follow Disco? Or follow Ian? Both courses made more sense than remaining on the fence, literally, but she stayed sitting down with her paint spattered legs crossed. Seconds later a big red truck pulled up beside her.

Ian cranked down the window. "This is Hank," he said, motioning to the mammoth man sitting behind the wheel. "He's going to give us a ride into town."

Hank wore a Mariner's baseball cap and a polo shirt with gray chest hair poking through the button holes. His skin had weathered to a wrinkly rawhide, tan to the middle of his biceps, white beneath his the sleeves of his polo shirt.

Ian climbed out of the truck to make room for Laine. "I'll sit in the back."

But the back was full of chickens—dozens of them. They clicked their beaks against the wire cages and clucked, chuckled and shook their downy feathers at

Ian.."Where?"she asked. "You need a beak to sit back there."

"There's plenty of room up here," Hank called out, smiling at Laine.

Ian and Laine looked at each other. It'd be a squeeze. She'd have to wedge between Ian and Hank. Ian would never fit in the middle, not with the stick shift. A chicken looked at Laine with one black eye. What had happened? Had it been born that way, with one eye closed?

Laine climbed in the cab. It smelled of mud and grease. Ian climbed in beside her and put his arm across the back of the bench seat. To keep from touching Hank, Laine pressed herself against Ian's side. He felt warm and solid against her goosepimply skin. By necessity his thigh ran alongside hers.

"Are you selling your chickens?" Laine asked, attempting small talk.

"Yep," Hank said, looking her squarely in the eye. "Tomorrow being the Lord's day and all, I try to do all my trading on Saturdays." He flashed a quick glance at her multi-colored thighs and turned his attention to the road. His big beefy hand rested on the stick shift inches from her knee.

"Are you a commercial chicken farmer?" Laine asked.

"Heck no," Hank said. He shifted from second to third gear and his hand grazed Laine's thigh. She scooted closer to Ian. "I just raise a few chickens on the side and trade my leftovers to the Rooster Inn over in Clydesdale.

He looked from Laine's legs to Ian's face. "You two married?"

Neither spoke. Finally Ian said, "Yes."

He chuckled and shifted into fifth. Laine crossed her legs, trying to avoid contact with Hank and the stick shift.

"I can always tell," Hank said.

What was that supposed to mean? "We're separated," Laine put in.

Hank's grin didn't fade. He shot a quick glance at Ian's thigh pressing Laine's. "Not for long, I'm guessing."

Was Hank a Dr. Phil in overalls? He knew nothing about either of them. Laine tried to pull away from Ian, but that brought her knee closer to Hank's hand resting on the stick shift.

"You're separated, but still traveling together?"

You don't have to answer him, Laine mentally told Ian. *We paid for a ride, not a counseling session.*

"'Cause you're not separated at this moment," Hank continued. "You're clearly very much together."

"This isn't a pleasure trip," Ian said, parroting her

words.

Hank snorted and threw Laine a quick glance. "You look like pleasure on a Popsicle stick."

Laine stiffened. *Again, what was that supposed to mean?* She'd just been insulted, but she didn't know why. Wouldn't anyone with bright-colored legs at least look like fun? She didn't speak until they pulled up at a stop signal next to a tavern called the Angry Bull. Disco sat on the wooden porch, tied to a bench made out of a split log and four branch-like legs. Laine ignored the dog. She didn't want to confront the man who had stolen her purse.

"Thanks, Hank. We'll get out here," Ian said, opening the door and pulling Laine out with him. He slammed the door and waved as Hank drove away.

"Wait, why here?" she asked Ian's retreating back. He was already climbing onto the porch.

"I didn't like Hank," he said over his shoulder. He stopped beside the tavern. "Did you? Were you comfortable with him pressing against your thighs every time he shifted?" He waited a beat. "I didn't think so. We'll use the phone and get road side service."

Disco, who had been resting on the porch, sat up and cocked his head at Laine as if to say, *Hey, I know you.* Laine gave the dog a brief nod. She didn't want Ian to know she'd already met Disco, and that perhaps her purse was inside the bar. She began a mental calculation of the value of her purse and its contents. Nothing was worth getting hurt or causing a scene. *The leopard print panties and bra.* She shook herself. So what? Helene had taught her a long time ago to keep spare underwear in her purse when she traveled--that way if she ever got separated from her suitcase, she'd at least have clean underwear. So, the purse snatcher would discover the matching panties and bra. No big deal.

Ian pushed through the tavern doors. The room was full of tattoos, smoke, beer glasses and pool tables. He walked up to the bar, but Laine stopped at the threshold and backed out. It was early afternoon and the sun outside was sparkly and clear, but inside the tavern could only be described as dim. The air smelled of stale smoke, flat beer—Laine's stomach rolled. She'd wait outside with Disco. Let Ian make his telephone call. She didn't want to see the Disco Dude again, even if that meant never seeing her purse again. Although, she really liked that purse—soft leather, brushed silver details.

Laine sat down on the bench and Disco gave her a pleading look. What if she untied him and let him run away? Passive aggression. She was too chicken to ask for her purse back, so she'd take it out on the dog? Thinking of Disco wandering around, lost and hungry made her feel slightly sick and angry with herself for even considering letting him go. She scratched him behind the ears. It wasn't his fault his owner was a thug.

Raised voices. Swearing. Something crashed. Laine stood and peered through the window in time to see Disco's master flying across a pool table.

CHAPTER 14

Laine pushed her way into the bar, moving aside a guy with his gut hanging over his belt. He shifted beneath her hands and she recoiled from the touch of his bare, pimply arm. Someone else stood between her and Ian—a small man, pale, skinny, all collarbones and ribs. She elbowed him to move.

Cheers and hoots filled the room as Ian cocked back his arm for a right hook. Disco Dude grabbed him around the middle and the two men crashed to the floor. Laine shoved her way through the crowd, yelling, "Ian! Stop! What are you doing?" Noticing her purse and its spilled contents on the wooden floor, she scooped it up and shoved the leopard print underwear inside.

"Please, Ian." Laine pleaded, but he ignored her. She sent the bartender an imploring glance—he watched the fight with an amused smirk.

Ian had the thug on the floor, wedged between his knees, but Thug had his hands around Ian's throat.

"Somebody stop them," Laine called to the crowd.

The tattooed guy next her folded his arms across his

chest and nodded at Ian. "He deserves it. Came in here acting all snobby and then suddenly flies into a giant hissy fit." He laughed. "Came unglued when he saw the leopard panties." He leered at her. "Those yours?"

Laine fluttered between the horrible realizations that everyone in the bar would know that the underwear belonged to her and that stopping the fight rested securely on her shoulders. None of the people surrounding the grappling men on the floor seemed inclined to break them up. This was probably better entertainment for them than the two professional wrestlers prancing in tights on the TV screen.

Ian and Disco's master grappled at her feet. Ian was on top, and then the thug, and then Ian; Laine couldn't tell who was winning, for both appeared to be losing. Their fists flew around them and occasionally landed with a sick thud. Ian managed to ease away and tried to stand, but Disco's master grabbed his ankle. Ian went down with a bellow and then quickly retaliated, catching a hold of the thug's shirt and bumping his head on the floor.

"Ian!" Laine called. She kicked Ian's shoulder and he sagged onto Disco's master who wrapped his fingers around Ian's throat. Then Ian had his throat. Within seconds, both their faces turned motley red.

Such is the power of leopard spotted panties, Laine thought. Frantically looking around, she saw a pitcher of beer on a nearby table. She poured it over the two men, ignoring the protests of the beer drinkers. Disco's master hollered and Ian sputtered. Laine grabbed Ian's collar and pulled him up with one hand. She smacked the bottle on the table and the bottle broke in two.

With her arm around Ian's waist, she brandished her new weapon at Disco's master who was struggling to his feet. "Back off," she said, her voice sounding small and apprehensive.

Disco's master laughed, pushed past Ian, scooped Laine up and tossed her over his shoulder. Laine waved the broken bottle in the air while the men around her hooted and laughed. Seconds later, her captor's knees buckled. Ian caught Laine before she fell to the floor. Ian carried her out the door amidst the catcalls from the crowd inside.

Laine wiggled in his arms until he let her go. She stumbled back, away from him. They stood at the edge of the woods. The highway, a distant rumbling of cars, was on one side of them. The tavern with its laughter and noise was on the other. She looked at Ian as if she'd never seen him before. His shirt hung in two shreds. Blood dripped from his nose and a cut above his eyebrow. He touched his bloody, sweaty forehead with the cuff of his shirt.

"Who are you?" she asked, pointing the broken beer bottle at his chest.

Ian jerked his head at the road. "Shall we?"

Laine lifted the bottle toward the tavern. "Don't you want to talk about—I mean, what just happened?"

Ian stepped toward her. "Where did you get the panties?"

Laine backed away. "That's what you want to talk about? The underwear?"

He caught up to her in two long steps. "Yeah, that's exactly what I want to talk about! Where did they come from? I haven't seen them before—believe me, I would have remembered."

She turned away from him and headed for the highway. He captured her elbow, despite his now obvious limp. "You're hurt," she said, watching him.

He didn't answer, but gimped along beside her, his feet crunching the gravel in angry staccatos.

"It wasn't worth it, you know." When he didn't respond, she continued, "There really isn't anything all that valuable in the purse."

"Is it all there? Did you check?"

Laine obediently checked her purse. Perfume, dead cell

phone, lipstick, credit cards, a few dollar bills, the offensive underwear. "None of this was worth risking your life. You could have been killed."

"Would you have cared?"

She turned to him and stopped walking. Reaching out, she tried to wipe away the blood on his forehead. He jerked away.

"Let me see," she said, coming closer.

He stepped back.

"Ian?"

He nodded at a church on the corner.

Sunlight sparkled on the raindrops clinging to the trees, casting the scene at the chapel in a warm morning glow. Madeleine and a very young Sid stood on the front porch. Madeleine wore a bright blue dress and even from a distance, the sapphire necklace glinted in the sun. Sid wore a dark suit that hung on his slim frame. Laine caught her breath. She didn't remember her grandfather being so strikingly handsome. Of course, she hadn't known him young. And yet, there he was. Undeniably Sid. A young Sid. A Sid in his prime.

Madeleine also looked beautiful, but she didn't look happy. Neither of them did. Were they arguing? Laine watched them.

"I wonder if this is the right church," Ian said.

"Oh, I'm sure of it."

He sent her a quizzical look. "How can you be so sure?"

She tried to smile at him. "I just think he is."

Ian lifted his eyebrows at her and then winced.

"Here," Laine grabbed the panties and pressed them against Ian's wound. "They're clean," she told him.

He smiled. "I know that. You'd never carry unwashed panties in your purse." He took them from her and their fingers brushed. An electric shock tingled up Laine's arm and to distract herself, she looked around for her grandparents. They'd disappeared. A sick knot formed in her belly. What if she never saw either of them again? What if Madeleine returned to the next life with Sid without saying goodbye?

Laine told herself that going to heaven—or where ever it was that Madeleine wanted to take him—would be a good thing. Even if it meant leaving without saying good-bye. But if that were true then why did she feel miserable?

She realized with a start that she would miss Madeleine. Terribly. She knew she could live at the cottage with Madeleine, but what if Madeleine left? Could she live there by herself?

Laine followed Ian up the steps of the chapel and he opened the doors. The scent of gardenias wafted out. A harp played a Bach fugue, a priest stood in the nave, and the congregation turned to stare.

Ian tried to get her through the doors and she resisted. He motioned his head at the chapel, and she shook her head. Dragging her, he maneuvered her to a back pew and then pulled her down beside him. She landed half in his lap. Scooting away, she gave him a nasty look and then a sheepish, embarrassed one to the wedding party who had turned to watch.

The harpist stopped playing and the pastor picked up a book from the pulpit and began to read.

The bride was young, *maybe* age eighteen, but she looked like she was twelve. The groom looked pubescent. Who would allow these babies to marry? The father standing near the bride had a sprinkling of gray in his hair. The mother of the bride sitting at the edge of the pew had bouffant hair typical of the 1990's and Laine realized with a jolt that the parents could be her same age. She and Ian could have had a bride or a groom child if they'd had a baby in their twenties. Laine clutched her tummy.

"And the Lord God said, it is not good that the man should be alone; I will make him an help meet for him," the pastor said.

"Therefore shall a man leave his father and his mother, and shall cleave unto his wife: and they shall be one flesh. And said, For this cause shall a man leave father and mother, and shall cleave to his wife: and they twain shall be one flesh. Wherefore they are no more twain, but one flesh."

Twain? Had she and Ian ever been *twain?* If she wanted to get biblical, she and Ian had failed at the commandment to go forth and multiply. Laine sank a little deeper into the pew, thinking that things couldn't get much worse. Why had Ian dragged her into the chapel? They couldn't look for Sid during a wedding ceremony. Ian shifted beside her. She knew he shared her discomfort.

A woman got up to sing. She stood in the shadowy chapel, light from the stained-glass window shining all around her. Her pink, chiffon dress looked like she wore a pink Pepto-Bismol bottle, but despite the ridiculous dress and the yellow frizzed hair, tears came to Laine's eyes as the woman sang. Breathless kisses, a night for forever, etched memories—the song performed at her parents' wedding and at her own.

Laine looked at Ian from beneath her eyelashes to see if he recognized the music. Of course he did. He stared straight ahead, his eyes focused on the stained glass, his jaw tight. With his mussed hair, his unshaven chin, and bloody smeared forehead, he looked very different from the boy she married. He seemed a very different man from the one she'd talked with in Seattle just the day before. Had he really changed so very much? Had she?

He still had the panties clutched in his hand. Reaching over, she pulled them loose. Startled, he let go and she tucked them into her purse. "They're Bette's," she whispered in his ear, smelling him. He reeked of the beer she'd thrown over him. He'd never been much of a drinker and the smell surprised her. She hadn't realized that she'd grown so accustomed to his scent.

He smiled, looking relieved, surprised and a little skeptical. "I don't believe you would wear someone else's underwear."

"It's true. They were brand new. Some guys on the football team gave them to Gregg as a gag gift."

"But still—why did they end up in your purse?"

The audience stood and cheered, the organ burst into celebratory chords and the bride and groom hurried past. Laine and Ian also stood and it wasn't until they were alone, after the wedding guests had filed out, that Laine realized Ian had hold of her hand.

***

"I'm sorry," Pastor Pike said, after the introductions. He wiped his eyes with the back of his hand and let out a satisfied sounding sigh. "I always get a little teary-eyed after such joyous occasions, But you two, I understand, are here on a much sadder errand."

"Yes," Ian said.

Laine didn't trust herself to speak, so she nodded. Now that the wedding party had moved outside and the stillness filled the chapel, she heard her grandparents. Their voices floated through the floorboards. They must be in the basement.. She had thought she'd never see or hear or grandfather again, but there he was—his bass voice unmistakable. Laine's knees felt weak as she followed Ian and Pastor Pike down the nave.

Sid and Madeleine were fighting. Laine only caught snippets of the conversation, but their voices were raised and they sounded angry. How sad—they hadn't seen one another in fifty years. Laine followed Ian's broad back down the stairwell. The gloom in the basement quickly disappeared when Pastor Pike flipped a switch and fluorescent lights flickered on.

"Yes, that's him," Ian said after the pastor lifted the lid of the black coffin.

Yes and no, Laine thought. That was the Sid she had known, but was that really him? Or was the real Sid the young, handsome man arguing with Madeleine in the corner. Neither of her grandparents looked at her, but she found herself studying them, straining to hear what they said.

"We can't stay here," Madeleine said

"I can't leave," Sid argued.

"You must. You have to move on."

Sid's attention drifted to Laine. Breaking free from Madeleine, he crossed the room to Laine and wrapped his arms around her, engulfing her in a cold that seeped into her bones and took her breath away. Her knees buckled and she slipped from her grandfather's embrace to the floor.

CHAPTER 15

"Lainey?"

She blinked open her eyes. Why was Ian hovering above her? Who was that man with the abundant nose hair? Her head hurt. The tile floor–chilly and hard. Had she hit her head when she fell?

"Seeing a loved one who has passed can be distressing," the nose-hair guy said. *Pastor Pike,* a voice reminded her. "Is she prone to dizzy spells?"

"No, not at all," Ian said, lifting her shoulders and cradling her against his chest. "But she does have low blood pressure, and she hasn't eaten this morning."

"Oh! The poor thing," Pastor Pike crooned. "Let's get her some wedding cake."

Laine tried to stand despite her shaking knees and pulled away from Ian.

"Okay?" Ian asked. He still smelled of beer and blood.

Laine fought a wave of nausea, but she nodded. Rubbing the back of her head, she felt a knob forming beneath her fingers. What happened to Sid and Madeleine? Someone had moved the casket and her grandparents must have gone with it.

Ian led her up the stairs and out through a back door to the wedding party. A four piece band played on a makeshift stage set up on the concrete beneath a basketball hoop. Vases of sunflowers sat on picnic tables covered in white cloths. The singer in the Pepto-Bismol dress scurried around the tables with a tray of food. Ian led Laine to a chair in the shade.

"We can't just crash their party," Laine whispered to Ian. He didn't answer, but left her there.

"Oh, they won't mind," Pastor Pike said. "Those two are so in love, they won't even notice you're here. The real lions in charge are my wife and her sister, Margo." His eyes twinkled. "I'll go talk to them, but I won't be telling them your secret, or else they'll be all over you like a quilt on a winter's night."

My secret? What secret? And then she felt it, the warm Chinook wind. *Once one secret is told, no secret is safe.*

Ian returned with a plastic cup filled with water. He handed it to her before sitting down on the grass near her feet. "Better?" he asked after she obediently drank.

She nodded. "I don't know what happened. It's not like I was feeling sick. I was there, looking at Sid and then you were there, looking down on me." She rubbed the bump on the back of her head. "It doesn't make sense."

Ian smiled.

"It's not funny."

His smile faded. "No, it's not. It's just so unusual to see you flustered. Do you want to go to the doctor?"

Laine shook her head and it hurt. "Not here."

"Do you want me to call Sean?"

"No," Laine said, holding her head very still. She did not want to see Sean.

A young man in a poor-fitting suit joined the band on the makeshift stand. He picked up the microphone and it squealed in response. After the equipment's complaint, the band began.

Moments later, Pastor Pike arrived carrying two plates heaped with food. Green Jell-O mixed with whipped cream and pastel-colored miniature marshmallows, tater tots in a creamy sauce that reeked of mushrooms—Laine's stomach rolled.

Ian, watching her face, took the plates and thanked the pastor profusely.

"I'd get her some cake, but they won't be cutting it for another hour."

Another hour? The music played soft and slow while Laine tried to sort her emotions. She wanted to be mad at

Ian, but somehow she'd lost the energy. Part of her wanted to be young, newly married. Newly married to Ian. She didn't want to be with anyone else.

The sun sank beneath the canopy of trees—only a pink glimmer of daylight remained. The candles on the tables cast small puddles of light. Twinkly lights hung from the trees, tacky and yet, lovely. Sweet.

"Actually, roadside assistance won't be here for at least another hour," Ian said.

"In time for the cake," Laine said. "How smart of them. When did you call?"

"Just a minute ago while I was getting the water."

Laine picked up the fork and toyed with the pink and yellow marshmallows before taking a small bite of the Jell-O. It didn't taste as bad as it looked. She licked the whip cream off her fork and then saw Ian watching. Her fingers trembled and she put down the fork.

The bride took the microphone. "I want to thank all of you for helping us celebrate—" she began.

"What happens now, with Sid?" Laine whispered to Ian.

"The mortuary will pick him up on Monday."

"He'll be cremated then?"

Ian held her gaze. "Of course," his voice soft.

The groom took the microphone. He was a little drunk and his words slurred.

Laine sniffed. She knew Sid was to be cremated, but what she didn't know was if Sid and Madeleine would then disappear. Madeleine had Sid, she had what she'd come for, so she'd leave. Right? Forever?

Forever. What does that really mean? What happens next? She really should have pressed Madeleine for more answers. Laine realized she'd been given this incredibly unique opportunity to talk to someone from the afterlife and she'd blown it, or most of it, by being mad. Mad about what?

A spotlight flashed on Ian. He jumped to his feet when a man dressed in a plaid dinner jacket handed him a microphone. Ian shot Laine a please-help-me look. He was so incredibly handsome, even with the ripped and stained shirt and the blood smeared on his forehead and cheek. Laine did her best to smile at him. She hadn't been paying attention to the ceremonies going on around her. The reception had been little more than background noise to her thoughts.

"You're supposed to offer words of marital advice to the bride and groom," Pastor Pike whispered to him.

What would Ian say? And did he speak for both of

them, or was she also supposed to speak as well? Ian gave her another, much longer, look. He cleared his throat—a rumbly noise in the microphone.

"Today would have been my grandparent's 70th wedding anniversary," Ian said. He cleared his throat again. "They married young, very young, and stayed together for sixty years. They parted when Grandpa Jay died. I believe they'll be together again. Everything I've learned about love and marriage, I've learned from a life time of watching them care for each other."

Ian passed the microphone back to the man in the plaid jacket and sat down on the grass at Laine's feet, carefully avoiding her eye. He really hadn't offered advice. It was a lovely thought, but it was more statement of fact than advice. Maybe, given the state of his own marriage, he didn't really feel like he could offer advice. Laine's heart twisted. She really did love Ian. She didn't want him to feel as if he'd failed anything, let alone their marriage. She knew so much about him, could read him so well.

I'd do anything to make up that lost time, Bette had said. And then just moments ago, Laine had thought, *I'd been given this incredible opportunity and I wasted it by being mad. Mad about what?* She'd been thinking about Madeleine, but couldn't the same question be asked of her marriage? She'd been given this incredibly opportunity to love and be loved, and she'd wasted it. Laine reached out and touched the back of Ian's neck where his dark hair curled around his collar. She knew he was ticklish in that one vulnerable spot.

He slowly turned—his expression unreadable.

The well-wishes and marital counsel ended and the band resumed.

"*When I fall,*" the young man in the poor fitting suit sang. "*It'll be forever.*"

"Want to dance?" Laine asked, knowing that her question held so many more questions than just that one.

As they melded on the concrete basketball court/dance floor, with the stars and the tacky twinkly-lights shining down on them, Laine thought of all the nights behind them and all the nights ahead of them, and told herself this night was just one in a very long string of nights spent together.

***

They didn't talk on the drive to the ranch, but Ian held her hand. The Mercedes headlights pierced the dark as Ian nosed the car through the gate and down the dirt driveway. They bumped over potholes and stopped in front of the house. Once the headlights blinked off, the only light came from the moon and stars.

"Do you think she's already gone to bed?" Laine asked.

Ian answered with a slight shrug and his eyes misty. The ranch had once teemed with life. Dogs, horses, cats, chickens, a couple of cows and lots and lots of dark haired, blue-eyed children—where had they all gone? The animals, one by one, had died. The children had grown up.

Laine and Ian had spent every Christmas here for years. Aunts, uncles, and cousins usually joined them and they would party for days. Grandma supplied candy and food. Grandpa provided games and tucked little gold envelopes filled with money into the tree. They had stopped coming after Grandpa's death. Ian's siblings had families of their own and hosted their own large, noisy parties. Grandma rotated through their homes for the holidays. She seemed happy enough.

Ian and Laine, unhampered by children, usually spent their holidays traveling, visiting cities and hotels. Laine wondered where she'd be the upcoming Christmas—if Ian would be with her.

A faint jingle of music drifted toward them from the back of the house. Ian and Laine followed it. Dozens of candles flickered in the dark night. Ian looked over at Laine and smiled, hesitant and unsure.

"Grandma Ivy isn't sick, is she?" Laine looked around at the candle studded patio. A small table draped in a lacy table cloth stood in the center, with a bottle of sparkling cider a single rose in a silver bud vase and candelabra with a host of burning candles on top. The smell of steak came from the kitchen. "She's not even here."

Ian slid his arm around Laine's waist and pulled her close. "Dance with me?"

We're trespassing, she thought, feeling like they were interloping on a very personal moment, someone else's private moment, but she knew this was her moment. Her moment of decision. The rest of her life depended on this moment. What she said, what she did, right now would alter the course of her life. She could chose Ian or walk away. If she left, she knew Ian's pride wouldn't let him return. She relaxed against him, touched by his efforts. "You hired someone to do this."

He nodded, his chin rubbing her cheek. "Kelsey and Sarah, the most romantic of my nieces."

"Where's Grandma?"

"Florida, with Val and Leonard."

The stars sparkled down on them and beyond the candles lay the countless acres of pasture and woods. They were completely alone. Laine smiled and moved with the rhythm of the music. She felt a sudden shift in Ian and she knew she had his complete and undivided attention.

At this moment, she could do a number of things. She could resurrect the tired adoption argument. She could press him about Carly—mention the book of poetry she'd found. Instead, she leaned against him and murmured, "Who's going to do the dishes?"

Ian kissed her temple and whispered in her ear, his voice seductive, "Brian, tomorrow when he comes to feed the chickens."

"That is the most romantic thing I've ever heard," she said into his chest.

She could feel Ian smile.

"I didn't know if this would work," Ian said, his lips trailing down her neck.

"You've always worked—in that regard," she said.

He lifted his lips from her so that he looked her in the eyes. "I haven't worked in weeks. Six weeks."

She smiled and touched his lips. "Does Grandma Ivy still have the baby-maker quilt?"

Ian scooped her into his arms. "That doesn't work either. We've tried."

"That's okay," Laine said, smiling up at him. "It's always fun to try."

***

Is it a dream, or is it real? She wakes in the hospital bed, listening to a baby cry in another room, knowing or believing that it belongs to her. The nurse apologizes that the hospital is full and that she has to share a room. There's a tiger-striped fur coat hanging on the chair. Plastic surgery, the nurse tells her. Why would the baby need plastic surgery? What could possibly be wrong? But then she realizes the tiger striped coat belongs to the woman in the next hospital bed, the woman who had plastic surgery. The baby crying isn't hers. No, her baby died weeks before it could even cry. She saw it still, motionless, a peanut sized creature without a heartbeat. An almost baby. The only baby she'll ever carry. She rolls to face to the window and watches the ships in the bay, knowing that for her there is no sailing away.

Ian pushes a wheel chair to the car and takes her home. He carries her up the stairs and lays her in their bed. He holds her while she sleeps. She feels his tears falling on her skin, but the drugs and pain are so deep, she can't leave the state of numbness to comfort him. Even if she wanted to. Even if she had something to give.

Laine woke to the smell of smoke. She kept her eyes closed, unwilling to let go of the warmth and comfort of sleep. Memories of last night flooded through her and she relived them in detail.

"This is not a good idea," she had thought, her face pressed against his chest.

But that hadn't been a time for ideas, good or bad. She hadn't been able to think at all. For so many months and years their love had been on a schedule, dictated by a calendar, passion relegated to a recipe of calculations, medications and temperature readings. A recipe that had always failed.

She'd forgotten how good it felt to just *be*.

She peeked open one eye. Ian stood shirtless before the fireplace, stoking a smoldering flame. She watched him, liking how she could see his muscles move. She tried to reconcile her feelings for him with the vivid dream memory of only moments ago. He sat on the stone hearth and blew into the fire. Despite the past fifteen years, the Ian of today looked remarkably the same as the one in her dream memory. What had happened? What had gone so wrong? If he hadn't changed, why had she?

He must have felt her eyes on him, because he turned, a small, tentative smile on his lips. She saw his nervousness. "Good morning," he said, still looking uncertain.

Laine hitched the quilt higher, tucked it beneath her arms. "Good morning," she returned.

"Is it?" he asked, running his fingers through his already tousled hair.

She cocked her head at him and smiled.

"Don't do that, Laine, or I swear there will be a repeat performance of last night."

"And that would be bad?"

"No… I just think we need to talk first."

"Maybe we've talked too much."

"Don't do that, either," Ian sat back down on the hearth.

"Do what?"

"Don't shut me out, Laine."

Laine twitched the quilt and she saw Ian notice. His eyes flicked away from her bare shoulders. She looked out the window. Ian must have pushed it open to air out the smoke from his struggling flame. Mist hung in the air. The mountain air was cooler, thinner. Its cold stung her bare arms and left goose-pimples.

"There's never been anyone for me but you," Ian said, coming and sitting beside her on the bed. He picked up her hand and toyed with her fingers.

She believed him, but she didn't know how to resolve

her pain. She didn't know how to make Ian look at her the way he looked at Carly. She didn't doubt that Ian loved her, but she worried that he might love Carly more.

"I want to come home, Laine."

"I think that's a good idea," she said slowly.

He leaned forward to kiss her, and she backed away. "I've moved out to the cottage."

Ian sat back, surprised. "The cottage?" His jaw hung slack for a moment. "Permanently?"

"Why not?"

"For one thing, it's filthy—"

"You know, it really wasn't that bad. Sure, it was dusty."

"Not that bad? Laine—you're a clean freak!"

"Thank you," she replied, even though she knew he meant it as a statement of fact and not a compliment. "I don't believe it's been abandoned for—how many years did you say?"

Ian's scowl pushed down his eyebrows. "I didn't say."

"Someone's been living there and taking care of it, I'm sure of it."

"So I can come home, but you're not going to be there."

"Hmm."

"I get the pleasure of Cheshire's company but not yours."

She nodded. "I'll tell Gemma. She's been taking care of him."

Ian's voice turned hard. "Gemma knew where you were?"

Laine picked at the quilt, not meeting his eyes. "No. Not really. She just knew I was away."

"Why don't you want to live with me? Is it Carly?"

When she didn't answer right away, Ian leaned toward her. "I've told you, there isn't anything between us. It's just you and me." He took her face in his hands and held it inches from his. "You are it for me. You always have been."

Laine closed her eyes, trying to shut out the memory of Ian holding Carly in his arms, whispering in her ear the same way he whispered to her. Maybe he'd said different words, but from her distance, which at the time had seemed immense, she couldn't hear. All she knew was how the sight of them together made her feel.

"Ian, if we really want to try to rebuild, I think we need to take it slowly. I don't just want to jump back to where we were. I want to stay at the cottage and fix it up. I want to write my grandparents' life stories. I want to build a butterfly garden."

"A butterfly garden?" Ian shook his head. "What are you not telling me?"

"I'm telling you I need some space."

"And I'm telling you that I need you."

She smiled at him. She loved him, but she wasn't ready to step back into their old life. Not now. Maybe not ever. She didn't know how to create a new life, especially one without Ian. The thought of leaving Ian behind terrified her. She couldn't do it. She *wouldn't* do it. Somehow she'd create a life that made sense, but right now her life was complicated by ghosts. Not only her grandparents' ghosts, but also the ghosts of her former marriage and her unfulfilled hopes.

If they were as close as they'd once been, she'd tell him about Madeleine. She'd tell him about Sid. She'd confide that she was afraid she was losing her mind. But she didn't trust him. What had happened to her trust? Had it been killed by disappointments? Medications? Infertility treatments? Acupuncture? Last night there had been an obvious physical connection, but even that had been missing for years. She wondered if he could feel that same rush if she left him and he turned to Carly.

She couldn't think about Carly, and maybe if she

stayed at the cottage, she wouldn't have to.

"I need you to stay at the house and take care of Cheshire." Reaching out, she laid her hand on the side of his face and he leaned into her. "But come visit me at the cottage, often," she said. "I think you'll love it as much as I do."

***

A swell of pride rushed over her when Ian pushed open the door. Because of her hard work, the cottage gleamed. She took a deep breath. The place even smelled good. She loved the mingled scents of lemon oil, glass cleaner, and ammonia.

Ian took her hand and reluctantly said, "It's beautiful. I can't believe it's been vacant for years." He stepped into the living room and ran his hand over the fireplace mantel.

"I don't think it was. I think Sid used to come here. In fact, maybe he was coming here on the day he died."

"What's all this?" Ian asked, stopping in front of the collection of journals, letters and photographs on the dining room table.

"Remember, I told you I was writing about my grandparents." Laine picked up a photograph of Madeleine. "This is my grandmother."

"She's pretty, if you like that petite, porcelain look."

Laine smiled. "I know. She's beautiful, but she doesn't look like me at all." She paused. "It's funny, since coming out here and starting all of this—" she motioned to the memorabilia on the table, "I really feel like I know her."

Ian leaned over and kissed the top of her head. She knew he understood her longing for a large, close-knit family. They had both wanted a large family for different reasons—Ian, because he had loved growing up surrounded by siblings, aunts, and uncles, and Laine because she'd disliked being an only child. Ian pulled her into his arms and laid his chin on top of her head.

"Who are you?" Missy asked.

Laine jumped away from Ian as if she'd been caught in a guilty act.

"A better question—who are you?" Ian asked Missy, who stood in the doorway.

The girl stepped into the room. "I'm Missy and this is Bettina." She held up a baggy holding a tiny white moth. "She's my first butterfly. I caught her on my way over. Luckily, I had this full of oranges."

Laine considered the baggy holding the moth and the smear of juice from the disappeared orange slices. "I don't think that's a very kind place to keep your moth."

"Bettina the butterfly," Missy corrected her.

Laine considered the moth. "Bettina probably doesn't like orange juice and I'm pretty sure she's not getting enough air."

Missy looked concerned. "I didn't have anything else to hold her in."

"What happened to the oranges?" Ian asked.

Missy looked at him as if he was the stupidest creature on the planet and then ignored him.

"Let me see if I can find something more hospitable for her," Laine said, heading toward the kitchen. She listened to Missy and Ian's conversation as she looked through the kitchen cupboards.

"Do you collect butterflies?" Ian asked.

"In jars, but just until the butterfly garden is finished," Missy said.

"Butterfly garden?" Ian asked.

"Laine and I are building a butterfly garden. We checked out a bunch of books on butterflies from the library and my uncle Alec is donating a ton of the wood."

Laine found a large pickle jar under the kitchen sink. It would work, but first it needed to be rinsed out.

"A butterfly garden, huh?" Ian said.

"Are you Laine's boyfriend?"

Laine squirted dish soap into the jar and turned on the

water.

"I'm her husband."

"Then why don't you live with her?"

Laine swished a rag inside and outside of the pickle jar, trying to hurry as the questions became increasingly embarrassing.

"That's a very good question," Ian said.

"Are you going to live here too?"

Laine slammed through the drawers, searching for a clean dish towel. All the drawers were empty. She knew that because she'd cleaned them out on Friday. Giving up, she tried to dry the jar with the hem of her t-shirt.

"No," Ian said. "I want her to come live with me."

"But she can't."

"No?"

"No," Missy said with stern resolve. "She has to take care of Bettina and the other butterflies."

Laine stopped in the doorway when Missy said, "Maybe she doesn't like you anymore. That's why Rochelle's dad left. *He* said he left because he had important other things to do someplace else, but Rochelle heard him tell Ben's dad that he hates Rochelle's mom."

"That's a very sad—" Ian began.

"Laine *probably* doesn't hate you, because she's very

nice, but you must have done something that made her want to live here with Bettina and not with you." Missy looked at Ian, as if trying to assess his niceness. "Unless you live in a cave, or something. Or a shack. Della's grandpa lives in a trailer. Do you live in a trailer? Laine probably wouldn't like a trailer. Or a tent. She hates camping because she said it's dirty."

Ian's expression looked pinched. "I know she doesn't like to be dirty."

Laine decided she needed to rescue Ian and hurried into the dining room to show Missy the pickle jar. "See, it has this lid so Bettina can't fly away. She just needs some air." She held it out to Ian. "Maybe you can find something to punch some holes."

Ian took the lid from her and stomped into the mud room where he began to open and slam cupboards and drawers.

"Let's get Bettina out of the baggy," Laine said to Missy, carefully taking it from her and trying to upend the moth into the jar. The moth was plastered to the baggy. *This does not look good,* Laine thought. Finally, after a lot of shaking, the moth fell to the bottom of the jar where it lay, tiny and lifeless.

Missy looked at it in horror.

The sound of violent pounding came from the mudroom.

"She might be tired," Laine said. "She probably found the trip here pretty exhausting."

Missy looked ready to cry.

"She'll probably like her new place better if it seems more like what she's used to outside."

"I shouldn't have tried to keep her," Missy said. "I should have just left her alone."

Ian came back into the room carrying a lid riddled with holes.

"Why don't we try looking for flowers and leaves?" Laine suggested again.

"Okay," Missy said, sounding almost as morose as Ian looked.

Ian twisted the lid on the pickle jar.

"Come on," Laine said, touching his arm.

A window slammed and a horrible noise came from behind a closed door.

"Not. A. Gain!" Missy said, running for what Laine now knew as the bathroom.

Ian followed her and pulled open the door. "What the—"

"Don't open that!" Laine and Missy both yelled at the

same time.

A white duck flew at Ian's head.

"Max!" Missy hollered.

Laine ran to the window and called to Max's backside retreating into the woods, "I told you that this house is not your personal zoo!"

Max didn't look back, but his friends did. A skinny kid with hair that stood up straight without the use of hair gel gave her a wide-eyed look, and a tall, fat kid with a beanie pulled down around his ears, tripped as he tried to run away and simultaneously look at her.

Suddenly, a small elfin looking woman appeared at the edge of the wood. The boys saw her and ran back to the house, screaming.

The crazy lady, Laine thought, before correcting herself. *Charlotte Rhyme, the artist.*

The boys thundered toward the house, pounded up the porch steps, and flung open the front door. Laine hurried to the living room and watched Ian, Missy, Max, and his two friends trying to capture the duck. The only one with any degree of calm was Bettina the moth—she'd finally picked up her wings, and stood fluttering on the bottom of the jar. Laine sank to the floor, laughing.

Ian stopped chasing the duck and looked at her as if

she was the crazy person, and then his lips twitched as he watched the three boys, Missy, and the duck play tag in the living room.

The duck squawked, the kids yelled instructions to each other, and Laine sat in the corner, holding her side, laughing. Ian joined her.

"You'll have to re-mop the floor," Ian said, between gulps of laughter.

"If the duck poops, I'm getting a new carpet," Laine said, still laughing.

"I hope it poops," Ian said. "I don't like that carpet."

"I'll let you pick out a new one."

"Thank you." Ian leaned over and kissed her.

CHAPTER16

On Monday morning, Laine consulted her list—refrigerator, telephone and Internet service—while Ian got ready to return to his office. They'd had a lovely weekend, but now they had to resume real life, although Laine wasn't exactly sure what that meant. She'd yet to discover or define her new real life.

"Don't you think we should have at least talked about this?" Ian asked, frowning as he followed her and the two delivery men hauling in the brand new washer and dryer she'd ordered.

"It's mine, right? I own it."

Ian gave the delivery guys an intimidating glance, before he turned his frustration toward her. "It's not the expense, Laine."

Of course, she knew that. Handing him a bottle of window cleaner, she said, "You can stay and help, but you can't stay and lecture me."

He opened his mouth in surprise, and then shut it into a hard, straight line.

The delivery men plunked the washer and dryer down

in the mud room and fiddled with the hoses and wires. Laine turned her back on them and walked into the now spotless kitchen, admiring the new gleaming stainless steel refrigerator.

"My house, my rules." She hooked the spout of the window cleaner bottle on her finger and dangled it at him. He followed her into the kitchen, but ignored the window cleaner.

"Washington is a community property state."

"Don't be that person, Ian." She took the window cleaner by the bottle's neck and wrapped her fingers around it, fighting the overwhelming temptation to squirt a blue streak onto Ian's silk tie.

"What person?" He folded his arms across his chest.

"Our marriage isn't just about who owns what, who earned what."

"What marriage? How can we have a marriage if you're here and I'm...where I belong."

"Who's to say that this isn't where I belong?"

He took a step closer, leaning in. "You belong with me."

"Uh, excuse me," the delivery guy with the nose ring said.

"Yes?" Laine said, ignoring Ian's eye rolling.

The delivery guy handed Laine a clipboard and pen. "If you could just sign here." He pointed at a line on the paper with a finger as fat as a sausage. Laine did as he asked and then handed the clipboard back to him.

After the two men disappeared through the dining room, Ian turned back to her. "Okay, spend the week with me, at home, and we'll come here on the weekends."

Laine considered him. She did like having him around, but the thought of returning to Seattle was like a concrete block on her chest, cutting off her breath. In some ways, it'd be so easy to slip back into her old life, and yet—

"I have to go to work and I want you to come with me."

Laine shook her head. "I can't. I've got the window washers coming. The floors are being buffed this afternoon. I'll see you when Sid is—"

Heavy footsteps announced the delivery guy's return. "Uh, excuse me."

Ian scowled at him.

"Your car is blocking us in."

"This house sits on ten acres." Ian almost yelled. "How can there not be room for you to drive around?"

"We don't want to drive through the mud and get the van dirty."

Ian turned back to Laine. Taking her face in his hands, he gave her a quick hard kiss. "We'll discuss it more this afternoon."

"Hey." A man in jeans and suspenders stuck his head in the door. "I got a delivery for wood here."

"Oh good!" Laine hurried to the door. A truck with a pile of lumber in its bed stood behind the appliance delivery van.

Ian came to stand beside her on the porch. He raised his eyebrows, questioning.

"Butterfly garden," she told him, feeling incredibly happy. Wrapping her arms around his waist, she pulled him against her. "I love you, but I want to stay here. Just for a while."

***

Drapes and drop cloths spun in the rinse cycle. A crew of men with squeegees worked on her windows and the brand-new dishwasher hummed. Laine sat at the gleaming dining room table and considered her grandparent's photo albums, journals and letters. The collection was the only messy spot left in the house. She'd conquered cobwebs, chased away dust bunnies and scoured sinks—now, the hard part started. She started with two piles—one for Sid and one for Madeleine.

Where were they? Had they passed on? Wouldn't Madeleine at least say goodbye? But wasn't that just like death? When a death is sudden—there isn't time. No one gets the luxury of hugging or kissing goodbye. There isn't time for apologies.

But none of that held true for Madeleine. She'd played by different rules. Laine didn't understand the rules, but she guessed Madeleine had broken more than a few. Not that she would have wanted Madeleine hanging around yesterday—yesterday she'd only wanted Ian. Over and over again.

But now he was gone and the house was finally clean. She had a collection of memorabilia staring at her and she wished Madeleine would reappear. With the two piles created, she started trying to assemble a time line.

The doorbell interrupted her.

"Hey." Bette stuck her head in the doorway and then whistled in appreciation. "This place is gorgeous!"

Laine shrugged away the compliment, but looked around the room in pride. "I know its horribly dated."

"I love 1930's furniture," Bette exclaimed, coming in and standing in the center of the living room.

"The wood pieces are great, but I'm going to replace anything upholstered."

"They look good," Bette said, running her hand over the back of a sofa.

"The fabric is worn thin and every time I sit down I'm swallowed in a cloud of dust."

"No one likes dust envelopes," Bette agreed.

"Exactly," Laine said. "Although, you know, I'm sure the house hasn't been empty since my grandparents'time. Someone has been taking care of it. It was dusty, but it wasn't decayed."

"Maybe your grandfather?"

"Exactly what I'm thinking," Laine said. "But how odd that we never even knew of its existence."

"Almost as odd as you promising to be here on Saturday and then—" She spread out her arms in a question. After a beat of silence, she continued, "So, where were you?"

Laine flushed.

"I knew it. You went back to Ian!"

"Well, yes and no."

"What does that mean? And if you're back with Ian— why are you here?"

Laine bristled. She wasn't good at sharing emotions, especially ones she hadn't really explored. Ones she didn't quite understand. The messy ones, with all sorts of unanswered questions. "I have things to do…like build a butterfly garden."

Bette seemed to understand, which was good, because Laine wasn't sure if she did. "Actually," Bette said. "I've come to ask you about that."

"The butterfly garden?"

"Yes. What would you think of holding off on that and using the lumber for a haunted house?"

"But Missy—"

"It was Missy's idea. Every year the Boy Scouts hold a haunted house as a fund raiser. In the past, they've always used the old Rhyme house, which, as you know, is the newly completed library."

"So they want to hold it here?"

Bette looked sheepish. "It is rather perfect. You wouldn't have to do anything. The scout committee would set everything up and take everything down. They're pros. They've been doing this for years."

Laine opened her mouth to protest.

"You said you wanted to replace the furniture. I bet I can find someone to take it all away for you."

Laine thought about strangers paying money to come into the cottage. Really, she had to stop calling it that. It was much more mansion than cottage. She had her own personal mansion and she hadn't done anything to earn it. Sharing it was the least she could do. *We have what we have to share and to bless,* Madeleine had said. Besides, this would be a great way to get to know her Rose Arbor neighbors. "Okay," she said, without stopping to think that her stay at the cottage mansion was supposedly temporary.

"Really?" Bette asked. "You won't mind? It'll mean having a haunted house set up in your barn for three weeks."

"The barn?" She'd thought Bette was asking for the house. The barn would be easy. She wouldn't have to move her research upstairs. Ian could come and stay.

"The haunted house would only be open on the weekends."

How ironic—she'd gone from having a real ghost to only a pretend ghost. And a swarm of Boys Scouts. She didn't know which she feared the most.

Her stomach clenched when she thought about the ghosts she hoped to see this afternoon—Madeleine and Sid. She hadn't seen Madeleine since they'd found Sid in the church.

"Laine, are you alright?" Bette laid her hand on Laine's arm.

"I'm fine. I'm just—well, today Sid's being cremated

and I'll probably bring his ashes home with me, and I'm hosting a haunted house—" A nervous laugh caught in her throat.

Bette frowned, looking concerned. "Maybe this isn't a good idea."

"No, it's a great idea. I'd like to get involved in the community, get to know people."

Bette folded her arms across her chest. "I thought you were just visiting."

"Even visitors can be friendly."

"What about your job?"

Laine touched her forehead with her fingertips. How had she forgotten about her job? She hadn't thought about the foundation for nearly a week. How had something that had once been so important to her completely disappear from her thoughts. She thought about her co-workers with a twinge of guilt. Without cell service at the cottage, she'd let her phone batteries die. She really needed to talk to Gemma.

But Bette was talking. What was she saying? Nothing she said even registered or made sense. Something about cookies. No, a bake sale.

***

Laine sat in the foyer of the mortuary, blinking back

tears.

"I'm sorry, Lainey," her father said. "I didn't think this would upset you. Cremation had been on the schedule since the beginning. I thought you were okay with that."

"Of course, I am," Laine said, hugging her purse to her chest. "I mean, I know what we had decided—"

"We're just a week behind schedule, that's all." George sat beside her, patting her knee.

A week? Had it really only been a week? She'd met Madeleine only a week ago and somehow she'd become a huge part of Laine's life. She couldn't explain to her father that her tears were for Madeleine and not for Sid. She accepted Sid's death—her fear was that with Sid's body cremated and gone Madeleine would also be gone. Without saying goodbye. Laine wanted to thank her. She couldn't say exactly what for, but she wanted to say it. She felt she owed Madeleine at least that.

"Would you like to hold onto the ashes until Saturday?" George asked.

"Say yes," Madeleine materialized beside George. She wore a black chiffon dropped waist dress, a long string of pearls and a pinched expression.

"Yes?" Laine's answer came out as a question. She also wanted to ask where Madeleine had been, but she didn't know how with George sitting beside her. Relief at seeing Madeleine washed over her. She felt braver and stronger with her grandmother close. She swallowed. "Saturday is when—"

"We scatter the ashes at sea," George said.

"What would you think of doing that at the cottage?" Ian asked.

Laine jumped. She hadn't seen him come in. He placed his hand on her shoulder. The warmth of his hand steadied her and she leaned into him.

Madeleine nodded her approval of Ian's suggestion.

"The haunted house—" Laine began.

"It's haunted?" Trudy asked, her eyes wide.

"No, of course not," Laine said, but mentally added, *sort of.*

"Tell them you'll scatter the ashes on the beach," Madeleine said.

Laine's thoughts scrambled. "I told the Boy Scouts that they could host a haunted house fund raiser in the barn."

"Boy Scouts?" Madeleine asked. Really, for a ghost, she wasn't very omniscient.

"Boy Scouts?" Trudy raised her eyebrows. "Are you crazy?"

"Yes," Laine said. "I think I am."

Everyone laughed, except for her.

"But there is a beautiful beach down the bank," Laine said. "Far away from Boy Scouts, scout masters or bossy librarians."

Mr. Ketchum, the mortician, appeared in the doorway and greeted the family. "If you'd like to follow me," he said in a sonorous voice that seemed completely incongruous with his tiny frame and shocking red hair. He sounded so practiced, so *reverent,* that Laine wondered if he'd learned to talk like that in mortician school. He looked like a leprechaun and sounded like Orson Wells.

Trudy and George followed, but Laine stayed in her chair. To her surprise, so did Ian. He reached out and touched a tear on her cheek.

"Don't be sad," he said. "We're going to be okay."

Laine nodded and sniffed. She didn't know where she and Ian were going, but she knew she wanted to be with him, even if she didn't know anything else. Did she want to live in Seattle? Did she want to continue her work at the foundation? She didn't know, but she did knew she loved Ian.

Madeleine stood watching and Laine looked at her from beneath her eyelashes. "Sid refuses to leave," she said, folding her arms and tapping her foot.

"Can I see him?" Laine asked.

Ian took her hand. "Sure, although you picked out the urn, so I'm sure it won't be much of a surprise."

Madeleine shook her head. "No, you won't be able to see him."

Laine had to bite back the question, *But why not? I can see you.* She squeezed Ian's hand.

Ian looked into her eyes, questions reflected on his face. She stood and pulled him up with her.

"What happens now?" Ian asked.

"Sid and I will go back to the cottage," Laine said. "You come and visit as often as you can." *Maybe we can create the happiest times of our lives,* she thought.

***

He's being ridiculous," Madeleine complained while Laine worked on props for the haunted house.

"I'd really like to see him." Laine secured a plastic skull on top of a broomstick wrapped in an old quilt and then, using white electric tape and strips of white cotton, she fashioned a mummy. She'd already made a number of paper mache bats and spiders and they sat on top of the kitchen table, looking like a black and hairy feast. "If you see him, tell him I miss him."

Madeleine folded her arms across her chest. "I can't

see him anymore than you can. Maybe he'll want to talk to Ian."

Laine frowned at her mummy. He looked lopsided. She punched the quilt into a different shape.

"Is Ian coming back soon?"

Laine nodded. "Tonight."

Madeleine looked at the pot simmering on the stove. "Ah, that explains the coq au vin."

Laine blushed as she twirled the white cotton strips around the mummy's mid section. "Yes. Ian loves coq au vin."

"And the lemon meringue cookies?" Madeleine snagged one cookie off the counter and Laine frowned at her.

"Those are for the Boy Scouts." Although, Ian also loved lemon meringue cookies.

"More Boy Scouts?" Madeline stopped mid chew.

Laine laughed and glanced out the window at the cars parked in the driveway. "I think there are a bunch of them here now. We'll be seeing a lot of Scouts in the next few weeks. After all, they're building and manning the haunted house." And it struck her how odd it was to be casually talking to a ghost about a haunted house. She needed a dog named Scooby.

"I don't think I'll be here that long."

Laine paused twirling the cotton strips. She didn't want to think about Madeleine leaving. "You said Sid doesn't want to go."

Madeleine paced across the kitchen tile. "Of course he doesn't want to go! That's the problem."

"I don't know why that's a problem." Laine propped the mummy up in a corner and looked him over. He needed hands. Maybe she could find some at the Dime Store. "He doesn't want to leave—I want him to stay. So stay."

Madeleine scowled at her before fading away into a patch of late afternoon sunlight.

Laine rolled her eyes at her grandmother's disappearing act, left the mummy standing in the corner, and gathered her collection of bats and spiders. Pushing out the door, she was surprised to see Ian's car parked alongside the pick-up trucks and vans that belonged to the Boy Scouts' parents.

Juggling spiders, bats and a large ball of string, Laine headed toward the barn and the sounds of hammering and nailing. The crisp autumn air smelled of sawdust and dying leaves. Laine carried her collection into the dim barn and stopped to watch Ian hammering two-by-fours into a coffin. He had his tie tucked into his buttoned shirt and his shirt sleeves rolled above his elbows. He must have felt her gaze, because he stopped, looked up and smiled. Sawdust sprinkled his dark hair and clung to his suit pants. Beads of sweat dotted his forehead.

"Hey," he said, leaning toward her.

"Hi." She kissed him, acutely conscious of the stares of the Boy Scouts who milled about the barn.

"What you got?" he asked.

She showed him her spiders and bats.

"Spooky," he said.

She motioned toward the hayloft. "I've got to hang these."

"I've heard stories about haylofts—maybe I'll join you."

CHAPTER 17

She shook her head, laughing. "Later," she said over her shoulder as she climbed the ladder to the loft. At the top, she sat down with the spiders and bats intending to string them on the cord, but watching Ian instead. He'd returned to hammering and she liked watching him hammer.

"He's beautiful, isn't he?" A voice spoke in her ear.

"Grandpa!" Laine twisted her head to see her grandfather sitting beside her. Of course, she'd never known him young, but he'd always been handsome. She hadn't realized how much he looked like Ian, with his dark hair and strong jaw. His legs dangled through the trap door and he wore the suit she'd chosen for his burial, but he'd lost the jacket and tie. How did that work? Was he cremated in his clothes—or in the nude? Was he wearing "ghost" clothes? Laine shook all the ridiculous questions from her mind. All that mattered was that he was here, right now—she didn't need to think about anything other than this very moment, because she didn't know how many moments with her grandfather she had left. According to

Madeleine, not very many.

"I'm so glad you two have worked things out."

"It's…I'm not sure what we've worked out," she faltered.

"But he's here and you're here."

"Yes."

"And that's good, right?"

Laine nodded, biting her lip. "How about you—are you good?"

Sid held out his arms, considering them as if they were foreign objects. "I feel fine. I don't feel dead at all."

"I wonder how that's supposed to feel."

"Maybe just like this—I've never had anyone to ask, before."

"You don't look dead."

Sid ran his fingers through his thick mop of dark hair. She'd only known him with silver hair and she had to fight the temptation to touch it. "I miss you," she told him.

"I've missed you, too." And for a moment, he sounded old again.

"Where have you been?"

Sid scowled. "It took me awhile to figure out where I was—the hospital, the morgue, the mortuary—that church and a whole bunch of people I didn't know, crying and carrying on, like somehow I was responsible for their lost uncle Barry.'

He sounded so much like himself, the Grandpa Sid she'd known and loved that she smiled. Holding herself upright, she had to fight the desire to lean against him as she had as a child.

"And then your grandmother showed up."

"And that was good, right? I mean you hadn't seen her in so many years."

Sid shook his head and then let it fall, as if it was too heavy to hold. "I didn't know I'd see her again…I would have done things differently if I'd known we'd be reunited."

"I think she understands that," Laine told him. "Better than either of us—she knows what it's like to die." She leaned toward him. "She still loves you, despite all the stupid things you've done."

He sniffed. "I'm so embarrassed."

"Go talk to her. That's all she wants."

Sid looked uncertain and then he wavered, suddenly translucent, like a flickering hologram.

"Lainey?" Ian poked his head through the trap door, the exact same place where her grandfather had sat just seconds ago. "Are you talking to someone?"

Laine sat up straight, smiling. "Just singing." And she began to sing. "If you ever laugh when a hearse goes by, then you will be the next in line to die. They wrap you up in bloody sheets and bury you down about six feet deep."

Ian joined in. "The worms crawl in, the worms crawl out. They eat your brains. They eat your nose. They eat the jelly between your toes—"

"Oh—I made dinner," Laine said. "Do you want some?"

***

She didn't see Sid at all the next day and she wondered why not.

"It's difficult," Madeleine had tried explaining to her. "He hasn't learned how to control his visibility yet."

"What? You mean whether or not to be seen is like something you learn in the ghost master class?"

Madeleine smiled. "Something like that."

"And since Sid is a rookie ghost—"

The chandelier above the dining room table suddenly, violently swayed.

Laine smiled, "Oh, I get it. Sid doesn't like being called a rookie ghost."

"He'll always be a rookie ghost if he refuses to pass on."

A door slammed shut.

Laine returned her attention to the photo albums. "I think he knows that."

"No, he doesn't," Madeleine said. "If he understood, we could leave."

A window blew open, scattering the photos across the table and mussing Laine's careful organization.

"I don't think you're helping," Laine told Madeleine as she tried to capture the fluttering photographs. "You're just making him mad."

"He's mad that he can't eat your snicker-doodles."

"But why can't he? I thought you could eat."

"*I* can."

"But he can't?"

Madeleine nodded. "Once Heaven's trust is earned, privileges are granted."

This led to so many questions, Laine couldn't decide which to ask first. She really wanted to know about heaven, but she picked one she thought Madeleine could answer. "Snicker-doodles are a privilege?"

"Just one of a million that you take for granted."

"Who are you talking to?" Trudy stuck her head in through the open window.

"What's this about snicker-doodles?" George asked,

coming up behind his wife.

Laine jumped out of her chair. "What are you guys doing here?"

"We just came to see your new digs," George told her, beaming.

"Can we come in?" Trudy asked.

Laine gave Madeleine a pained look and mouthed, "Sid?" before opening the door for her parents.

"I'll try to make sure he behaves," Madeleine said to Laine before turning her attention to the air behind Laine's shoulder. "Maybe you can have cookies. Have you tried? Honestly, you're like a two year old."

Madeleine faded as Trudy and George bustled into the room, but Laine heard her yelling in the kitchen. Fortunately, her parents did not. As Laine returned her parents' hugs and accepted their compliments on the cottage, she tried to tune out her grandparents arguing.

"This place is just fantastic!" Trudy exclaimed, standing in the center of the living room and turning in a slow circle to take it all in.

Laine flushed with pleasure. She really did love it. "The upholstered furniture is threadbare—I'm going to replace it."

Trudy's face lit up. "You can buy some of Sid's

furniture!'"

"Sid's furniture?" Laine echoed, feeling like she'd missed a beat.

Trudy nodded and George looked at his shoes.

"We're going to put it on Craigslist as soon as the house sells," Trudy said, as she walked past the baby grand piano, trailing her fingers along the lid.

That her parents even knew about Craigslist was almost as surprising as their plan to sell the furniture.

"Why not include the furniture in the sale of the house?"

Something crashed in the kitchen, making Laine think that Sid didn't want the house sold. Well, too bad. If Madeleine had her way, George wouldn't have any use for it and if her parents would rather have the money than the house, that was their decision and Laine supported it.

"What was that?" George asked, swiveling toward the noise.

"I—um, don't know," Laine swallowed. A lone, disembodied arm floated in the kitchen. She hurried to steer her parents into the living room, but George headed toward the sound. Laine hoped that if Sid couldn't control his body parts that he'd at least hide.

George pushed open the kitchen door and the snicker-doodle smell rolled out. He scratched his head and turned back to Laine, his expression pinched.

"So you're going to sell Grandpa's house?" Laine repeated. It made sense, no matter what Sid thought. Her parents didn't need a second home two blocks from their primary residence. "And you'd like to sell me the furniture?" She found this more surprising than the Craigslist bomb. Her father had always been generous to a fault. The thought of him trying to sell her anything boggled her. He had always given her whatever she wanted.

"Just if you can use it, dear," Trudy said, walking around. "You know the down sofa would look really lovely right here." She scooted the big arm-chairs away from the fireplace. "Imagine curling up with a book in your grandfather's wingback in front of the fire!"

Laine had always loved her grandfather's big chair and it would look good there. "I don't know—I'll have to think about it. Ask Ian."

"Ian?" Trudy wandered into the dining room and glanced at the photographs and journals on the table before going to stand in front of the French doors that led to the stone patio. She stood staring out at the view of the Sound and then turned around and waved her arms, encompassing the whole cottage in her gesture. "I thought all this meant that you've separated with Ian for good."

"All what?" Laine asked.

Trudy imitated Vanna White showing off a prize. "All this. This gorgeous home you've created for yourself. Away from Ian."

"I—" Laine didn't know what to say, because she didn't know what she wanted. She loved the cottage and yes, she wanted to stay, but she also wanted Ian. She wanted Ian much, much more than she wanted the cottage.

"We've heard the rumors," George said, coming and sitting down at the dining room table. He folded his arms, making Laine wonder what was happening with Sid's arms. She gave the open kitchen door a nervous glance. No sign of Sid's anything.

"Ian's behavior has pained us greatly," George said.

Laine opened her mouth, tempted to defend Ian, but since she didn't know what her parents had heard, she didn't know what to say.

Trudy nodded in agreement and placed her hand over her heart. "We not only understand—we applaud your decision. In fact, we were wondering why he was at the funeral home yesterday."

"I...don't know what you heard, but Ian and I—"

Laine stuttered. She ran her fingertips along the dining room table, absently stirring her grandparent's photographs.

"Oh sweetie," Trudy rushed forward and placed her arm around Laine's shoulders. "You don't need to be brave in front of us."

"I'm not being brave." Her mind went back to the evenings, nights and mornings she'd spent with Ian at the cottage and the memories of their hours in bed made her tingle. She looked down at the photographs on the table to hide the blush creeping up her cheeks.

Trudy stared at Laine, as if trying to read her expression. Laine couldn't look at her step-mother or father. She didn't know where this discussion could possibly be headed.

"I would love a tour of your new home," Trudy said.

An abrupt change of subject, Laine thought.

"Yes dear," George stood. "Why don't you take a look around, while Laine and I talk business." His words came out so smoothly, Laine knew they had to have been rehearsed.

Business? Her father hated business. He avoided it at all costs.

George pulled out a dining room chair and motioned for Laine to sit down while Trudy trundled out of the room.

Laine looked in the kitchen. It was quiet. Her grandparents
had stopped arguing. Did that mean they'd simply moved
their fight to another place? Was Trudy going to stumble
over them? Laine took the chair her father offered and
watched as he settled into a chair directly opposite her. The
photographs and journals lay between them. This bothered
Laine. She wanted him to at least notice the pictures of his
parents. A small sign that he cared—that's all she wanted.

"We have a buyer for Leon Land," George said.

Laine wouldn't have been more surprised if he'd said
he had mice in his pocket. "You want to sell some of the
company's land?" Why would he be talking to her about
that? He knew she didn't have anything to do with their
land holdings.

"Not the land, the company." George fidgeted with his
gold cufflink.

"You want to sell the company?"

Cupboards and doors began swinging and slamming in
the kitchen.

"What the—" George, startled, jumped out of his chair.

So, her grandparents hadn't taken their fight elsewhere.
They were listening and obviously, Sid didn't like what he
heard.

Laine's thoughts rushed. She decided to ignore the

kitchen drama, pretend that she couldn't hear or see, what was going on in the next room. George bolted into the kitchen and the slamming and swinging stopped. He returned looking confused and flustered.

"What was that?"

"What was what?" Laine asked. "You mean the snicker-doodles? They're for the Scouts coming over tonight, but you're welcome to have one." She folded her hands on top of the table to keep them from shaking. "Now, what were you saying about selling the company?"

"Well, I just thought that since you and Ian are separating—"

Laine didn't interrupt her father, but a flying snicker-doodle did. It whizzed past George's ear and landed on the table beside him.

Laine gulped as her father's face turned red. "You should try a cookie—they're very good." Struggling to regain composure, she said, "What about the employees? The foundation?"

Standing, blinking and surveying the kitchen, George gripped the back of his chair and faced her. "You didn't see—"

Laine kept her face impassive. "See what, Daddy?"

His face softened. She rarely called him Dad, let alone

Daddy. He'd been George to her ever since he'd married Trudy. He shook his head. "Maybe this isn't a good time to talk."

"Yeah. This is a bombshell." Laine rubbed her forehead. "I can't believe you want to sell the company."

More swinging doors, slamming, and at least five flying cookies—Laine worried she wouldn't have enough for the Boy Scouts and their families if Sid didn't stop using them for pitching practice. Laine tried to ignore it all, but George stood transfixed, his gaze shifting from the spectacle in the kitchen to Laine's pokerfaced expression.

He can't sell the company, she thought. *He needs me to do that. Maybe, probably he even wants me to leave Ian so he can have control of the proceeds.* She shook her head. Nothing made sense. He had a generous salary. When the house sold, he'd have at least another million. Why would he want her to sell the company? And *if* she sold, and she was pretty sure that she never would, the money would be hers. Right? Slapping her hand on her forehead, she really regretted not attending the reading of the will.

After a brief knock on the door, Missy let herself in. She stood in the foyer, a scowl and tears on her face.

"Missy!" Laine greeted her, glad for the distraction. She stood to introduce Missy to George and explained that

Missy had been a great help cleaning the cottage.

Missy blinked back tears and George said nothing more than, "Ah."

Laine knew that George wasn't happy about the interruption, but really, Laine couldn't agree to sell the company on her father's recommendation alone. She knew her parents. If they had unlimited access to almost inexhaustible funds, they would blow through the money in minutes. Were they in a pinch? Is that why they were selling furniture on Craigslist?

Laine turned her attention to Missy. "What's the matter, sweetie?"

Missy sniffed. "I have to be a banana or a gorilla!"

George, still seated in his chair, snorted. "I'd choose to be the gorilla—that way you won't get eaten."

"Halloween costume," Laine murmured to her dad.

"Ah, right… People still do that?" George asked.

Missy's shoulders shook with pent-up emotion. She ignored George and gave Laine a long, pitiful look. "I have a choice between Max's last year's costume or my costume from the school play on the food pyramid." She sniffed and wiped her runny nose with the back of her hand. "My mom said we can't afford anything more."

Laine squatted so she was on eye level with Missy.

"Well, what would you like to be?"

"A butterfly."

Of course. "Maybe I can help," Laine said.

George lifted his finger. "Darling, I think we have more important things to discuss—"

Trudy came back into the room with something tucked beneath her sweater. "We need to go, George."

"But you just got here," Laine said, but even to herself her voice sounded off. She wanted her parents to leave. She couldn't possibly discuss selling the company—she could barely even stand to think about it. She'd have to talk to Sid. He'd know what to do. Instead, she said to her parents, "I'm making pecan chicken for dinner. Ian's coming. You should stay and talk to him about selling the company."

"Ian's coming?" George asked, his eyebrows lifted. "I thought you two were separated."

Trudy looked impatient and headed for the door. Her heels beat a swift staccato on the hardwood floors. "Sweetie," she said over her shoulder. "We have to leave. Now." She didn't even acknowledge Missy and that small breach of politeness surprised Laine almost as much as the thought of her parents selling furniture on Craigslist.

As her father's Lincoln Town Car pulled away, Laine

was pretty sure they were hiding more than whatever Trudy carried beneath her sweater.

CHAPTER18

"You can help me?" Missy said, her voice quivering as she sank into a chair beside the fireplace. "I just can't wear Max's gorilla suit—it reeks of pee. He said he didn't pee in it, but I don't believe him. He probably really had to go—"

"Would the banana suit be so bad?" Laine asked, settling down on the ottoman next to Missy.

Missy rolled her eyes and leaned back into the chair with a giant sigh. "P-l-e-a-s-e."

"Okay," Laine said, smiling, reaching out and patting Missy's knee. She thought for a moment and then had a wonderful idea. "I found a trunk full of my grandmother's clothes and it's got a real ball gown made of the most amazing material. Come on, I'll show you." She led Missy up the attic stairs and knelt in front of the huge trunk she'd found. One by one she pulled out the clothes for Missy's admiration.

"You should wear these," Missy said, fingering the fine silk of a blue dress.

Laine laughed. "Oh, I couldn't."

"Yes, you could." Missy held up a beige cotton blazer

with a rounded collar piped with a silky cobalt blue trim. "I bet these would all fit you." Laine considered the clothes. She was several inches taller than her grandmother, but just as lean. If she let the sleeves and hem down…She shook her head. When would she need a rounded collar or a blue silk dress? She always dressed very conservatively at work—wool suits, sturdy leather pumps.

Laine pulled out the ball gown. It shimmered in the attic's dusty light.

Missy let out an appreciative gasp.

"We could cut this up and use the fabric to make wings."

Missy, who had been sitting cross-legged on the floor beside the open trunk, jumped to her feet. "You *can not* cut this dress up into pieces. I won't let you! It's much too beautiful! It'd be a—" she sought for the word and came up with one. "A desecration!"

Laine laughed, folding the dress and placing it on her lap. "Okay, calm down. Let's look and see what else." She rustled through the trunk and pulled out a swatch of fabric that matched the ball gown.

"What's that supposed to be?" Missy asked.

Laine stood and held it up. It swayed and shimmered in the breeze like a live thing. There had to be about two yards. "Maybe it's nothing. Madeleine, my grandmother, probably had the dress made and this is the left-over material." She raised her eyebrows at Missy. "Can your mom sew? This would make a pretty cool dress."

Missy bit her lip. "And an awesome pair of wings."

***

Hours later, after Missy and Laine had found some wire and cutters in the barn, their wing building was interrupted by a knock on the door.

Missy ran to answer, while Laine tried to glue the fabric to the wire.

Gemma followed Missy into the kitchen.

Laine looked up from her work, pleased. "Gemma! I've missed you!"

Gemma frowned at the wings and then raised her gaze to Laine's. "Not as much as I've missed you!"

A twinge of guilt pricked Laine, but then she burnt her finger with the hot glue gun and stopped feeling guilty.

"Have you forgotten about us?" Gemma wailed. "The masquerade ball is in two weeks! The caterers—"

Laine put down the gun and tried to peel the hot glue off her stinging fingers. She never should have let Cheryl talk her into using it. She had suspected Cheryl didn't like her, and this proved Laine's suspicions correct. Friends should not let friends use glue guns. She looked up at Gemma. Her red curly hair quivered with emotion.

"Gemma, you are completely capable—"

"No, I'm not!" Gemma folded her arms tightly across her chest, hugging herself.

"Yes, you are. You can talk to the caterers." She pulled out the kitchen chair beside her. "Here, sit down."

Gemma looked like she wanted to argue, but after a moment, she sat down and sniffed. "But the band—"

"You can talk to the band or get a new one."

"I miss you," Gemma said. "It's not fun without you."

Laine sighed. "How did you find me?"

"Jane told Mike where you were."

Laine nodded. Jane knew everything. Laine picked up the glue gun, feeling a new sense of resolve.

Gemma nodded at the wings. "If I finish whatever that is, will you come back?"

"Those are my wings," Missy said.

Gemma turned and smiled at Missy, her frustration obviously slightly dissipating. "Oh, are you a fairy?"

"A butterfly," Missy said in a tone that had the word duh attached.

Gemma took the gun from Laine and began to work.

Laine watched Gemma work with dexterity. "You

know how to use a glue gun?"

Gemma laughed. "Of course. Doesn't everyone?"

"If you can make butterfly wings, you can certainly organize the masquerade ball. You've been helping me run it for fifteen years. That's longer than any of my father's marriages." She bit her lip, surprised at her own outburst. She should not have said that.

Gemma paused the gun over the wings. "Everyone's saying that you've left Ian and that you're not coming back. Are you? Coming back, I mean?"

Laine looked at Madeleine standing in the kitchen. When had she shown up? Madeleine smiled, but Laine couldn't return the gesture.

"I don't know," Laine said slowly. She really needed to face some hard decisions about her work. "But I do know that you can be in charge of the masquerade ball."

Gemma opened her mouth and then closed it. She finished her gluing and then held up the completed wings for Missy's approval.

"They're beautiful," Missy breathed in unmasked pleasure.

"Go try them on with your dress," Laine urged.

Missy gathered up the wings and dress and scampered to the downstairs bedroom.

Gemma's smile faded when Missy disappeared. She turned to Laine, her expression serious and more than a little sad. "If I have to work for Carly—I won't work there. It's you or nothing."

"Don't say that, Gemma," Laine said, her voice catching in her throat. "You love the foundation almost as much as I do."

"I can't do it without you."

"Can you at least do the masquerade ball?"

Gemma looked so pained that Laine laughed. "It's been planned for weeks and weeks, and yes, small things always go wrong at the last minute, but I know you can handle anything—"

"I can't handle—"

"Yes, you can."

"No."

"Yes."

Gemma scowled. "Okay, maybe. But you'll at least come, right?"

"I don't have a costume," Laine said.

"You can wear my dress," Madeleine said. "And Missy's wings."

"It won't fit," Laine said.

Gemma looked confused and Laine corrected herself.

"My costume…I'm not sure it will fit. If I had one."

"We'll get you a costume that fits."

"I don't want one."

"That's a ridiculous reason not to come to the ball."

Laine laughed and shrugged. "It's the only reason I got." She couldn't, wouldn't admit that she didn't want to see Carly.

***

Laine sat on the bed in the quiet, dark bedroom. Through the window, she watched for Ian. He'd gone running on the beach and she expected to see him sprinting up the bank and crossing the lawn at any moment. The moonlight cast a shimmery glow in the room and suddenly, Sid appeared out of the shadows.

Laine lifted her hand to her throat in surprise. Someday, maybe, she'd get used to her grandparents' sudden appearances. "Grandpa, you scared me."

He came over and sat down beside her. The mattress didn't shift beneath his weight. She wondered if he *had* any weight. "That's one of the very few pleasures of this in-between state."

"Scaring granddaughters?" Laine smiled. She still struggled with the desire to touch him. Not ever having a physical relationship with her grandmother, Laine hadn't thought about touching her. But

she'd grown up sitting on her grandfather's lap and holding his hand and a small part of her ached to feel his arms around her.

Sid chuckled. "Among others. I had that Max kid running scared this afternoon."

"What did you do? He's really not that bad, you know."

"Not that bad for a hellion," Sid grunted.

"He's not a hellion."

"Tell that to the chipmunk he had trapped in crab cage. Who would give a kid like that a crab cage? He's likely to try to squish his sister inside."

"I'm glad you're here," Laine told him. "I need to talk to you—"

"I don't want to talk about selling the company," Sid said in a sharp and authoritative voice.

Laine looked at him in surprise. She knew her grandfather had a reputation for being a ruthless business man, but he'd only ever spoken to her with love laced.

Sid sighed and raked his fingers through his hair. "I'm sorry, Laine, I can't tell you what to do, but I will tell you that at this point in my life...or my existence...or whatever state or plane I happen to be in or on... I care about you. I care about Ian. The company…well, that's up to you and Ian."

Laine fingered the lace on her nightgown's sleeve. She'd never thought she'd hear her grandfather say he didn't care about the company. Leon Land had been his life's work, his passion."But George, Daddy—you care about him and he wants me to sell."

Sid's shoulders sagged. "I love George. I want him to be happy and I can tell you that selling the company won't bring him any sort of happiness. Have you asked yourself why he wants you to sell?"

Laine chewed on her lower lip, thinking, confronting the issue that had haunted her since her parent's sudden departure. "It doesn't make sense. If the company belongs to me—how can the sale profit him? He's much better off in his current bogus position, collecting a salary."

"Your father knows you." Sid looked at her until she squirmed. It was true, what he was saying, or implying—George knew she was an easy touch.

Laine stood and watched Ian running along the beach, a dark shadow in the moonlight.

"He's a good man," her grandfather said, coming to stand behind her.

"I'm lucky," Laine said, smiling. "And so are you.

Madeleine loves you very much."

Sid's expression turned soft. "I can't believe she's forgiven me. Of all the miracles of the last few days since my death—that, to me, is the most difficult to believe."

Laine swallowed hard, a lump forming in her throat. Scanning her grandfather's face, trying to read his eyes, she asked, "Will you go with her? I don't think you have to." She paused, watching him. "I want you stay here."

"I want to stay here," Ian said, coming behind her.

She whirled to face him. Damp with sweat, smelling of the Sound, he was so alive. Tangible in a way that her grandparents were not. He drew her to him, and she let him, despite his damp sweat. Laying her head against his chest, she listened to the steady thump of his heart and a long forgotten poem came to mind.

Age is opportunity no less
Than youth itself, though in another dress,
And as the evening twilight fades away
The sky is filled with stars, invisible by day.

When Ian began to kiss her, she forgot about her grandfather, and she forgot about the future of the company. She really couldn't think of anything other than how it felt to be surrounded by Ian.

***

On opening night, the haunted house looked great, almost as good as Missy's costume.

A local farmer had donated hay bales, corn stalks and pumpkins. Missy and Max came over to

help carve pumpkins and although Laine had been hesitant to give Max use of a knife, eventually she lost her fear of him carrying sharp objects. Cheryl came over with a pair of overalls, a flannel shirt and a pair of work boots.

"For Jack," she said.

Laine didn't know what or who Jack was, but she watched Cheryl and the kids stuff the clothes full of newspapers and create a headless man that they propped up in a chair by the barn's entrance. Missy took one of the pumpkins she'd carved, set it on Jack's lap and put a candle inside.

"Will you take a picture of us?" Cheryl asked Laine, holding out a small camera. Laine's throat felt tight as she took a picture of Cheryl and her kids. She'd yet to learn what had become of Mr. Clements, and she knew there must have been one at some point, but Laine had watched for evidence of him and he'd been a no show in any conversation or weekend or even Missy's soccer games. Cheryl single-handedly ran a successful fabric and craft store and a one parent household. At times, Laine found herself watching Cheryl, admiring her. She didn't always like Cheryl's bossy and outspoken personality and maybe the Mr. Clements hadn't either, but as Laine took the family picture, something a little like love touched her heart.

"Now let me take one with you and the kids," Cheryl said.

"Oh no," Laine shook her head. "I don't like having my picture taken.

"Nonsense," Cheryl said. "You look great in that costume and the haunted barn looks fabulous. We need to immortalize it."

Laine looked down at her costume. Madeleine had taken a break from fighting with Sid to put it together for her. Fish net stockings, tight black corset, pointy hat—it was perhaps the sexiest witch costume she'd ever seen. Certainly the sexiest she'd ever worn. She hoped Ian would like it.

Missy and Max both wrapped their arms around her and they posed beside Jack, his face glowing in the semi dusk.

"The cookies!" Missy yelped, remembering the last batch in the oven.

"Smoking hot dog poop!" Max yelled and he tore after

Missy toward the kitchen's back door. Laine and Cheryl followed, laughing.

Inside the warm, fragrant kitchen, they found all the cookies laid out on wax paper on the giant pine table in neat orderly rows. Hundreds of cookies in a variety of flavors.

"Wow," Cheryl said, admiring, "You take your bake sale items very seriously."

Laine shrugged. "I like cookies."

Missy and Max flung open the oven door to inspect what should have been a smoldering tray of cookies, but the oven was empty.

Missy turned and stared. "I thought…"

"I guess, we didn't forget," Laine said at the same time Cheryl said, "Maybe we have a real ghost."

Max rolled his eyes, Missy's eyes widened, and Laine smiled when she said, "One or maybe even two who love cookies."

CHAPTER19

A crunch of gravel in the driveway signaled the first guest's arrival. Laine looked at her watch. It was still too early to expect Ian—she knew he had a late meeting. She wrapped her arms around her waist, feeling a perfect surge of happiness and anticipation. Looking out the window, she watched a van full of kids in costumes swarm over her dead lawn. The boys ran around each other, yelling, waving plastic swords and light sabers while a couple of men in pick-up trucks unloaded folding tables and chairs for the bake sale items and entry fees.

When she'd worked at the foundation, all of her work had been for children and yet her actual interaction with them had been minimal. She'd thrown dinners, luncheons, art auctions, car shows and parties that raised millions of dollars for children and moms, but the moms and children hadn't been a part of the equation. They profited from the result, but they hadn't been a part of the recipe.

Her kitchen phone rang. Ian had the service hooked up a few days before. "I hate not being able to talk to you," he had said.

And, apparently, so had her staff, because they'd been calling several times a day.

"When are you coming back," had been the general, repeating chorus.

Laine tripped over Max on her way to the phone, noticing that he had a handful of cookies hidden beneath his Batman cape. Her gaze landed on the dining room table where her grandparent's letters and photographs lay in organized piles. She smiled, knowing she wasn't done with them yet. Someday she'd finish, but she wasn't in a hurry.

"We have to talk about the Huntington event," Gemma wailed when Laine picked up the phone.

Laine closed her eyes, thinking about how different the haunted house was to the masquerade ball the Huntington's threw every year. Yes, there were costumes and music and food, but that was where the similarities ended.

"I thought we agreed that you don't need me," Laine replied.

"We were wrong! In fact, I was right and you were wrong. The caterer just called—the price of shrimp has doubled since last year."

"So serve something else."

"Something else?"Gemma squeaked. "We always serve shrimp cocktail."

Laine closed her eyes, fighting back a wave of impatience. She just so didn't care.

Laine looked out the window hoping to see Ian's Mercedes, but stood up straight when she saw a Channel Two news van and her parents' car parked in the drive. When had they arrived?

"I have to go," Laine said.

"But wait—I haven't even told you about the band—"

Laine hung up the phone when she saw Kitty Carlisle, the Channel Two anchor woman, and a camera man standing on the lawn with her parents.

Boy Scouts tumbled out of the barn to inspect the new comers. Smoke from dry ice faded into the near darkness. Flickering candlelight from the jack-o-lanterns glowed. Organ music mixed with shrieks and moans sounded from speakers. Watching the news team, her parents and the Boy Scouts mingle on the grass, Laine knew all of this boded ill. She hurried outside, keeping her eye on the news team.

Kitty stood in the center of the lawn with the haunted house in the background."We're here in Rose Arbor where Troop 196 of the Boy Scouts is hosting a haunted house. Now, I understand that the troop has held a haunted house for years, but this year is different. Isn't that right?" Kitty held her microphone up to the hairy face of a boy dressed as a werewolf.

The boy howled in response.

Why would the news team be interested in their haunted house? Why would they come all the way out here? Laine looked for her parents, but they had disappeared. They had something to do with this, but even Trudy's love of the microphone and spotlight couldn't drag a news team all the way from Seattle for a boy scout's fund raising event.

"That's right," Kitty said, as the werewolf kid had said something astute. "This is the first year in the new location and some say this house is really haunted."

Wait. What? Of course it was, but no one knew that but Laine. She started toward the news team. She could throw them out, right? This was her private property and they were trespassing. A hand on her arm stopped her.

Cheryl beamed. "This is great!"

Laine hesitated. Part of her wanted to pick up Kitty Carlisle and throw her into her van and then use her magic wand on her parents to make them really disappear, and another tiny part wanted to listen to Cheryl.

"We couldn't pay for better advertising," Cheryl whispered.

"Have you heard that this place is really haunted?"

Kitty asked a girl in a fairy costume.

The fairy touched her curls and batted her eyelashes for the camera.

Where did she learn to do that? Laine wondered. She was all of six. Laine sought out her parents while half listening to the anchor woman.

"This house has a history of mystical activity," Kitty Carlisle said. "We have here with us Dr. Abbott, a professor of the paranormal."

A professor of the paranormal? Really? Laine stopped to listen. She remembered Dr. Abbott's name from her study at the library. And she suddenly realized what Trudy had been hiding beneath her sweater—her library books on ghosts!

Dr. Abbot looked familiar in that old classmate sort of way. Laine recognized his photo, which must have been taken twenty years ago, from the back of his book. Laine put her finger tips to her forehead to stop the sudden thrumming.

"Yes." Dr. Abbot cleared his throat and addressed the camera. "A haunted house can be any building occupied by disembodied spirits of decedents—"

Kitty pulled the microphone away from Dr. Abbot and said to the camera in a voice reminiscent of Elvira, "You mean dead people?"

"Yes, of course," Dr. Abbot said in a voice as serious as a heart attack. "Now the decedents may or may not have been former residents of the property, but they must have had an emotional tie to the home. Supernatural activity is said to be mainly associated with violent or tragic events in the home's past—such as murder, accidental death, or suicide."

"And in your research, have you found historical evidence of any such tragedies in this house?" Kitty asked.

"This house has a fascinating history," Dr. Abbot began.

"Nonsense," Madeleine spoke in Laine's ear. Laine jumped and placed her hand on her racing heart. She looked around to see if anyone else noticed her fright.

"We bought this house from a very nice family who made a fortune in the logging industry," Madeleine continued.

Laine shot her grandmother a small smile and returned her attention to Dr. Abbot.

"This house originally belonged to Captain Shirley. He built the house for his bride, Bridgette Glen, back in 1906. The legend claims that Captain Shirley's ship was lost at sea on the same day that his bride died in childbirth. Given the strange coincidental deaths, it is possible that the two love-lost spirits have chosen to live in their home, rather than join the spirit realm."

"Hokum!" Madeleine said. "We bought this house from Mr. and Mrs. Brown. Mr. Brown raised Jerseys and Mrs. Brown did cross stitch needle point. She'd covered every spare inch of wall space with her wall hangings."

"And you think that their spirits may still be here," Kitty Carlisle said.

Dr. Abbot nodded. "It's possible."

"And how do you intend to find out?"

Dr. Abbot laughed. "Ghost detection has come a long way since the days of Ghostbusters." He waved his arm in the direction of a group of men holding electronic equipment that looked like scary toasters and circa 1980 sound systems.

Laine's breath caught in her throat. Beside her, Madeleine laughed. "Don't worry, they can't detect us."

"Not even a rookie like Sid?" Laine whispered.

"Not even Rookie Sid," Madeleine assured her.

Kitty turned her attention to a woman standing in the crowd, watching. She wore a long flowing skirt, a loose red sweater, and hoop earrings. Her hair, close clipped, short and gray looked like it belonged on an aging business man and contrasted sharply with her gypsy clothes.

"Let me introduce Gigi Loyd," Kitty held her microphone to the woman. "Gigi, you are a self-professed medium, is that correct?"

"I am a channeller," Gigi clarified. "I'm a communicator for the dead. A link, if you will."

"Does that make me a channeller, too?" Laine whispered to Madeleine.

"Shh!" Madeleine hushed her.

"And what is your opinion of Dr. Abbot's scientific approach to ghost hunting?"

Gigi's smile turned superior. "It's totally unnecessary. If a ghost wishes to be seen, it will be seen. If not, there aren't any electronic doodads that can summon them."

"Ah," Madeleine said. "This one isn't all fluff."

Which Laine thought funny. Gigi certainly looked like fluff.

Kitty held her microphone in front of Dr. Abbot's face. "And how do you respond to that, Dr. Abbot?"

Before Dr. Abbot could respond a chorus of shouts erupted from the barn—the jack-o-lantern in the headless dummy's lap had overturned. Flames licked Jack's overalls and flannel shirt and leaned dangerously close to the corn stalks and hay bales. Kids screamed. Adults threw their jackets on the fire in unsuccessful attempts to smother the flames.

Cheryl demanded a garden hose and Laine responded by shaking her head. She had spent all her time on the interior of the house—she didn't even know if she *had* a garden hose.

A bucket full of water flew through the air and landed on Jack, who turned to a smoldering, smoking mess. The crises ended as abruptly as it had begun.

The crowd stood as still and as straight as the corn stalks surrounding the barn. Whispered murmurs rippled through the crowd.

"Did you see that?" several asked.

"Who threw that bucket?" someone demanded.

Laine wanted to take responsibility, but she was much too far away. No one would have believed her any more than they believed their eyes.

"Did you get anything?" Kitty asked her cameraman.

He shook his head, looking confused. "I got the fire and then the water. All I saw was a flying bucket."

"We'll have to watch the tape. Maybe we can edit something in or out." Kitty looked like a cat presented with a bowl of cream. "Change of plans," she announced. "There's more than a simple Halloween human interest story here. Let's milk it."

I don't think I want to be milked, Laine thought.

"Where are Mr. Brown's jerseys when we need them?" Madeleine asked.

"Did you throw that bucket?" Laine whispered to her.

"Bravo," Cheryl said, coming up and placing her hand on Laine's shoulder. "That really did look like a flying bucket from hell. That was one cool trick and a brilliant move to do it in front of a news team. We need to give you a silver plaque." She took a deep breath. "I don't know how you staged it, or how you pulled the news team out here— but this is probably the best thing that's happened in Rose Arbor for years. This tourist attraction will raise hundreds of dollars for the Boy Scouts and will also bring potentially thousands of dollars to the local business owners. You really are beyond brilliant."

Laine opened her mouth to protest, but Cheryl cut her off, shaking her finger in Laine's face.

"I heard about you. Bette told me you manage a charity foundation and raise millions of dollars for charity. You can't tell me you didn't jerry-rig this."

Laine smiled weakly. "Not me. The ghosts, right?"

"Who's your accomplice?" Cheryl demanded. Then she held up her hands. "No, don't tell me. It's much more fun this way."

Oh yeah, Laine thought, staring down at smoking Jack. *The fun just doesn't end.*

"We'll need to have the house open every night," Cheryl muttered as she turned away to confer with the other parents.

"Lainey," her father called out to her. He carried a clipboard and a pen and had both extended out to her. "I need you to sign these release forms."

"Release forms?" Laine took the clipboard and glanced down at the papers.

After another glance at the forms and then another at Cheryl, the other parents and all their happy expressions, Laine signed. Cheryl was right—the publicity would be good for not only the Scout troop, but also the town's merchants.

She gave her father a level stare, handed him the clipboard and stomped up the steps. She snagged a few snicker-doodles off the bake sale table and slammed through her front door. Leaning her head back against the door, she breathed in the quiet and let her shoulders relax. The peace of the house felt like a haven compared to the chaos on just the other side of the door. Would she be able to keep her grandparents' ghost hidden if her home became a focal point of media attention?

After a moment, she peeked out the window. Kids in their gaudy costumes lined up in front of the barn. The news team wandered around the property, deep in discussion with the two proclaimed ghost experts. Gigi had her head bent toward the anchor woman while Dr. Abbot fiddled with a large silver contraption that looked like a DVD player mixed with a bicycle pump. Where were her parents? She knew that they'd arranged for the news team

The clouds gathering out on the Sound matched her increasingly dark mood. She was happy to provide a haunted house, happy for the publicity and increased tourism for the town, but did she really want people coming and going through her property when she had two very real, live ghosts—no, they weren't alive, were they? That was just it. Sid faded in and out, crashing things.

Someone would notice. The wind picked up. It tossed the pines and fluttered the tops of the corn stalks. Laine let the curtain drop and headed toward the kitchen and a cup of cocoa. With whipped cream. She deserved it.

Poised over the kitchen table, a cookie hung in mid air. It disappeared bite by bite.

CHAPTER 20

"Grandpa Sid?" Laine paused in the doorway.

The cookie completely disappeared.

She'd wanted to talk to him for a long time and now she finally had an opportunity. She just wanted to relax with cocoa, but reason said she had to speak to her grandfather. "I know you're here. Even if I can't see you, I'm pretty sure you can hear me… I just want to know if you're happy. Are you?" She swallowed. "I'm sure you're scared. I know I would be, but Madeleine seems happy enough. Anyway, I love you. I've always loved you. I know Madeleine loves you, too."

"Who are you talking to?" Trudy emerged from the bathroom.

Lained swallowed hard. "I… I know it sounds crazy, but since I started writing Sid's personal history, I've felt close to him." She shrugged and laughed, embarrassed. "Sometimes I talk to him."

Trudy approached her slowly, almost cautiously, the way one would approach a rabid dog. "Do you think he's the one haunting this house?"

Laine shook her head, adamantly. "No, of course not. This house isn't haunted."

The air shifted, so subtly, almost indistinguishably, but Laine could swear her grandfather was laughing. A nervous giggle bubbled in her throat.

"Are you all right, sweetie?" Trudy asked.

"Of course… I just—"

"You've taken Sid's death hard, but really, he's been gone for some time now."

Laine nodded, suddenly conscious of her head nodding in agreement. She felt like a bobble head doll. The thought of her own plastic clone made her smile.

Trudy's frown deepened.

Laine took a deep breath. "I'm going to make some cocoa. Would you like some?"

Trudy looked at her through squinted eyes. "No. I don't think so."

Laine shrugged and took two mugs from the cupboard. Filling a pot with water, she resolved to order a microwave immediately after she got rid her parents and the two hundred kids filling her barn. She put the pot on the stove, willing it to warm quickly.

"You're probably wondering about the news team," Trudy said, settling herself in a chair at the kitchen table.

"And the Ghost Gurus," Laine added. She leveled two scoops of cocoa into the mugs.

"Yes, it was just too good of a human interest story to pass up."

"It must have been a slow news day," Laine said.

"Well, once Kitty heard the house's history—"

"Is the history true?"

Trudy looked shocked. "Of course, why according to Dr. Abbot—"

"When did Dr. Abbot get involved?"

"Well, after I called him, of course."

"And he just happened to know the history of the house?"

Trudy nodded.

"That's a little coincidental." Laine poured water into the mugs, stirred them and then retrieved the whipped cream from the refrigerator. When she had the mug to her lips, Trudy asked, "Dear, who is the other mug of cocoa for? Do you make food for your grandfather as well as talk to him?"

Laine choked on the hot liquid and sputtered. She'd gotten so used to making cocoa for Madeleine, her actions had been completely automatic.

"Ah, a familial ghost."

Laine slowly set down her mug and turned to face Dr. Abott in the doorway. Behind him stood the news team and the gypsy, Gigi.

"Probably the most common ghost is a friend or family member," Dr. Abbot said.

"Do you agree with this, Gigi?" Kitty hustled her way into the kitchen and stuck her microphone in the gypsy's face.

Gigi nodded. "Yes, of course. Although, I rarely interact with familial ghosts. Which is sad—they are, by far, the most endearing."

Laine shot Trudy a pained look trying to ask *How could you have invited these people into my house?* Could she throw them out even though she'd just signed all those papers saying they could stay? She thought of Cheryl and the Boy Scouts and sat down at the table and stared into her cocoa.

"Tell us about familial ghosts," Trudy said Dr. Abott.

She doesn't care two figs about familial ghosts, Laine thought. She just wants another chance to be on TV. For Trudy, her days on *The Passing Days* had passed much too quickly.

"This type of ghost is not only self aware and intelligent, but capable of interacting within the linear world of time and space. They can be seen, heard and touched."

"And tasted?" Trudy asked with a wicked, flirtatious smile.

Oh please, Laine inwardly groaned, but Dr. Abott didn't find it an absurd question.

"Of course. There have been those who claim to have sexual relations with the dead."

This was too much. "Excuse me," Laine interrupted. "We've a yard full of school children. Can we please keep this conversation family friendly?"

Kitty made a motion to the camera man. "We'll edit her out."

Laine frowned and picked up another cookie. She waved the snicker-doodle at the lot of TV people. "This is *my* house and you are here only as long as I say so."

Kitty looked surprised. "This is your house?" She raised her eyebrows at Trudy, looking for confirmation. "I thought—"

Laine faced her step-mother. Trudy looked out the window.

"This is *my* house," Laine repeated.

"Did you sign the agreements?"

When Laine nodded, Kitty dismissed her with a small

shake of her head, and returned to Gigi. "Now, why are your interactions with these familial ghosts rare?"

"Of all the sightings, familials are the most common, but are also the most short-lived. Usually, they are seen once, typically by a grieving spouse or parent. They are generally agenda driven. They come to say goodbye, or provide comfort, or offer a warning."

Dr. Abbot, not wanting to be ignored, chimed in. "Unfortunately, because they are often not seen more than once, and briefly, this makes them among the most difficult to confirm or study. Of course, sometimes familials will make more than a single appearance, though this is even less common." He turned his bug eyes on Laine. "Your grandfather—the sea captain—"

Laine shook her head. "My grandfather wasn't a sea captain."

"Interesting. So we have a sea captain and another ghost entirely."

"No. We don't have a sea captain."

Gigi lifted her finger at Dr. Abbot who opened and then closed his mouth, clearly thinking. "But we do have your grandfather. Why don't you tell me about him?"

Laine's eye twitched. "We only have my grandfather because his ashes are right over there." She pointed at the urn sitting on the fireplace mantel. "We don't have any ghosts," she said, her voice small.

"Nonbeliever," Gigi mouthed the word to Dr. Abbot and Kitty and crew.

Laine rolled her eyes. She'd never felt so completely misunderstood. What would they all say if she admitted that yes, she believed in ghosts? Not only believed, but conversed with them, made them cookies and cocoa and listened to their stories late into the night? Obviously, Dr. Abbot and Gigi wouldn't think her crazy—but what about Trudy? What about Kitty? What about the thousands, if not millions of TV viewers of the Channel Two News? Laine couldn't open up to any of them. She had to hold her secrets close. And then she remembered what her mother had said about secrets and the hot Chinook winds. *An eastern wind carries more than dust and ashes. It uproots secrets. And everyone knows once one secret is told, no secret is safe.*

"Just as human beings are capable of displaying a whole range of emotions and temperaments, so, too, is a ghost," Dr. Abbot said.

"Playful and loving or dark and angry—how would you describe your grandfather's ghost, dear?" Gigi asked Laine after sitting down beside her.

"Ashen," Laine said, frowning while munching her cookie.

"Depending on the cause of their death," Dr. Abbot said, standing at the head of the table as if it was a pulpit and he was preaching to a congregation of faithful followers. "They can have a full range of emotions— brooding, sad, melancholy. If they died with unresolved issues they can be full of rage, fear and jealousy."

"Maybe your grandfather is visiting you because he's worried about your selling the company," Kitty suggested.

"I'm not selling the company!"

Kitty raised her eyebrows again and Trudy, wisely, slipped out of the kitchen.

"I'm not talking about the future of Leon Land to a TV crew." Panic rose in Laine's throat. How had she allowed things to become so twisted?

"An encounter with a ghost may be either a pleasant experience or a frightening and disturbing one, depending upon the nature and temperament of the ghost and the circumstances of its manifestation as well as the emotional state of the observer," Dr. Abbot said.

Laine did *not* want to discuss her emotional state.

"Most ghosts are harmless and, in some cases, even beneficial," Dr. Abbot said. "You should treat your grandfather with respect and dignity—even if he's dead."

"Are you thinking what I'm thinking?" Gigi asked.

Laine didn't know what they were thinking, but she didn't think their thoughts could possibly be as full of cuss words as her own thoughts.

"A séance," Dr. Abbot said, smiling.

"No!" Laine said, crumbling the remainder of the cookie in her hand.

"Brilliant," Cheryl said, emerging from behind a camera man.

Laine turned to Cheryl with a pleading look. "It's not brilliant—it's hokum," she said, borrowing her grandmother's word.

"Hokum that will draw a crowd," Cheryl said. "Raise money."

Laine didn't want a crowd and she didn't need money, but she could understand Cheryl and the Boy Scouts' goals. She raised her fingertips to her forehead.

"Tomorrow then?" Trudy asked.

"Why not tonight?" Cheryl asked, her gaze scanning the room, landing on Laine last of all.

"Dear, are you worried what the ghosts might have to say?" Gigi asked.

"Could you please turn off the camera?" Laine said to

the camera guy. "Turn it off. Turn it off or leave."

He obediently pointed the camera at the floor.

"Are you worried, dear?" Gigi patted her hand and Laine fought the temptation to swat her away. "Do the dead make you nervous?"

"I don't think I'm alone in this," Laine said. "Plenty of sane people would be uncomfortable summoning the dead."

"It's not zombies, is it? Are you afraid of zombies?" Gigi asked. "You must know that zombies do not exist."

Laine's stomach churned. Zombies no, ghosts yes. This wasn't happening.

"Ghosts retain much—if not all—of their former earthbound personality," Dr. Abbot told her. "Your grandfather and the sea captain were good, honorable men. Wouldn't you like to see your grandfather again?"

What could she say? Why was the camera man's camera blinking? Hadn't she just told him to turn it off? Sure, he had it at knee level, but it was not only blinking but making a low, whirring sound.

"There's no need to fear, dear," Gigi said. "Your grandfather is clearly a familial ghost, while the sea captain is possibly an imprint."

"A what?" Laine asked.

"An imprint," Dr. Abbot murmured. "Of course."

"An imprint is human in appearance and mannerisms, but appears and acts as though it is entirely oblivious to its surroundings."

Dr. Abbot nodded. "They have a tendency to repeat the same actions—such as walking down a set of stairs or sitting in on the edge of the same bed—as though they are actors in play that is being performed over and over again."

Gigi chimed in. "They live an automated existence, very similar to the patterns they repeated in their living years. Any effort to communicate or interact with an imprint in any way is always met by silent indifference, as though we are the ones invisible and imperceptible."

"If they're invisible and imperceptible, then how do you know they're there?" Laine asked.

Dr. Abbot looked offended, but Gigi smiled patiently. "It is possible that an imprint isn't a ghost at all, but rather a reflection of a person's daily activities that have somehow been imprinted into their past environment."

"While this theory has some plausibility and is growing in popularity with paranormal investigators," Dr. Abbot said, "It leaves questions unanswered. Can such a ghost interact, and is it simply choosing not to interact?"

"You're calling them ghosts, when the argument is that they're not." Gigi picked up a cookie and took a bite.

Dr. Abbot ignored her. "Then there is the question of whether it is possible such a ghost may even be aware it is visible to the still living; in effect, it may not be trapped in a prerecorded visual 'loop' but may simply suffer from an inability to perceive the living any more than we are usually able to perceive the dead. In such a case, then, the tendency to repeat the same actions may be no more remarkable then our own tendency to repeat precise routines day in and day out in our own world; we often walk through our home via the same route, open and close the same doors in order, sit in the same chairs, gaze out the same windows, with similar regularity, so there is no reason an earth-bound ghost—especially if it wasn't aware it was visible to the living—might not keep the same routine it had while alive."

That was me, Laine thought. Before Madeleine, before the cottage—her life in Seattle, she'd been walking through her days via the same route, caught in precise routines, a constant disappointing cycle of infertility. Sure, she'd shaken things up by throwing Ian out, but had he really been the problem? Or had the problem been the waiting, the relentless surviving until the day she conceived and was free to move onto the next stage of her life? Motherhood. And what if that day never arrived? The routes, the routines, would they make her insane? Had they already?

"No!" Laine shouted.

Her outburst surprised them all. "If we're going to have a séance, then it will be strictly on my terms." She looked around the room at the startled faces. "One week from tonight."

"Halloween?" Trudy asked.

"Brilliant," Cheryl said, clearly in awe.

Laine nodded. "We'll open it up to the public but charge a hundred dollars to attend—all the proceeds will go to my foundation."

***

The wind blew and the windows rattled. Thunder cracked, announcing the flash of lightning. It had been stormy all week, but Laine really hadn't minded. The wind and rain had postponed the formal ceremony of scattering Sid's ashes. Madeleine had already warned her that when they scattered Sid's ashes, it would be time for them both to go. Laine hoped the storm would continue indefinitely.

"Then, I'll just keep him," Laine had said, only half in jest.

Madeleine had given her a sad smile. "It's time."

As Laine put on her black dress and hose, the same dress she'd worn to Sid's viewing, she thought about all that had happened in the last two weeks. She'd made friends with her grandmother, reconnected with her grandfather, made friends with Cheryl, Missy, Max and a crew of Boy Scouts…and Ian.

Ian had been commuting from Rose Arbor, spending his days at the office and the nights in her bed. Neither one of them had asked how long they could or would continue, but their marriage had turned a corner. As if by an unspoken agreement they didn't talk about babies—either making them or adopting them. They didn't talk about what would happen when Laine finished writing her grandparent's story. They didn't talk about Ian's work or Laine's foundation. Instead, their evenings fell into a pattern of quiet dinners followed by the crazy, sometimes insane bustle of the Boy Scouts and the haunted house. While Ian worked in Seattle, Laine spent her days writing and laughing and talking with her grandparents. She knew things couldn't continue as they were, but she loved it all too much to think about letting it go.

"Tomorrow?" Madeleine's image shimmered in front of her.

Laine sighed and fingered the necklace around her neck. "Tomorrow," she said. "But what if it's still rainy and miserable?"

Madeleine looked wistful. "It's time to say goodbye."

"No, it's time for a séance."

"For a bogus sea captain," Madeleine said.

"At a hundred dollars a pop!" Laine chimed as she pulled open the bedroom door and headed down the stairs.

Bedlam reigned in the living room. Laine quickly did a head count. Of course, the two Ghost Gurus and the television media wouldn't be paying, but even after subtracting them, Laine guessed that close to a hundred people filled the room.

Cheryl stood in the doorway, addressing both the inside and outside crowd. "Three hundred for a seat at the dining room table, two hundred for a place in the living room, one hundred for standing room in the kitchen, mud room, foyer and hall."

"One hundred for the mudroom?" Laine whispered to Madeleine.

Madeleine shrugged. "It's better than standing outside in the rain." She motioned to the faces on the other side of the windows.

Laine shivered. "This is craziness, right?"

Madeleine laughed. "Is it?"

Laine paused at the top of the stairs, acknowledging that she probably wasn't the best person to judge sanity.

After all, she talked to her grandparents' ghosts and she had invited half the town of Rose Arbor into her home, plus a news team. And Ghost Gurus.

The house, despite the crowd, looked beautiful. Hundreds of candles flickered from every available surface—the mantel, the piano lid, every table, every window sill. She'd filled vases and glass jars full of dried leaves, fallen branches and gathered berries.

Gigi, who would be conducting the séance, had dressed for the part in a long velvet skirt and lace blouse. Dr. Abbot wore his customary tweed jacket with leather elbow patches, but had added a plaid bow-tie for the occasion. Gigi sat with her eyes closed and her back ramrod straight in a wingback chair. Sleeping? Pensive? Conversing with the dead sea captain? Gigi's eyes flew open an a hush fell over the crowd. Slowly, she rose from the chair and lifted her hands above her head, swaying. Although her mouth appeared closed, she chanted softly. Other than Gigi's song, the room was dead still.

Dead still? What a funny and yet relevant term. Laine wondered who first coined it and why.

"She's communing with the other world," Trudy said in Laine's ear.

Laine started at her step-mother's voice. She hadn't

seen her parents come in. "Such bad traffic," Trudy whispered. "I was worried we wouldn't get here on time."

Traffic? Is that what was keeping Ian? Of course he could be in the crowd and she just hadn't seen him, yet.

Trudy squeezed her hand. "What a brilliant idea. Think of all the money you're raising."

"Yes," her dad said, leaning across Trudy, "You couldn't pay for better advertising. I bet those Boy Scouts won't know what to do with all the money pouring into their coffers from their haunted house."

Gigi, with hands held high, headed for the dining room and the crowd parted for her, much like the waters of the Red Sea. "Please be seated," she said. She pulled a large candelabrum from her bag, and placed candles in a variety of shapes and heights upon it. She turned her back and suddenly a brilliant light flashed. The candles lit.

The crowd gasped and murmured their appreciation as those who had paid settled into their chairs around the table. Gigi motioned for Laine to sit at the head of the table. When Laine refused, Gigi said, "As the owner of this house, you must take your rightful place."

Laine sighed and pulled out a chair between Trudy and a man she recognized as the mayor.

"Please join hands," Gigi said. Those seated placed

their elbows on the table, their joined clasped hands turned toward the ceiling, imitating Gigi.

"Spirits of our fathers, hear our words this night," Gigi began, her voice low. The crowd fell to complete silence. Outside, a dog howled and the wind blew.

"Accept our poor oblations, transform us with thy might. Open our minds. Purify our hearts. Take us where thy spirits have fled. Reunite us with our kindred dead."

Just then the door from the kitchen pushed open and a man's dark silhouette stood in the light. Trudy screamed.

"I'm sorry," Ian whispered. "I didn't mean to interrupt." He cleared his throat. "I, um, guess I destroyed the mood."

Dr. Abbot glared at Ian, but Gigi considered him through lowered lashes. "It's you," she said after a beat of silence. "The spirits recognize you. Powerful, passionate— you are the energy filling this space. You are the master in this game."

Ian looked around, grabbed a chair from the kitchen and carried it into the dining room. People scrambled to move out of his way.

"Hey," the mayor complained as Ian wedged his chair next to Laine. "We paid good money for these seats."

"Sorry," Ian said, not sounding at all contrite. He

leaned over and whispered in Laine's ear, "She said I'm the game master." Laine heard the smile in his voice and squeezed his hand to quiet him.

"Shh!" Trudy hissed, sounding like a bicycle tire losing air.

Gigi repeated her chant and then began to hum. After a moment, she said, "Captain Brown, would you speak to us?"

"Lainey," Madeleine said, hovering mid-air, shimmering in the candlelight. "I'm afraid we have to go." She stood on the far end of the dining room, just behind the seated Gigi.

"No," Laine said.

Ian looked at her questioningly and the others in the room swiveled their attention from Gigi to Laine. A flush crept up Laine's neck.

"I'm sorry, sweetie," Madeleine said. "I thought we could stay until tomorrow, but the time is right."

Laine bit her lip so hard tears sprang to her eyes.

"Captain Brown speaks!" Gigi rose from her chair, her face shining and her hands raised to the sky. "He is trying to tell us something! What is it, Captain?"

"Lainey, remember we love you," Madeleine said. "We'll never leave you completely alone, although you probably won't be able to see us."

"Why?" Laine asked.

Ian rubbed his finger on Laine's wrist. She knew he wanted to speak to her, ask her why she was crying, who she was talking to.

"You don't need us anymore. You already have everyone and everything you need to be happy."

Laine bit back a small cry, but with Ian holding her hand, she realized that Madeleine was right. She had everything, everyone she needed for happiness.

"He's telling us not to sell," Gigi said. "Sell what, Captain?"

"Oh, this is nonsense!" George said, standing, looking around at the room. "I want to call this off right now!"

Just then, Sid's urn fell from the mantel. A man in a green sweater tried to catch it, but it fumbled in his hands and landed with a crash and a puff of ash on the hearth.

Several people screamed while Sid's ashes hung in the air. The French doors blew open and the storm swirled into the room, carrying Sid's remains outside.

Crying and shaking, Laine stood and watched her grandparents float out the French doors. They passed through the crowd until they reached the Sound's dark shore. Holding hands, they headed for the cloud shrouded moon.

Ian held out his hand and Laine let him pull her to him. Her days of saying no, of pushing him away, were gone. As were Sid and Madeleine. She sagged against him, grateful for his solidity and strength.

"Well, that's just bogus and buggers," George declared, standing, his face mottled and red. "And that's my father you just tipped over for dramatic effect!"

While George ranted about suing and trespassing and attempted to throw everyone out of the house and off his property, Ian led Laine through the French doors and into the night.

All around them the storm blew, but Ian led her into the barn, into the depths of the haunted house. They passed skeletons in makeshift wooden coffins, zombies leaning in dark corners, and a headless man sitting on a bench. Ian directed her to a bale of hay and pulled her onto his lap.

He held her as she cried and told him that she missed her grandparents.

CHAPTER 21

Laine woke the next morning, tangled in bed sheets, her face puffy and red from last night's cry. The smell of cinnamon French toast came from the kitchen.

Outside, the sun shone bright, as if trying to make up for its previous bad behavior. Laine sat up, pushed her curls off her face and looked at the mess outside her window. Smashed pumpkins, tossed corn stalks, fallen branches and bent trees. She flopped back down and put her pillow over her head, thinking about the ashes in the living room. *Sid.* How could she clean up? Not with a vacuum. A broom and dust mop? She felt ill.

Steps plodded up the stairs and Helene pushed open the door.

"Hey, what are you doing here?" Laine asked, eyeing the enormous breakfast tray in Helene's hands. French toast, strawberry jelly, a cheese omelet—what did it mean? Besides Helene wanting to fatten her up?

"Ian called me. That boy's worried about you."

"But I thought you were going to Florida—"

"You thought wrong. How could you be thinking I'd

be going to Florida?" Helene sat the tray down on the bed beside Laine.

"Because you told me you were going." Laine eyed Helene, trying to read her.

"Well, I'm not. I'm staying here."

"Here? At my house?"

Helene shook her head. "I'm buying a café in town, but that doesn't mean I won't have plenty of time to check in on you."

Laine's head spun with the news. A café? Helene diagnosing and treating the citizens of Rose Arbor with her emotion-altering food? Laine picked up a fork and toyed with the French toast. She had so many questions, but she asked the first one, the most important one. "Where's Ian?"

"He had to go into the office." Helene scowled at her. "You should know that. You should know what's what in that company. After all, it is mostly yours."

Laine took a small bite of a strawberry. Her stomach rolled. She knew she should care about Leon Land, but she never had.

"Is Ian paying you to check on me? Make me breakfast?" Laine swallowed hard. "Because you don't have to do as he asks, you know. You don't work for him anymore. He can't just tell you what to do and expect you to do it."

Helene folded her arms across her chest. "Baby, I'm here because I want to be here. I'm not going anywhere."

Laine considered this news, tried to wrap her mind around it and make some sense of it. Finally she said, "Thank you. This is incredibly sweet. In many ways. This is also an incredible amount of food."

"And you need it."

"Have you seen the...living room? Are there...ashes everywhere?"

"No ashes."

No ashes? The wind must have carried Sid away. Completely.

"A little girl came to help me clean. Now, how come a child that age isn't at school on a Monday morning in November?"

Laine brightened. "You met Missy? She and her brother Max are homeschooled."

"Is home school the same as no school?"

Laine laughed. "I'm going to give her an education in butterfly gardening. Want to help?"

Laine could tell from the look in Helene's eyes that she most certainly did. Tucking into the huge breakfast, Laine listened to Helene's plans for the café.

"It's on the main road and there's an apartment right above it and best of all, there's a small yard. I can plant a vegetable garden!"

Laine bit into the French toast and thought that the best thing of all was that Helene was going be less than two miles away. Putting down her fork, Laine placed her hand on her belly. Minutes later, she was vomiting into the toilet.

Helene leaned against the door frame, watching, compassion etched in her eyes. "Baby girl, when are you going to acknowledge what's going on inside of you?"

Laine sat back on the tile and leaned her head against the wall. The cold seeped through her nightie. "I can't be."

"Sure you can."

Laine shook her head, slowly, careful not to arouse the nausea. "No. It's only been a few days since—"

Helene frowned at her and Laine remembered. She did some mental math. Ten weeks ago. A whole month before she'd thrown Ian out. "Do you think?"

Helene smiled. "I'm pretty sure I know."

Laine's emotions flew and dipped like a kite without a tail. This had only happened once before. That hadn't ended well. The baby had died at eight weeks. She was already two weeks past that sad, unobserved anniversary.

"There's someone else who should know," Helene

said.

***

Before she could tell anyone, before she could let her secret out into the world, she had to know for absolute, proof positive herself. As Laine drove over the bridges on automatic pilot toward her home, she found it telling, interesting, that when she'd left Seattle her period would have already been late. How late? She did some calculations. Why hadn't she thought about this? Why hadn't she packed tampons?

She was never late.

Once she had been late.

All the rounds of infertility treatments could never slow or hinder her ever-regular cycle. Laine gripped the steering wheel, remembering. They had talked about adoption. Of course, they had. They believed in adoption, applauded those who "got pregnant on paper," as some of their friends had done. Together, they'd visited their friends who had adopted, those who had paid thousands to go through a private firm, or those who were paid by the government to go through the Russian roulette of being foster parents with the hope of someday calling a borrowed baby their own. Laine had seen first-hand the pain of loving and losing a foster child—that she knew she couldn't do it, but why not adoption? Why hadn't they done more than just talk about it? Laine knew why.

It was Mic, Ian's older adopted brother. A blond in a sea of dark haired Collins. The kid who didn't look, didn't act and didn't perform like his siblings. Because he couldn't. Because he didn't have the same intellect or skill set. Ian had seen Mic's hurt and his parents' frustration and he didn't want to do that to a child—especially since Ian still believed that they would someday have children of their own. She had thought him foolish for holding out hope and had often told him so. And now, maybe, he'd be able to say *I told you so.* If it was true, if Ian was right after all, she would never mind being proved wrong.

Although she'd only been gone a week, it was an odd homecoming. The house felt different to her, like it belonged to another person, trapped in another life. Cheshire came to wrap himself around Laine's legs. She scooped him up and held him against her chest.

"I've missed you," she whispered into his fur. The cat purred his appreciation. Holding him tight, Laine ran up the stairs to the bathroom and took out a pregnancy test with shaking hands. In the early days of her marriage she'd used the tests at any given sign of encouragement. One day late? Pee on the stick. Tender breasts? Pee on the stick. After she'd been properly schooled and conditioned for disappointment, she'd used the kits more judiciously. She'd developed a rule—no tests until her period was five days late. So, it didn't surprise her when she found the test in the back of the cupboard beneath her sink covered in a fine layer of dust. After blowing it clean, she opened the box with trembling fingers. Such a kit had only had good news once, and that good news had quickly died.

When the first strip tested positive, Laine threw it away and tried again. Cheshire jumped onto the sink to watch. Her heart raced. She started to cry. Then she started to laugh. "I'm going to have a baby," she told Cheshire.

The cat sat back on his haunches and licked his paw. Laine picked him and holding the cat and the stick, she began to dance around the room, humming the Frank Sinatra tune Ian had played that night at Grandma Ivy's. She had to tell Ian. Immediately. Dropping the cat onto the bed but still carrying the stick, she ran down the stairs.

Running through the kitchen, she skidded when she heard a sound coming from his office. Had he come home? Dashing into his office, she stopped short.

Not Ian.

Carly. She stood behind his desk, looking through his drawer. Her expression darkened when she saw Laine. "I thought I heard someone," Carly said, her tone impatient.

How could she have *not* heard someone? Hadn't Laine just flushed the toilet not once but twice?

"What are you doing here?" Laine asked, not liking how small and tremulous her voice sounded.

Carly sighed as if Laine shouldn't have to ask. "Ian asked me to come by and pick up some things." She rested her fingers on a stack of papers and gave Laine a hard look. "You do know that this is a pivotal time for the company, right? You are, at least, aware of the countless people hoping for Leon Land to crumble so they can pick up our droppings. No?" Carly's voice turned hard. "I didn't think so. Even you should have understood that the company needs Ian's undivided attention. At a time like this—he shouldn't be spending the weekends in Soap Lake—"

"Who needs Ian's attention, Carly? You or Leon Land?" Laine leaned away from Carly's attack, hating her for spoiling her happy moment, wishing that Carly would leave so that she could return to her happy plans. Laine braced herself in the doorway.

Carly swung toward her. "You don't get it, do you? You've had everything handed to you your whole life— you've enjoyed one long pleasure cruise with all you can eat and drink buffets. You're so used to getting what you want you can't even see that the Aubusson rug you've been standing on is about to be ripped out from under you."

Laine crossed her arms across her chest, holding herself tight. But she didn't flinch from Carly's fury and raised her voice in return. "Are you the one pulling my rug?"

Carly's face registered surprise. Laine knew she had a pussy cat reputation. She also knew that if she didn't act carefully, that reputation would be destroyed. Shredded in a cat fight. Right now. "What I have is my husband—the one thing that you want the most."

"What *I* want isn't important. This isn't about you or Ian—the company needs—"

A sudden calm washed over Laine and for once she felt composed, secure in who she was and what she wanted. She looked Carly in the eye. "You want Ian and you're using your position in the company to get his attention. You and I really have nothing to discuss. Ian's attachment to you is professional, emotional or both. Those are his decisions. Not mine." Laine paused and then pointed at the papers on the table. "Make sure you get everything you need, because you won't be invited back into my home. I'll tell Ian that you are not welcome here."

"He won't listen to you," Carly smirked.

Laine turned from Carly and said without looking back. "He won't have a choice."

"Ian will choose me," Carly called after her, her voice tinged with desperation.

Laine swung back around. "He might, but only if I let him go. Only if I tell him that our marriage is over. Ian has loved me most of his life. Anyone else, including you, will never have our shared history. Ian has invested so much emotion into our marriage that he will never willingly walk away from it. And that means that anyone else, including you, will always be Ian's second choice. Ask yourself this, Carly—do you really want to be the consolation prize?"

"I'm not the runner-up," Carly said, gripping the desk and leaning over it. "You are. You're refusing to see what everyone else already knows. Ian has out grown you. He needs someone who can match his strength, be his equal— someone who shares his interest in the company."

As Carly's words sank in, Laine took a step back.

"Just because he shares your bed, for the moment, that doesn't mean you hold his heart, or even his interest." As Carly stepped around the desk, Laine had the horrible realization that Carly had a valid point. She had a responsibility, not just to Ian, not just to her marriage, not just to herself, but to all the employees at Leon Land, to their business partners and to the charities supported by the foundation. She couldn't hide at the cottage nor could she spend her days building butterfly gardens.

Madeleine's words sprang to her mind, *"We have what we have so that we can share and bless others."* Stunned by the sudden insight, Laine said, "Thank you." And then she turned away, filled with an overwhelming resolve.

"Thank you?" Carly called after her confusion and hurt in her voice.

"Yes." Laine stopped in the doorway, smiling. "Thank you."

Laine then did something she knew she should have done weeks ago.

She went to see Uncle Harry.

CHAPTER 22

Laine knew that if she went to the Leon Land offices her chances of meeting Ian were high and the chances of someone telling him that she was in the building were even higher, so she called Harry and invited him to lunch. Her stomach clenched with nerves as she sat waiting for her grandfather's closest friend and attorney in a restaurant overlooking the Sound.

She'd asked for a quiet table near the back and ordered a glass of wine for Harry and a ginger ale for herself. She stood when she saw him walk in. His designer suit, silk tie and well-combed hair did little to disguise his advanced age. He looked old, stooped shouldered and tired and she suddenly wondered why a man of his years and wealth was still working. Guilt flashed through her. Was he not being paid enough to retire? She gave herself a small mental shake. The man had a house on Lake Sammamish and a collection of vintage cars making her think that employment had to have been a choice rather than necessity.

She stood to hug him and kissed his weathered cheek.

His returning smile was weak as he handed her a folder. The will and financial statements she'd expected, but when a small silver DVD slipped out, she asked, "What's this?"

Harry looked pained as he took his seat. "This is something that we need to discuss." He put the menu to one side without looking at it. "Have you ordered, dear?"

Laine nodded and looked through the will and financials while Harry told the waiter that he'd like blackened salmon and a lobster bisque. She found the paperwork straight forward.

Laine set the file down. "I don't understand. According to this, the company has the means to withstand the pressures of a down economy for decades. Why the panic? The need to sell?"

"What I'm going to say will undoubtedly cause you tremendous pain, so let me apologize before I start." He looked at her with his watery eyes and Laine saw the handsome man he used to be—the gentle, kind man with a wicked sense of humor who had made her grandfather laugh, even during the thick of his divorces. Placing a protective hand on her belly, Laine braced herself.

Harry slid the DVD toward her.

"What is this?" Laine asked, her voice trembling.

"This, my dear, is a video of you."

"Me?" Her voice squeaked.

Harry nodded.

"Why…what?"

"It's a video of you at Sid's old place in Rose Arbor. In it…well, you are talking to yourself. Rather animatedly, I'd say."

Laine's mouth dropped open. "How—"

"A Dr. Abbot set up video equipment—"

"For the ghosts—"

Harry looked ill. "Yes." He cleared his throat. "The ghosts."

"Oh! But I never believed—" Her mind spun, grasping for reasons and explanations that didn't sound crazy or insane.

"Your parents—" Harry began.

"My parents?" Not Ian. Not Carly, but her parents? Her parents what?

"They want you to leave Ian."

"No, that doesn't make sense. They want me to sell the company."

"Yes."

Laine put her fingertips on the DVD, realization dawning. "If I divorce Ian and sell the company—"

"And if they can prove your mental incompetency, all

the proceeds of Leon Land will be theirs."

"My parents…my dad—he loves me. He would never…" Oh, but he would. She knew he would. Not on his own. Not without help. That's why he'd confided in Harry.

"Does Ian know?"

"No one knows."

"And this video?"

Harry shook his head. "I'm afraid there's little we can do about that."

"Can't I just explain I was writing my grandfather's personal history and talking to him was a part of the creative process?"

Harry smiled and for a small moment looked relieved. "You weren't talking to ghosts?"

"No. Well, sort of." Laine laughed and it sounded off to her own ears, but Harry seemed convinced.

"The video serves no purpose as long as you retain the company. I would never encourage you to stay in a loveless marriage, but your marriage to Ian further ensures your financial safety. You know that, don't you? That you can trust Ian financially, if not emotionally?"

Laine nodded.

Harry looked stern. "Even if you were to sell, and even if you were found mentally incompetent, as your husband

Ian would control your inheritance."

It went without saying that her father had no interest in the company if he had to run it. He liked money, but he wasn't interested in managing it.

After their lunch had been cleared away, Laine looked at Harry and said, "What would you do, Harry? How would you manage Leon Land?"

Harry smiled, leaned back in his chair, and told her what he thought she should do.

***

After a long day spent accountants and financial analysts, Laine returned to Rose Arbor. Of course, it was ridiculous to think she could just step in where Sid had left and come to a sudden and complete understanding of the machinations of a company as large and complex as Leon Land, but she could learn. She would learn, she promised herself, and the idea stirred and excited her.

When she turned onto Olympic Avenue she noticed a big white moving van parked in front of an empty store front. Seeing Helene outside ordering around harassed looking delivery men, Laine parked her Volvo and climbed out. She wasn't the only one with big business plans.

"Hey sweetie," Helene said, wiping her hands on her white apron.

"Hi, is this your new place?" Laine looked around at the giant glass windows and double Dutch door. Despite the gaping holes where there had once been booths, the space had a friendly, open-armed vibe.

Missy stood on a stool washing down a giant wooden counter top. "Hi, Laine," she called, waving a rag in her direction.

While Helene gave Laine a tour of the about-to-be café, Laine reported on her conversation with Harry.

"I hate to burst your bubble, honey," Helene said as they climbed the stairs to the new apartment above the café. "But you don't know the first thing about running a massive company like Leon Land."

"I know," Laine said, following Helene. Her mouth began to water even before Helene opened the door.

"They're for Missy," Helene said as she put on pair of hand mitts and pulled a tray of molasses cookies from the oven.

"She works for cookies?"

"Why not? She already has her butterfly garden."

"Not yet."

"But soon, right? You promised her a butterfly garden." Helene put her hands on her hips and faced Laine.

"A butterfly garden, your work with the foundation, a

baby—girl, you don't have the time, let alone the know-how, to run a company."

"But Ian does."

Helene narrowed her eyes at her. "Do you trust him?"

"Yes. Yes, I do."

"Then you got to show him that. And tell him."

Laine knew they were no longer talking about the company.

"I'm going to tell him tonight at the masquerade ball."

Missy ran up the stairs, her footsteps loud and urgent. "Quick! Hide the cookies before Max and his goons get here!"

"Now why would I do that?" Helene asked. "When I can use their help, too."

"You want their help?" Missy asked, her voice tinged with disappointment.

"Missy, would you help me?" Laine asked.

"Sure."

"Can I borrow your butterfly wings?"

***

Laine stood on the steps of the McCain mansion watching the cars file past the valets, searching for Ian's Mercedes. Twilight lingered over the Sound. A smattering of clouds hung above the dark water. The sun also hovered, as if it hated for the day to end. Laine took a deep breath, bracing herself. She knew what she had to do. She knew what she had to say. Would it be easier behind her mask?

No. She had to take off the mask, face the music and confront the company. In her grandmother's dress with Missy's attached butterfly wings, Laine knew she looked beautiful. Bette had arranged her hair and Helene had tucked a couple of homemade biscuits into her purse to keep her nausea at bay.

No one recognized her as she passed through the grand doorway, which didn't surprise her. Her past costumes to the masquerade ball—Raggedy Ann, Little Bo Peep, a mouse and even once a bunch of grapes—had been more about humor than beauty. Sending a prayer of gratitude to Madeline for all the beautiful clothes that had been left behind, Laine wandered through the crowded ballroom to the head table.

Carly, standing by the bar and nursing a cocktail, wore a Glenda the Good costume. Eddie wore the same Spider Man suit he wore every year and there was Harry, dressed as Gandalf. She didn't see Ian.

Laine placed her faux diamond studded clutch on the table beside her name card and looked around the room. Black table cloths, tall glass apothecary jars filled with bright green Granny Smith apples, hundreds of glittering candles in all shapes and sizes. The band, dressed in tuxedos, tuned up their instruments. Moments later, the saxophone began to play Moon River. Gemma, dressed as a pirate wench, hustled toward her.

"Wow, Laine—is that you?"

Laine laughed. "You can call me Monarch," she said, referring to her wings.

"I bet those wings didn't look as hot on Missy." Gemma's eyebrows raised a notch higher. "You look—wow. Just wow."

Laine put her arm across Gemma's shoulders and squeezed. "Same to you. Everything looks perfect. I knew you could do it."

Gemma let out a happy sigh and launched into a laundry list of all that had gone wrong. "And then the caterers said they couldn't do shrimp—" Laine only half listened. She knew and understood the difficulties of planning large events. That was why she wasn't going to do it anymore. She leaned toward Gemma's ear and whispered, "Congratulations, you've been promoted."

Gemma stopped mid sentence. Her mouth half opened, and for once, was still. "Wait. What?"

"You're the new president of the Leon Foundation."

"But—" Gemma sputtered. "That's your job. I want to work for you."

"Oh, you will be."

A mix of emotions fleeted across Gemma's face.

"Are you ready, my dear?" Harry said, bracing himself on his wizard staff.

Laine's hesitation and nervousness froze when Ian entered the room. Even a Phantom of the Opera mask and cape couldn't hide his striking beauty. The chiseled jaw, the bright blue eyes—he made her heart stop. He always had. Ever since the first day she saw him in that long ago PE class, he moved her in a way no one else ever had. Ever could.

Yes, she could walk away from him. She could support their baby on her own. Carly had been right. Financially, her life had been one long pleasure cruise. But all that money could never fill the hole left by her mother's early death, her father's careless indifference, or the absence of siblings. Would she deny her baby close and daily contact with a devoted father?

Because, she knew Ian would be a devoted father. Just as he was a devoted husband. Handsome, charming and yet constant. Laine took note of Carly's reaction to Ian. She simpered, leaned forward, perked up her breasts. For Ian, there would always be a Carly, a girl on the street, or a woman in the park, ready to fawn, giggle and flirt. Ian would never know what it was like to walk down the street without attracting attention. The Carly's, the women, didn't matter to her, until they mattered to Ian. Watching him angle away from Carly, his eyes searching for her own, Laine knew Ian wasn't looking left or right. He was looking straight at her.

And nothing else mattered. Nothing and no one else ever would.

Harry cleared his throat. "Now?"

Laine started.

"Are you sure you're ready, dear?"

Gemma gave her a questioning look.

Laine took a deep breath. "Yes, of course. I can do this." Although, she wasn't sure that she could.

Harry signaled for the band to stop and escorted Laine to the microphone. It screeched as she began addressing the crowd, just as she'd seen her grandfather do for countless years.

"I'd like to thank you all for coming." Her voice sounded weak, so she braced herself and picked up her volume. She didn't have any notes. She knew what she wanted to say. She was afraid that if she had notes she'd spend the entire address looking at them rather than her assembled employees. Her employees. Her responsibility. And Ian's. Together.

She told them of her grandfather's love for them and for the company they had created. "My grandfather truly felt that Leon Land's most valuable asset was not the property holdings or the investments but the talented individuals who worked alongside us and shared our vision and passion. There have been rumors of the company's dissolution. They are unfounded. I will carry on my grandfather's work."

A murmur ran through the crowd. Laine held up her hand for quiet. She met and held her father's eyes. "Leon Land will continue as it has since my grandfather bought his first property. He is no longer with us, but we remain. As does the company."

She took a deep breath and turned her gaze to Ian. "We are much better together than we ever could be apart."

The crowd burst into applause, but Laine didn't notice. All she saw were the tears in Ian's eyes. She returned the microphone to its stand with shaking hands.

"Well done," Harry said, applauding.

Gemma smiled at her through watery eyes.

Within moments she was wrapped in Ian's arms.

Epilogue

The Chinook wind stirred the leaves on the old brick walk. *An eastern wind carries more than dust and ashes,* Laine's mother had told her; *it uproots secrets. And everyone knows once one secret is told, no secret is safe.*

Hers included.

Laine paused in front of the Queen Anne Hill Chapel doors. The sun, a faint pink glow over the eastern hills had yet to shine, but Laine hadn't any doubt that it would rise to another beautiful summer day. She looked out over sleeping Seattle. The dark gray Puget Sound stretched away from her. On the horizon, distant ships bobbed and sent quivering beams of light out over the water.

She turned her back on the ships, thoughts of sailing away far from her mind. The chapel, built in the 1930s, had a musty, empty smell. She stepped into the cool shade of the foyer and the door swung shut, closing with a click that echoed through the cavernous room. The morning sounds—birds, crickets and insects—disappeared when the doors closed. She'd come early, hoping for this moment alone, this time of peace for prayer and thanksgiving.

She turned her face to the stained glass, remembering how she'd first met Madeleine. Slipping into a pew, she bowed her head and began to pray.

The next thing she knew Bach resonated through the chapel. With a sleepy start, Laine lifted her head to see Bette at the organ and Pastor Clark behind the pulpit. Turning, she saw Ian walking in, carrying Sidney in his arms. Dressed in a tiny white suit complete with a silky bowtie, the baby nestled in the crook of his father's arm. Madeleine followed close behind in her grandfather's arm. Her lacy dress hung to George's knee. Behind him trooped Ian's large, boisterous family. Laine caught and held Grandmother Ivy's eyes. Ivy winked.

They shared a secret, but the secret Laine held closest was the one in her heart while she nursed her babies. In her life-time she would never see Sid or Madeleine again, but she saw them every hour of every day in her children's eyes.

The Rhyme's Library

By Kristy Tate

Brobdingnagian \brob-ding-NAG-ee-uhn\ , *adjective*:

Of extraordinary size; gigantic; enormous.

CHAPTER 1

Blair brought her finger down on a random word. Brobdingnagian—she wrote the word and definition on the chalkboard above the circulation desk and came up with her own sample sentence. *Drake Isling is a brobdingnagian twit.* And because she gave each of her library patrons a chocolate for every sample sentence they gave, she took one for herself, even though Brobdingnagian was technically tomorrow's word. Today's word was tenebrous: dark; gloomy. *Tenebrous describes the weather and my mood,* she thought and then realized that she deserved a chocolate for her second sample sentence. *My thighs will be brobdingnagian if I don't stop eating these chocolates.* Another sentence—another chocolate.

Outside, the wind whistled and moaned around the library, tossing branches and bending trees. A near human-like scream tore Blair's attention away from the open dictionary, but after a moment of wind listening, she returned to her work, collecting words and definitions for the upcoming week. Opprobrious, vitriolic, and vituperative—she looked for derogatory words that could easily be made into Drake-descriptive sentences.

The bell tower on the nearby Lutheran Church tolled five. Finally, she could close the library. *Stop eating chocolates,* she told herself, *drive to the university and confront Drake in front of the students lingering after his American Lit class.* She knew that there would be a handful of coeds hanging around Westchester Hall waiting to talk to him. She knew that because she used to be one of them.

Well, not anymore. She'd never wait for Drake again. After today, of course.

The lights flickered a warning. Wind storms and power outages were common in tiny Rose Arbor. Flickering candle light, a roaring fire and a good book were only enjoyable at home. But she wasn't going home. Gathering up her things, she debated her plan. Confront Drake or wait out the storm in front of a fire with a Mary Stewart novel? Fight sluggish traffic, wind and rain for the hour drive to Bellingham or cuddle under a quilt and read? Her resolve wavering, she locked the heavy wooden doors and headed for the light switch.

Knocking. Someone at the door or the wind? Looking over her shoulder she watched the door knob rattle. It took a moment to unlock the heavy wooden doors. The storm's cold wet wind flew in the library, and Blair looked in confusion at the pitching trees and driving rain. Gray skies cracked with lightning. She was about to go back inside when she saw a huddled figure at the side of the porch.

Dressed in a ratty brown coat and mud caked jeans, Will Harris crouched in the flower bed, his head bent low to the ground. He appeared to be kneeling in prayer in the storm. Will, a regular attendee at the library's story hours, lived on a farm just outside of town with his brother and grandmother. Because of his rapt attention to her stories, his quiet lisp, and unkempt hair, Blair both loved and pitied Will. Not even school age, he typically walked to the library for story hour unattended and now here he was alone in the middle of a storm. She knew it was hard to live with an aging parent, and she guessed Will's older brother was his primary, albeit reluctant, care giver.

Blair ran to the edge of the porch and yelled over the storm's noise to get Will's attention. Rain pelted his matted hair and rolled down the shoulders of his jacket. He knelt in the dirt between a rhododendron bush and the side of the library, his face inches from the mud and his hand inserted into a drain pipe.

Rain spilled over the side of the library and beat upon Will's face and mingled with his tears. Blair came around the porch, pulled her sweater tight across her chest, and ignoring the mud and rain, she knelt beside Will.

A tiny, whining meow echoed inside the storm drain— cries and claw scratching barely discernable above the storm's racket.

Blair lowered her face down toward Will and he looked at her with big brown eyes that welled with tears.

"Diddlebrain, Todd's dog, killed all of Midge's kittens but this one here," Will said between bighting back sobs, "and my grandma won't let any of the cats in the house."

Blair frowned at the rusted pipe. It could probably be cut by a sturdy pair of gardening shears, but she guessed that the easiest, quickest form of rescue would be to unclog the drain.

"Could you keep him? I can't take him home. Diddlebrain will get him, just like he got the rest," Will said.

She didn't know if she wanted a kitten, but she did know she didn't want to squat in the rain. After giving a Will a quick pat on the shoulder, she went to the office to fetch a plastic shopping bag and umbrella.

Will trailed after her, talking. "Everyone knows how you live alone and have nobody and but your crazy aunt. And now they say she ain't talking no more and of course, there's only whispering at the library. No real talking going on 'round here—"

A small community, an insane artist of small renown—of course people talked. They talked about anything and anyone, and Aunt Charlotte was interesting. Parading through town in her nightie, throwing apples at passing cars, spraying painting neighborhood dogs, Charlotte provided entertainment the town couldn't get on the local cable stations.

"Of course, cats can't really talk," Will said.

"And that's a good thing," Blair said, returning to the porch. Quickly, she explained her plan to Will. His gaze followed her outstretched finger to the roof, a window, and the trellis that ran up the wall.

After giving Will simple instructions, she ran up the stairs, threw open a second story window, climbed out onto the ledge and tentatively stuck a toe of her penny loafers onto the trellis.

Will watched her with wide eyes, and she waved at him. Grabbing the trellis with both hands, she gave it a tug to test its strength, and swung out into the storm. *This is a brobdingnagian mistake,* she thought, promising herself another chocolate.

Rain beat on her head and trickled down her neck. Her straight skirt hampered her climb, and she pulled it up to increase her range of motion. Dormant rose vines plucked at her socks, snagged her sweater, and scratched her hands as she scaled the wall. When she reached the roof, she shot a jubilant look at Will. Todd, Will's brother, had the child by the arm and leered at her.

Suddenly conscience of the skirt bunched around her hips and the red panties she was quite sure that Todd and Will could see, Blair called down to the boys. Todd grinned back.

"Nice seeing you, library lady," Todd yelled at her, his tongue ring making his words slur. He tugged Will away.

Blair watched the two figures, one dressed completely in black leather, the other splattered in mud, disappear into the woods that edged the grounds of the library. The bag that Will was supposed to use to trap the kitten lay in the dirt like a deflated balloon.

Blair stuck her hand into the muck that clogged the drain and threw it at the retreating boys. The dead leaves, mud and sticks felt slimy and cold, but she hurriedly mucked out the drain while balancing on the trellis. A whoosh of water washed the kitten out into the garden bed. It stood on shaking stick legs—its fur matted to knobby, protruding bones. It stared, frozen in place, as she climbed down the trellis.

Blair jumped and landed hard on the grass, her hands breaking her fall. She stood in time to see the kitten tear into the library through the wide open door.

At least it's a smart cat, Blair thought as she went after it. She tried to brush the dirt and leaves off her skirt, and she slipped off her muddy shoes and soaking sweater and left them on the front porch.

Standing in the doorway, searching, she called, "Here kitty, kitty." A tail, gray and rat-like stuck out from under a rack of books. She lunged toward the bookcase, and her stocking feet went out from under her.

Finding herself on the wooden floor, Blair turned to see the kitten watching her with one blue and one brown eye. She placed one hand in front for the cat to plainly see, and snaked her other hand behind the creature. The cat tried to dart away, but Blair grabbed it.

Rolling onto her back she held the squirming, skinny kitten in an outstretched hand in the air above her face. She considered the small, gray, and rodent like animal. Thinking of Drake, she said, "I'll call you either Mouchard or Rat-fink," she told the cat.

Blair rolled over, held the clawing cat to her chest and went to the basement in search of a box. Clutching the kitten with one hand, she slipped her silver bookmark into her novel, gathered her raincoat and umbrella and headed toward the door that led to the basement. She cradled the kitten in her arms and he held onto her sweater with tiny claws.

It had been less than a year since Blair had converted the Greek rival style home that her grandparents had bequeathed to the town into a library. Her grandparents' generosity had stopped at the bestowal of the house and property. Money for upkeep or improvements hadn't been a part of the will, and an outdated monster of a furnace that needed to be adjusted manually, heated the house.

A blast of cold air hit Blair when she opened the basement door. Somewhere an unlatched window thumped. *Odd*, she thought as she made her way through the dank and dimly lit basement, maneuvering through stacks of books, magazines, and old newspapers. *Who would open a window down here?*

Damp and moldy, the basement was a breeding ground for mildew and fungi that aggravated her allergies. What else might breed in the basement, she didn't want to know. Rodents, undoubtedly. She looked at the kitten in her arms that had finally stopped squirming, and now shivered against her. "Are you a mouser?" she asked. "Because I believe this basement could be a rodent smorgasbord."

She'd been avoiding the basement. As a child she had been terrified of the roaring furnace, and nervous about the dark, cobwebbed corners. As an adult she was overwhelmed by the flotsam of a family that she had never really known. Blair sniffed and then sneezed. The basement really needed cleaning, but for the moment she was grateful for the clutter because she soon found a fishing creel and an old towel. She dropped the towel in the creel and then placed the kitten in the newly created cage and secured the lid with a leather strap. The kitten mewed pitifully at her.

"Sorry, but I can't have you roaming free on the ride home," she told it.

Clutching the basket she went to turn down the furnace. The natural gas furnace was almost her height, and many times her width. It coughed and burped as if it suffered from a digestion problem. Blair turned the heat down and then glanced around to find the open window.

The wind howled, and for a moment the lights flickered. She took a deep breath, and followed the thumping noise. It came from a room behind a heavy wooden door. Someone had locked it. Why? She fumbled for a moment with the outdated latch and then wrenched it. The latch broke in her hand and the door swung open.

A window beat to its own erratic rhythm. Little more than an air vent, the window was scarcely six inches high and a foot wide. From the outside it sat just above the soil and hid behind a lilac bush, but from the inside of the basement it was high above Blair's head. Standing on tiptoes, she secured the window at the same moment lightning flashed, a roll of thunder shook the house, and the electricity went out.

The meager light from the window filled the basement with a soupy darkness. Blair jumped and dropped everything except for the creel. Her spark of frustration matched a flash of lightning. Her books and raingear lay at her feet, but not the keys. Squatting, she patted the dusty, cold cement with one hand. The basement floor sloped toward a center drain. Although she couldn't imagine the keys rolling, she moved along the floor in that direction.

A flash of lightning followed by a crash of thunder showed a gleam of something white wedged between stacks of boxes. Feeling along the floor, Blair pushed against the clutter, hoping to find her keys, but instead found a white sock tucked into a familiar pair of ked sneakers, a dark straight pant leg, and a man's white shirt.

Aunt Charlotte. She lay on her side; her head lolled at an awkward angle. Blair touched her, and then peered into blank eyes. "Charlotte?" Gently, Blair spoke her name, and picked up a limp, cold hand. Blair began to shake. Putting down the creel, she knelt beside her aunt, and tried to lift her into her arms. Wildly, she thought of CPR, but Charlotte remained wilted and unresponsive. Blair knew that she was dead.

Why had Charlotte come to the basement? How? Typically, the manor called when Charlotte managed to escape her room.

A rustling in the bushes outside distracted Blair. A rat? No, a human face with a sharp nose, barely distinguishable through the mud splattered window. Rain slid off a black slicker, and the tears of rain on the window distorted the features.

Blair called to them for help, but the person stood in a swirl of slicker and disappeared. She thought the nameless face would come to help, but after a moment of huddling in the dark basement, holding her lifeless aunt, and hearing no one approach, panic set in. With tender awkwardness, Blair returned Charlotte to the floor. She picked up the kitten's creel before bolting toward the stairs.

Stumbling through the gloom and maze of boxes of debris, Blair tripped once over a viola case and tore another hole in her socks. Righting herself, she plunged through the dark to the top of the stairs and finally reached the phone and caught her breath. She picked up the receiver and knew immediately that it, too, was dead. She scrambled through her purse for her cell phone before remembering she hadn't been able to pay her last bill and her service had been cut. She couldn't call anyone for help. Bolting, she took about three steps into the storm before returning for her shoes. Where were they? She had left them by the front door.

Inexpensive, dirty, size six shoes that no one would possibly steal.

Blair gazed into the library. Charlotte dead, a face in the window, her shoes missing. Was she alone? Somewhere from inside the library a door slammed. The wind, Blair told herself, but when the kitten cried, Blair darted down the library steps.

Staggering more than running in a straight skirt, Blair cast a backward glance at the library high on Olympic hill. Rain beat against her face and soaked her blouse as she ran toward Main Street and downtown. A streak of lightning cracked the gray sky; thunder rolled with an intensity that shook the sidewalk. Above her, wood cracked as a pine bough broke in the wind. It tumbled to land in a heap beside her. Fallen twigs and branches scattered on the sidewalk poked her feet. Clutching the kitten's creel, she ran the quarter of a mile to the first house.

Blair paused at the gate of Audrey Mortenson's home to catch her breath. Audrey's windows were dark, not surprising given the power outage, but the chimney didn't curl with smoke and the house wore a vacant, empty look. The gate creaked as Blair pushed through. Bracken and large, green slugs littered the walkway. She pounded up the steps and banged on the door, but her knocking sounded hollow.

The rain trickled inside her shirt, soaked her shoes, and filled her eyes as she continued running and stumbling down Main. She could barely see, but it didn't really matter. Aside from her brief years in college, she had lived in Rose Arbor since Charlotte's accident. Blair knew the streets well.

She ran into a large, warm expanse of flannel. For a small moment a rain slicker engulfed her, and then she tangled with an umbrella. In her efforts to extract herself, she slipped on the wet pavement and fell with thud on her rear. The creel landed beside her and the cat cried in protest.

Blair looked and saw a pair of heavy boots, Levi jeans, a flannel shirt and an unbuttoned dark green slicker. Rain and embarrassment washed over her. She pulled the creel onto her lap and checked its strap.

"Are you all right?" A tall man with wavy, honey colored hair gazed down at her and stooped to take her hand to pull her upright. His large hand swallowed hers. "You're shaking."

Stepping out of the umbrella's protective canopy, the rain beat against her. Large, wet maple leaves cart wheeled by and attached themselves to her legs. Blair shook herself, managed to run a trembling hand through her hair and stammered at the man, "I am so sorry."

"No, I'm sorry, here, let me help you." He held the umbrella over her.

"No, thank you," she murmured, stepping away from him.

"Don't you have a coat, or anything?" He followed her, sheltering her with his umbrella.

Blair shook her head as she fought the rain. Wind whipped through her hair, and tugged at her wet blouse.

"Wait!" he called, hurrying beside her. "Would you like a ride?"

"I'm not going far." She pressed on.

"Let me come with you," he said, easily overtaking her and blocking her path. He looked pointedly at her bare feet. "Let me help you." He bowed his umbrella toward her. His eyes traveled over her. "Have you been fishing?" he asked.

"What?"

He pointed at the fishing creel.

"Excuse me, please." She pushed past him, but he easily kept pace. *I don't have time for this*, she thought and the words became her internal mantra.

"Where are your shoes?"

Blair tried to match his face with the one at the window. It could have been him. She pressed into the wind, trying to ignore the man, but when she stubbed her toe on an uneven bit of sidewalk and dropped the creel again, he was beside her.

The kitten shot out of the creel. Blair tripped toward the escaping kitten and stubbed another toe on another bump in the sidewalk. "Bugger," Blair swore and the man laughed.

She looked into his good-natured face, and fought the temptation to smack him. With a throbbing toe, Blair limped after the cat now scrambling up a trunk of a maple.

"Kitty, kitty," Blair called. The cat scampered out of

reach, lost in a maze of branches.

Rain and tears trickled down Blair's face.

The tone of the man's voice softened. "I'll get her. What's her name?"

"Mouchard."

"Moose-what?"

"Mouchard." Blair closed her eyes and immediately saw Charlotte lying on the floor of the basement. Her knees buckled and she reached out to brace herself against the tree trunk.

An old Ford wagon splattered up the street, and stopped at the curb. "Blair?" Emily rolled down the window.

Blair looked at her old friend. "Can you take me to the police?"

"Of course, dear," Emily said as she climbed from the car. The wind ruffled Emily's gray curls and teased her lace collar. "You look a fright."

Blair glanced at the kitten and then at the man.

"I'll save the cat," he said.

"We'll get the police to find your shoes," Emily said over the car roof. "What happened, Blair dear?"

A flash of lightning, a face through a mud splattered window disappearing in a swirl of a rain slicker.

"Can I help?" The man asked.

"I'm alright," Blair lied as she climbed into Emily's ancient Volvo station wagon.

A cold limp hand, a straight black pant leg at an unnatural angle. Unseeing eyes.

"Are you sure there's nothing more I can do?" the man asked. The door slammed but Blair could still hear the conversation.

"No thank-you, Mister-" Emily began.

"Rawlings, Alec Rawlings."

"I've known Blair since she was a little girl. She'll be very comfortable at my house. It'll be like old times. I was her piano teacher for years."

"Aunt Charlotte, she's dead." Blair said, as Emily climbed back into the car. Blair leaned her head against the cracking leather.

"What's that, Blair?" Emily asked, adjusting her seatbelt.

"Aunt Charlotte. She's dead. I saw her in the basement."

Emily stared at her, her mouth open and her eyes wide. "Are you sure?" she asked, her tone hushed.

"I saw her." Blair nodded, feeling like a bobble head doll—a babbling bobble headed doll. "In the library basement. She was just…I don't know what she was doing there. And then someone must have taken my shoes." Blair put her hand on her forehead, her skin felt as cold and clammy as Charlotte's had. She shivered.

"We need to call the authorities." Emily clucked her tongue, and then patted Blair's hand. "What else? Should we go and wait for them there?"

"It seems wrong to just leave her there, but—" Thinking slamming doors and her missing shoes, Blair shivered again.

"What a nightmare," Emily clucked. "You must be frantic. Let's get you cozy at my house. I'll make you some of my Granny Hilga's tea and we'll call Floyd. Let him take care of things."

***

Because her head was groggy and her eyes slipped in and out of focus, it took Blair a moment to realize where she was. Dark maroon walls, a large, black baby grand piano where she'd spent many hours running scales and learning arpeggios. Not much had changed since Blair's primer days. The basket of needlepoint supplies seemed the same. Gilded frames with photos of Emily's husband, Geoffrey, and only son, Floyd, lined fireplace mantle.

Shelves filled with travel books dominated one wall.

The Glory of Spain, Ancient Africa, The Hidden Himalayas, and it struck Blair as sad that Emily would become an armchair traveler. Geoffrey, Emily's husband, had exorbitant medical fees. Blair knew Emily couldn't afford to travel on her piano teacher salary.

How long had she slept under a comforter on Emily's couch? Sophia, a toy poodle, curled beside her. Her cup of tea had long grown cold and the night sky had filled with stars. Her head ached and Blair carefully pushed her fingers through her hair, trying to put together the events that had brought her here. Emily had called Floyd, he'd said he was on his way, Emily had made her tea. Shaking. Shock, Emily had said. Yes, she'd gone into delayed shock. A blanket, tea. Charlotte. It made sense. Sort of.

"I must have slept."

"Only for a minute," Emily said, settling beside her.

Blair glanced at the grandfather clock that had once timed her piano lessons. It read six-forty. She tried to do the math, but her thinking grew fuzzy, and her head ached from the effort.

"Where's Floyd?"

"I think I hear his car now," Emily said, glancing out the window.

***

Floyd McDonald and Blair stood in the dark of the basement. His flashlight made small yellow circles on the cement floor. Blair watched him try to suck in his dangerously protruding belly. Blair had known Floyd most of her life. He was the son of her piano teacher and she knew that he had gone to school with her mother. She had always liked Floyd, and she had always thought the feeling was mutual. Until now.

"I saw my aunt. She was lying right here. Dead"

Blair's hair, normally securely fastened in a tight knot, was loose and wild. Floyd stared at it and ran a thick paw through the sparse prickles of his crew cut.

Blair folded her arms across her chest, trying to hold herself together. "Are you listening to me?"

"Blair, I've heard everything you said. And I followed you here. Hell, I called the emergency response people, who have to come all the way over from Pinewood, despite the fact that this storm is causing emergencies to all sorts of real live folks. And then I had to call them back and say— we don't know where Charlotte is. We rarely know where the hell Charlotte is." He paused, and muttered, "Although being dead would be a new trick."

"Trick?" Blair's voice screeched.

He held up his hand to stop her objections. "Calm

down. Let's call the manor to see if they've managed to keep Charlotte in her room today."

Blair rolled her eyes, "You don't believe me."

"I didn't say that, honey," Floyd said.

As he punched in the number he had probably long since memorized Blair knew he was thinking about Charlotte, who managed to escape her room and cause some sort of a nightmare at least once a month. Her last escapade had included the garbage bin from the Morton's Fish Shop and a parade of alley cats.

The manor must have admitted to having misplaced Charlotte, because Floyd asked, "Could you please look for her, and call me back when she's found?"

"They aren't going to find her," Blair said trying to control her chattering teeth. "At least not alive. I saw her. She was here and she was dead."

"Well, she ain't here now," Floyd said as he flipped his phone closed, dismissing her. "Listen, Blair, assuming your aunt is dead, you need to reckon that as a blessing—" He held up his traffic hand when Blair sputtered a protest.

"Maybe not to you, but to her. Her life has been skidding downhill ever since that accident."

Blair's anger slipped and her shoulders hunched as she muffled a sob.

Awkwardly, Floyd placed his beefy arm around her shoulders. She found his warmth discomforting and alien, the smell of his aftershave repugnant. "She's been gone for a long time," he said. "Let me take you somewhere. Do you want to go home?"

When Blair shook her head he squeezed her shoulders before he turned to lumber

through the messy basement.

Blair saw his pity for her weighing down his massive shoulders. She read his thoughts in his heavy footsteps. *That whole family was a little off—Charlotte, Vivian and Blair—three generations of loony-tunes.*

Blair knew what he thought. She knew what everyone thought. She often thought it herself.

***

Although the storm had eased, the wind and rain hadn't completely stopped. Blair stood on the corner of Main and Third, soaking up rain like a sponge. Grumbles of thunder and the whoosh of the water being swept down the drains filled the air.

She needed to find Charlotte, and although she was very used to searching for her when Charlotte was alive, now that she was dead Blair didn't know where to begin. She could go back to the library and look for her keys. She remembered the yellow circles from Floyd's flashlight and knew she would never find her keys in the dark. Besides she was scared.

The face she had seen at the window—that person must have moved Charlotte. Which meant that her aunt couldn't have just died in the basement, or else why bother to move her? Someone had killed her. But why?

Feeling sick and lonely, she considered calling Drake, because even though she was incredibly angry with him, she still wanted him. He would be at the college. She could drive to his house and wait for him to finish chatting up co-eds. That seemed a better plan than sitting at home alone. She remembered her confrontation plan and dismissed it. Despite the fight—he'd still be a soft shoulder. Her soft shoulder.

But she couldn't walk to Bellingham so she headed to the Bluebird café. Most of the shops on Main Street looked dark and empty and the Café wasn't anymore warm or inviting than any of the other places of business, but through the window she saw Andrea and Meagan sitting in a booth, back lit by candlelight.

Andrea and Meagan's chatter stopped immediately when Blair and a blast of cold air entered the cafe.

"Hey," Andrea looked up, the smile of welcome on her

face fading when she saw Blair.

Blair tried to stop shivering.

"What happened to you? How did you lose your umbrella and shoes?" Meagan asked.

Blair ran a hand over her hair and tried to tie it in a knot, but she'd lost the clip and the hair wouldn't behave. "Charlotte—" She caught herself. Although she trusted Andrea, she didn't know Meagan very well. A beat of silence filled the cafe.

"What happened? Are you alright?" Andrea asked, leaving the circle of candlelight to make Blair a cup of cocoa before Blair could answer. She poured water from the coffee pot. "This is still warm," she said, stirring in the cocoa before pressing the mug into Blair's hands.

"Did you hear about Drake?" Meagan asked.

Andrea shook her head at Meagan and scowled.

Blair looked from Meagan to Andrea, feeling like she'd missed an important bit of conversation. She turned to Andrea, trying to read her. They'd been best friends since high school—Blair could usually pick up on Andrea's thoughts, but at the moment, all she could really think about was Charlotte. Dead. In the basement. And then not.

The Rhyme's Library

Coming Soon

Acknowledgements

I belong to Orange County Fictionaires, a group of incredibly talented and diverse writers. I'm honored and humbled to be among them. Their wit and intelligence has made me a better writer and person. At a meeting last April we talked about doing a collection of short, interrelated stories. Here's the premise: All of the stories have to take place within 72 hours of 97 year old Sidney's funeral. There's a viewing, a memorial service and a scattering of ashes at the beach, although you don't need to place your story at any of these events. There's an open casket, but Sidney will be cremated. Set in Laguna, mid October, the weather is warm. We'd decided to take turns writing a story (beginning with me, since it was my idea) and committed to having it posted by the next meeting.

And for that assignment, I wrote what I now call Chapter One. I liked it so much I turned it into a novel. Some things needed tweaking—Laguna became Seattle, at first Laine was called Rainie, short for Lorraine, but once I changed the setting—I had to change her name. I couldn't have a woman from Seattle called Rainie.

I really didn't start out to write a ghost story. Like Laine—I'm not interested in the occult. I like to keep my feet firmly planted in the here and now. I've never been to a séance. I shy away from Ouija boards, fortune tellers and tarot cards. Can ghosts carry cookies? Drink cocoa? Summon killer dresses and shoes? I don't know. I don't really want to know.

My mother died when I was young, and at times I've missed having a mother acutely, but I've never tried to channel or reach out to her. There have been rare, sacred times when I've felt her near, but I've never sought her spirit. I wouldn't know how. I accept those moments as remarkable gifts for which I'm profoundly grateful. I don't ask for more.

So when Madeleine started talking, she took me by surprise. And she had things to say I wanted to hear. Now that her story is complete—I miss her. But I'm so grateful for the experience and the time I spent with The Ghost of a Second Chance.

Of course, as always, there's a host of real live people to who deserve my gratitude. My husband, children, amazing critique partners, writing group, beta-readers, editor, my incredibly generous formatter, and the mortician who patiently explained to me the world of "decedents" and how bodies really can be misplaced.

Most importantly I have to thank the source of all good

ideas. I believe there's a muse for every creative endeavor and I pay humble recognition to mine. I stopped believing in coincidences a long time ago and started having faith in a God that's concerned with giant and important things and who also has a sense of humor about stories, floating macaroons and cranky ghosts. I really can't adequately express my appreciation for His guidance in my life.

About the Author

Kristy Tate studied English literature at Brigham Young University and at BYU's international center in London. She's been happily married for a very long time and has been blessed with six children and one Schnauzer. She lives in Rancho Santa Margarita, California but her heart belongs in Rose Arbor, a fictional town in the Pacific Northwest patterned after her hometown of Arlington, Washington.

14854899R00219